I0891262

PRAISE FOR
Just Enough to Start Over

• • •

"This beautiful and deeply moving novel by Sara Gothelf Bloom takes us through a very hard time in history, but there is so much soul on display that one can only rejoice. Hanna is among the vivid characters in contemporary fiction, and she—with the Dubrovsky sisters from the earlier generation of this marvelous family—will stay in my mind. *Just Enough to Start Over* is an impressive achievement, one that reminded me at various times of I.B. Singer. A vivid chronicle, told with poetic specificity and hard-won elegance."

—Jay Parini, author of *The Last Station* and *Borges and Me*

"A gorgeously written novel, all at once profound, relatable, and wry. Something narratively miraculous is going on in this realistic, unsaccharine telling of the people, places, and talents that saved three beautiful sisters fleeing Nazi Germany. Woven throughout is the mystery of their stolen art—its plunderers and its fascinating journey. *Just Enough to Start Over* wowed me. Brava, Sara Gothelf Bloom!"

—Elinor Lipman, author of *The Inn at Lake Devine*

"Luminous with surprising detail, the lives here are powerfully inhabited. Very short chapters, glowing, gem-like, reminiscent of flash fiction, bring the war years to life, particularly the Jewish refugee community of 1940s Shanghai. The art world of the time is also thrillingly evoked, along with brilliant musings on the power of the self-portrait to shape the artist's understanding of the self: 'We paint with cold-blooded authenticity. That is the gift of old age, a blessing really.'"

—Grace Dane Mazur, author of *The Garden Party*

"Three generations of an extended family are driven from Mannheim to Shanghai to Brooklyn as their plundered art collection is dispersed from Amsterdam to Berlin and Moscow. Each episode of their story is sharply, poignantly focused on a single, telling event, like light glinting on a shard of shattered glass. Sara Gothelf Bloom's deeply informed, keenly observant, alert heart, attuned to danger and irreparable loss, yet also unfailingly aware of the comical aspect of things, cherishes what is left, which is just enough, 'the incomparable solace of ordinary life.'"

—Sarah Kafatou, translator of *With My Shadow: Selected Poems of Hilde Domin*

JUST ENOUGH TO START OVER

JUST ENOUGH TO START OVER

A NOVEL

• • •

Sara Gothelf Bloom

pdb

PAUL DRY BOOKS
Philadelphia 2025

First Paul Dry Books Edition, 2025

Paul Dry Books, Inc.
Philadelphia, Pennsylvania
www.pauldrybooks.com

Copyright © 2025 Sara Gothelf Bloom

All rights reserved.

Front cover image: *Still-life with Photo* by Marie-Louise von Motesiczky, 1930, © Tate

This is a work of fiction. Names, characters, places, and incidents either are products of the author's imagination or are used fictitiously. Any resemblance to actual persons, living or dead, events, or locales is entirely coincidental.

Printed in the United States of America

Library of Congress Control Number: 2025941192
ISBN: 978-1-58988-208-9

To Davy

The Family Dubrovsky

- Isaac 1804–1865 + Rebecca Berowicz 1809–1839
  - Leml 1830–1913
  - Chaim 1835–1920 + Tsipa Rudner 1843–1898
    - Alfred Ludwig 1865–1928 + Liselotte Hohenemser 1877–1970
      - Bertha 1904–1997 + Hans Erich Silberstein 1894–1964
        - Hanna 1944–
      - Annelene 1905–2001
      - Hilde 1912–1995 + Immanuel Häring 1890–1958
  - Herschel 1839–1918 + Malka Slonimer 1845–1926
    - Aron 1872–1954 + Deborah Fried 1887–1960
      - Gertrud 1912–2003 + Louis Cantor 1906–1988
        - Harvey 1936– + Shoshanna Kalisch 1938–
        - Neil 1938– + Ellen O'Donaghue 1942–

Three Sisters

• • •

Bertha is the oldest. January 1940, she stands on deck with her husband, Doktor Hans Erich Silberstein, as the tall buildings of Shanghai's coast grow smaller, pull away, then disappear entirely. She is thirty-six years old and, again, without a home. Arriving in San Francisco, they continue east to New York, to their sponsor, the American cousin. Bertha is carrying a large leather suitcase. She struggles to keep up as they walk from the subway to the house on Marlboro Road. The suitcase contains a small part of her trousseau, eight linen napkins embroidered with the initials HE/B, and a matching tablecloth whose border threads she'd pulled, light articles, remnants of decent living. Beneath her two best blouses, the Chanel worsted, and warmest undergarments, lies a Peters Edition of *Beethoven Piano Sonatas* and a parcel of photos taken hastily from albums with gold leaf bindings. Bertha has added to them the photo of her performance at the Hongkew Refugee Center. Life had prepared her for marriage to Hans Erich, she is proud to be Frau Doktor Silberstein. Life had not prepared her for fleeing Mannheim, leaving behind the Bechstein grand piano, the Feuerbach, Spitzweg, Menzel, the Meissen porcelain, and the cut crystal vase, a wedding gift from the Mayor's wife. Life had not prepared her for Whangpoo Harbor, and life has not prepared her for Marlboro Road.

Annelene is next, born just a year after Bertha. Her suitcase is large and leather, too, and it is heavier than her sister's. In addition to clothing and other necessities, it contains a sketchbook with drawings of the voyage from Europe and the year in Shanghai, several tubes of oil paint, her best brushes, and two of her paintings taken from their stretchers and rolled up for transport. She hadn't been able to part with these, begun in the months she'd studied with Max Beckmann. There's an empty canvas as well, primed shortly before the voyage to America. On the deck of the ship, Annelene had imagined filling it with the frenzied charge of the ocean, white light curling up inside each wave. She recorded the yellow ochre of the sky at dawn and the color of the water along the horizon, a long smooth stretch of light-dappled Payne's grey. Once they've gotten settled, she'll lay out the oils on her palette. She'll need a large tube of Payne's grey in the new country.

And Hilde. The youngest by seven years, in a wild, secret affair with the Communist poet Immanuel Häring, Hilde and he have fled east to his family. Halfway there, they stop at Krakow's City Hall, she sets her suitcase down in a small chamber decorated with plaster of paris rosebuds and says *Tak* before resuming the journey as Pani Häring. In her suitcase is an envelope with poems she'd written at the rosewood secretary in her father's study, some finished, some still needing work. Tucked in among them, rolled in a silk scarf, is her grandmother's diamond ring. The last telegram from Podliszki, East Galicia: We are safe.

Bertha, Annelene, Hilde, the Dubrovsky sisters. Beautiful women, all who've known them agree. They have fine features, high cheekbones, blue eyes, their fair complexion dotted with amber freckles in summer when the sun adds strands of copper and gold to their long red hair. They are sometimes taken for Russian or Polish, but they are not. The Dubrovsky sisters are German Jews, Mannheim their birthplace, Alfred Ludwig Dubrovsky, banker and patron of the city's rich cultural life, their father. In November of 1928, Mannheim's most prominent citizens attend his funeral at the synagogue Alfred visited once each year on Yom Kippur, the synagogue his father Chaim helped build. Set on fire ten years later, its destruction is followed by the flight of Alfred's wife and daughters and the loss of the Bechstein grand piano, the Meissen porcelain, the paintings by Anselm Feuerbach, Carl Spitzweg, Adolph Menzel. Alfred is spared all this. He is spared, as well, the year in Shanghai, the passage to America, old age in exile.

Copper, Silver, Gold

• • •

A generation earlier, Alfred's family had traveled not east but west. The year is 1850, his uncle, Leml, has left Baranowitschi, he is twenty years old and living in a rooming house in the city of Mannheim. He's been there since February, sent by his father, Isaac, to make his way in the scrap metal trade. Isaac's other sons, Chaim and Herschel, will follow but, for now, Leml is alone. Contacts are what he needs. That evening, he's heard, there's a meeting at the local synagogue. Leml puts on a clean shirt, he's ready. Dr. Leopold Ladenburg, head of the Board of Directors, steps up to the *bima* and calls for quiet. The old rabbi has died, he says, it's time to enter the modern world. The members of Mannheim's liberal community are thriving. The Board is unanimous: a new synagogue will be built. Eighteen thousand guldens Ladenburg's asking. Leml holds his breath—eighteen thousand! In fact, after ten black marble columns lining the nave of the sanctuary have been crowned with byzantine gold capitals, after the sanctuary's walls and those of the gallery and choir loft have been decorated with gold-trimmed arabesque frescos, and the large rosette stained glass window and marble mosaic floors have been installed, the Jewish community's coffer is lighter by the sum of eighty-five thousand guldens. And as a good many of these have found their way to Leml Dubrovsky, purveyor of precious metals, it's Leml we see at the head of the procession, carrying the first of three Torahs down the aisle in June of 1855 in the ceremony dedicating them to the new synagogue. Five thousand citizens of Mannheim are in attendance: the Mayor is there, the City Council, prominent military officers, ministers, priests. The voices of a ninety-member synagogue choir, women and men together, are heard from the loft, accompanied by the organ that has caused so much controversy among the rabbis. But there they are, rabbis from the inner city, rabbis from outlying districts, rabbis from abroad, and they're all marching behind Leml Dubrovsky to the music of Hermann Levi, the fifteen-year-old composer who, in later years, will become the nation's foremost conductor of the music of Richard Wagner. Leml leads them all. The Torah he's holding is wrapped in maroon velvet with embroidered gold threads depicting two lions of Judah and The Ten Commandments. He's marching towards the Eternal Light, donated by Hohenemser, the department store magnate, and on both sides of the aisle, girls in white dresses hold garlands of flowers. It's the Sabbath. The rabbi delivers the sermon, *Wie schön sind Deine Zelte, Jakob.* How beautiful are Thy tents, Jacob. Leml's younger brother, Chaim, has come from Baranowitschi, sent by Isaac to assist Leml, and Chaim can hardly listen to the rabbi's words, he's stunned by the light of the gas candelabras, 220 flickering flames illuminating copper, silver, gold.

The New Objectivity I, 1925

• • •

Bertha and Annelene have left their wraps at the coat check and are heading for the powder room before joining their parents and Hilde in the Main Exhibition Hall of Mannheim's Museum of Art. Couples pause in their conversation and turn in the direction of the two figures gliding by. The young women's shoulders are bare. Their hair, opulent, abundant, has been coiled and pinned in place with mother-of-pearl combs, revealing long, graceful necks. Ascending the museum's marble staircase, they pause on the landing. No one takes notice of a tall, thin man who arrives just as the sisters have completed their ascent. He leaves his straw hat with the coat check but keeps his satchel, a black bag containing a stethoscope and medical supplies. He's come directly from the hospital. Excited, nervous, he smooths his hair and straightens his tie and, as he begins to climb the staircase, he looks up. There on the balcony diagonally across from him is a young woman with red hair. She is standing behind an iron grillwork railing, leaning against a marble column. The column is cream colored, the color of the young woman's skin, and its marble is crisscrossed with thin blue-black veins and uneven patterns of red and maroon. Rivers of blood, the doctor thinks, and his throat goes dry.

The woman looks down now, surveying the crowd. Her glance takes him in, sweeps by, and she turns to join a figure behind her, another red-haired woman, a more modest figure, it seems to him, smaller than the first, although the women, now that they're standing side by side, are obviously identical in height. The crowd parts before them as they turn to enter the exhibition hall, and Hans Erich, for that is the name of the doctor, Hans Erich Silberstein, hurries to catch up. He and the two women have come to the opening of The New Objectivity Exhibit. Otto Dix, George Grosz, Max Beckmann, artists as well as social critics, are here. It's been said that their "Objectivity" confronts those who'd profited from the so-called Great War, and those who are now profiting from the country's political and economic distress. Christian Schad, Rudolph Schlichter, Franz Radziwill, also exhibited tonight, are among the artists whose work is referred to as Magic Realism. This intrigues Hans Erich, the objective, the magical, seeming contradictions, how are they connected. He has discussed this with Siegfried Oppenheimer, one of his private patients, and Oppenheimer, a wealthy manufacturer of textiles, and a personal friend of the museum's director, has given him a ticket to the opening. For several weeks, he has been looking forward to the exhibit, he's changed his shift at the hospital in order to be free this evening.

Hans Erich enters the exhibition hall and stops in front of the first painting, a boy with a pale, emaciated face. The boy's ears stick out at an exaggerated angle from his head, his eyes are huge and desperate, his coat several sizes too large. Otto Dix, *Young Worker.* Hans Erich feels exhilarated, this is what he has come for. At the same time, he's aware that his attention is not undivided, he's not fully here with the boy and what is obviously his miserable life, somewhere in the hall there is a woman with red hair. He looks around, scanning the crowd. He knows no one. Unlike the woman with red hair whose pastel gown is long and elegant (he thinks he observed that as she stood by the railing), many of the women at the exhibit are wearing thin, rectangular, modern dresses that leave their arms and calves exposed, and their hair is bobbed or whatever it is they call that new hairstyle. A single feather sticks up from a thin velvet ribbon round the head of the woman next to him. Her mouth and cheeks have been painted an unnatural shade of red, and as Hans Erich moves through the exhibit, it occurs to him that many of the women look as if they've stepped directly from a canvas, from one of the Berlin street scenes, their elegance is hard and suspect. He loosens the knot of his cravat. The proximity of lightly clad women is having an effect on his senses. The night is warm, the hall is crowded, it's difficult to make out the paintings with all of the bodies posing and chattering before them.

Finding himself in front of a painting of two young women on a balcony, Hans Erich cannot move on. One of the women has draped herself precariously on the railing in a seductive pose. Her thin dress, revealing the outline of her body, comes just below the knee, and her long hair falls over one shoulder. Her mouth bright red with lipstick, cheeks with rouge, she's a passionate, sultry beauty. Her eyes look down on the scene below, and it seems to Hans Erich that she is bored by what she sees. Behind her stands the second woman carrying a tray with a teapot and one teacup. Her dress is long and modest, her gaze rigid, dutiful. A cat on the balcony gazes up at the first woman. Hans Erich feels his knees go weak. He's worked through the previous night, a coronary patient. The air in the hall is hardly circulating.

A triangle is sounding now, calling the crowd to attention. Hans Erich turns with the others towards the center of the room, where Dr. Gustav Hartlaub, the director of the museum, has begun to speak. Eight years from now, Hartlaub will be forced to resign. Right-wing nationalists have been gathering in number since the beginning of the decade and many of them hold influential positions in museums and galleries. On this evening in June of 1925, however, Hartlaub is enjoying a time of triumph. Aware of his critics and opponents, he begins on a conciliatory note, assuring his guests that the paintings in The New Objectivity Exhibit are not propaganda nor an attempt to discredit the work of the past and that which is traditional in German art. "The paintings on display," he tells them, "are an opportunity to experience a new wave of ideas sweeping the country. We live in a time of enormous creative ferment, a time in which radically new forms of artistic expression are thriving,"—and here Hartlaub, inspired by the boldness and festivity of the hour, injudiciously adds—"thriving despite opposition, even animosity, towards their very existence. Ours is a time in which artists must remain true to the essential characteristics of their trade, namely veracity and excellence."

Veracity and excellence. Hans Erich, applauding, is caught up in the brilliance of the moment when a portly man, pushing his way through the crowd, suddenly appears at his side. Oppenheimer. "Brilliant," he booms, as he grabs Hans Erich's elbow and pushes back through the crowd in the direction from which he's come, unaware of the bodies his bulk displaces, their scowls and disapproval. Hans Erich follows, mumbling Excuse me, please, sorry, terribly sorry.

Oppenheimer stops at a large canvas depicting a well-dressed civil servant with a fine mustache, a briefcase under his arm. His eyes are crossed. A low brick wall separates him from a one-armed man in uniform, obviously a veteran of the Great War, bent and walking with a cane. His mouth is pinched, his eyes downcast. Another man, his face without features, a shovel over one shoulder, walks behind the crippled veteran towards a factory. Black clouds rise from its smokestacks. "George Grosz," Oppenheimer says and, joining the group that has formed around the painting, "Herr Bank Direktor Alfred Ludwig Dubrovsky. Herr Doktor Hans Erich Silberstein." Hans Erich turns now and finds himself in the company of the redhaired beauty, in the company of both red-haired beauties, and his face suddenly feels hot and moist. His palms are moist as well, and he stammers as he shifts his bag to his left arm and reaches to shake the extended hand of the man Oppenheimer has just introduced. Dubrovsky nods his head. His smile is courteous, there's a gold chain across his vest, his white linen suit sits perfectly, his beard and mustache are thick and gray and cut in the style of the Wilhelminian era. He's Leml's nephew, Chaim's son, yes, but look how far he's come. Alfred is no peddler of precious metals. Born in a time of opportunity, he's a university-educated, modern gentleman. Despite rapidly rising inflation, he's the director of a bank that's holding steady.

"My wife," he says, indicating the woman to his left, "my daughters, Bertha, Annelene," the women bow their heads and smile politely, "and Hilde," he says, indicating a girl of twelve or so with long red braids. Hilde curtsies, and smirks. Oppenheimer tweaks her ear. He's known her from birth, watched Bertha and Annelene flower, he's the Dubrovskys' kind and eccentric adopted uncle.

"We've been discussing George Grosz," Oppenheimer is saying, "the Dubrovskys are divided. Our artist, Annelene, and, of course, Hilde, represent the leftwing flank, outnumbered by the conservatives."

"Here, here," Alfred protests, "we so-called conservatives are open to the modern, we see the necessity of moving on. Siegfried, you do us a disservice by locking us into a category. I was simply saying that Grosz has gone too far, he's ridiculed those who are dedicated to bringing our nation out of its current crisis. And I believe they will do so. I see no reason to lump them all together, to assume their efforts exploit the workers. And certainly no reason to reduce them to obscene caricatures."

"And those crossed eyes," Mutti adds, shuddering. Mutti, for that's what her children will always call her, is the former

Liselotte Augusta Hohenemser, an Eternal Light and a chain of department stores back up her sense of outrage. For Mutti, beauty is sacred, the exhibit is lacking in beauty.

"But Mutti," Annelene says now, and Hans Erich leans towards her, he follows her mouth as she forms the words, "Mutti," she is saying, "his crossed eyes are meant to be allegorical. Grosz believes that the civil servant cannot see the suffering around him. He does not wish to believe that through his arrogance and indifference, he is, in part, responsible for it. Don't you think so, Berti?"

Bertha has been fanning herself with the exhibition catalogue, there is no color at all in her cheeks, and she answers weakly, "Allegorical. Yes. I see what you mean, Leni. Still, I stand with Father. Grosz goes too far. I feel quite . . . shocked." Short of breath, she fans herself more vigorously. It occurs to Hans Erich that this young woman is not well, but before he has time to consider this, Oppenheimer has turned to him. "And you, Herr Doktor, where do you stand?"

Called on to speak, Hans Erich hesitates. With Annelene, of course, he stands with her, he'd always stand with her, of that he's sure, but it's her father whose permission he must request. "Wi-with all due de-deference," he begins, bowing his head to Herr Bank Direktor Dubrovsky, "I feel," and here he hesitates once more, wetting his lips with his tongue, "it is never correct to ca- caricature all members of a particular class, and yet," Hans Erich smooths back his hair and takes the plunge, "Grosz, it seems to me, stands at the forefront of The New Objectivity. I believe his work represents the principles of ve-veracity and excellence."

He's hardly finished speaking when Bertha topples forward, overcome by the heat. As she falls, he catches her and lowers her gently to the floor. Oppenheimer calls for the crowd to part. "Give us some air," he booms, and Hans Erich, supporting Bertha's head with one arm, opens his black bag, takes out smelling salts, and holds them to her nose. Hilde stands by, fanning her sister with the exhibition catalogue, and as Bertha opens her eyes and finds herself in the doctor's arms, she smiles. Hans Erich looks up. There's Mutti wringing her hands, Alfred saying something about gratitude, Oppenheimer pounding him on the back, Hilde skipping back and forth between her parents, and Annelene—Annelene is no longer there.

Hans Erich

Who is this holding her in his arms? Bertha wakes from her faint and looks up into the face of a dark-eyed stranger. She smiles. Quickly, he looks away. Modest, dignified, self-effacing, she thinks, although Bertha has no first-hand experience of men, she's recalling Goethe and Schiller, the romantic passages, and a Wedekind play attended recently at the theater in Mannheim. Hans Erich, likewise, has no first-hand experience, his knowledge of the female is derived from anatomy sessions with a particularly frightening cadaver, a short and unpleasant internship in gynecology, and afternoons poring over illustrated art texts in his grandfather's antiquarian book shop, stopping at the pages of nudes, dwelling on Botticelli's Venus, oh, the red hair. He is painfully aware now of being in an intimate position in a public place and, the worst of it is, he is holding the wrong sister in his arms.

But who is Hans Erich? Born in 1894 in a farming village on the outskirts of Mannheim, Doktor Hans Erich Silberstein's pedigree includes not a single rabbi or Talmudic scholar but, rather, three generations of cattle traders, the profession the family brought from Galicia when they settled in Germany in the early eighteenth century. His father, Isaiah, spoke the local Viernheim dialect mixed with Yiddish. Isaiah was not poor, the Silbersteins had done well in the cattle trade, and when it came time for him to take a wife, his family were able to match him with the daughter of a Mannheim bookseller, Hannelore Kahnweiler, a woman of culture and beauty. She was already thirty at the time, older than Isaiah by four years, her father's book shop was not doing well and, at this point, there are two versions of the story. One, that Hannelore's family were unaware of her illness at the time of her betrothal; the other, that her symptoms, even the diagnosis of her misfortune, angina pectoris, were known to all but the cattle trader who'd come for a *kuk*—a look at the lady—and had been taken with her beauty. Whichever version is true, a wedding did take place, and a year later, a daughter, Ruth, was born. Three years after that came Hans Erich, the pride and ambition of Hannelore's life. Her son would never be a cattle trader, never would he be a struggling bookseller, her son would be a doctor. Could it be she hoped he'd be the one to cure her? It could be. In any case, complications from her illness took her shortly after his bar mitzvah. She did live to see him enter Mannheim's academic high school in preparation, she reminded him, for medical school, and although her son was more drawn to books, particularly the art books in his grandfather's shop, than he was to medicine, there was no question of disappointing his mother.

When the Great War began, the war that killed his sister's fiancé, Hans Erich was far enough along in his studies to serve in a medical corps stationed near Brussels. On leave one day, he took himself to the Musée Royaux des Beaux-Arts. In one of the upper galleries, standing before a painting by Lucas Cranach the Elder, was a tall man with an imposing square jaw. His shoulders were rounded, his posture stooped. Hans Erich recognized him. It was rumored that this man, a volunteer medic with another unit in Flanders, was an artist. Some of the medics had seen him drawing soldiers and horses. His name was Max Beckmann. It was said he'd been reprimanded for sketching in an operating room, and someone had heard him speak of the "glorious pink and ashen limbs" of the wounded. Such lack of feeling was repugnant to Hans Erich, all the more so because he too had noticed the bright colors of blood and internal organs in the operating room when no other perception had been bearable. As if he felt Hans Erich's attention, Beckmann turned. The two men faced each other, silently acknowledged their common uniform, and walked in opposite directions. In that short encounter, Hans Erich noted the artist's bulging wild eyes, his trembling lips, and the word "breakdown" occurred to him. A week later, he heard that Max Beckmann had been invalided out.

In the months that followed, before his own discharge for similar reasons, as one mutilated member of his generation after another was carried into the lazaret, as he helped amputate an arm from one, a leg from another, and attempted to stem the flow of blood, Hans Erich became a political man. He resolved to ally himself with those who would prevent this abomination from ever recurring. He became a Communist and did his residency at Mannheim's Hospital for the Poor and Indigent. Attending late night political meetings and rallies for the workers, Hans Erich began to notice he was hardly sleeping, he'd developed eczema, acid reflux, bronchial pneumonia. A stutter, unavoidable in times of extreme stress, tore at his attempts to speak. He stopped going to meetings and, instead, sought refuge in his grandfather's book shop.

One day, while walking by the artists exhibiting their work outdoors along the Rhine, a small painting attracted his attention. It was not a political painting, it was not a nude or a landscape. It was a still life, a porcelain pitcher with a chipped handle, a bowl, a spoon, an egg. It was the simplicity of everyday life that Hans Erich had been drawn to and, approaching the artist, Hermann Adler, he purchased his first painting. He would buy several more in the years following The New Objectivity Exhibit, and each gave him pleasure, but the first, oh, the first, that was not to be compared with any other. The still life hung in the study just above his desk after his marriage to Bertha Dubrovsky, and every time he looked at it, Hans Erich was reminded of the incomparable solace of ordinary life.

The New Objectivity II

• • •

He thinks he caught sight of the back of her dress as she slipped through the crowd in the direction of—is that Beckmann? Hans Erich strains to raise his body. Still holding Bertha, he pulls them both to a standing position and sees, there, at the farthest end of the gallery, yes! Yes, it is. Max Beckmann, the most famous artist here tonight, famous already before the war. And there is Annelene, standing at the edge of the group that has gathered around him.

It must be he, she is thinking, she recognizes the artist from a photo in a monograph of his work. Annelene has also seen a self-portrait in the home of her cousin, Marie-Louise von Motesiczky. The thin lips, the large nose, prominent jaw, hooded eyes. Yes, it is he. Older now than in the photo, it's more than ten years since the monograph appeared, his hair's thinned, there are fleshy sacks under his eyes, and the space between them is deeply furrowed. Broad, tall, silent, Max Beckmann is a presence. No one who is here tonight will forget him.

Annelene studies the painting to his left. *Christ and the Adulteress*. A woman kneels at the foot of a man in a white robe, presumably the Savior. The woman's hair is red-orange, her breasts are exposed, her hands pressed together in prayer, her eyes and mouth set in an expression of determined piety. The man in the white robe stands between the woman and the soldiers who are mocking her. He is obviously protecting her. And he, with his prominent nose and chin, is none other than the artist himself, Annelene is sure of it. As she considers this, she turns to observe the people standing next to him and, who is that young woman with her arm linked to the arm of the famous painter? Her eyes flash as she bows to the crowd, she's radiant, as bright and fresh as the master is dour, and she's wonderfully turned out in the *garçonne* look, a geometrically patterned evening chemise that flattens and slims her tall body, framing it, rectangular and oddly seductive. A long rope of artificial pearls hangs from her neck and stops just below her waist, further elongating the impression of her body. At the center of a tiara, worn low on her forehead, is a red and green cloisonné brooch in the shape of a scarab, and it bobs up and down as she responds to her crowd of admirers with a coloratura laugh. Her wide smile reveals large white, slightly uneven teeth. The new wife. Annelene knows this from her cousin, in truth her third cousin, Marie-Louise. The new wife, Mathilde von Kaulbach Beckmann, known as Quappi. Two summers earlier, as a student at the Vienna Conservatory, Quappi had lived with the von Motesiczkys and made the acquaintance of their frequent guest, Max Beckmann. In a letter to Annelene, Marie-Louise had written: "Mother's furious. Quappi's won the heart of B and he's leaving his wife to marry her. I think Mummy wanted him for me." Scandal, divorce, Christ, the Adulteress, Annelene's head feels light. Impropriety rewarded, she is thinking, Quappi's radiant smile, her hand lying in the curved elbow of genius, proof of impropriety rewarded, and now Quappi is speaking, she's let go of her husband's arm and is walking towards her through the crowd.

"Why, it's a Josef Hoffmann," she's saying in her high, girlish soprano, "isn't it," she asks, stopping to examine the pendant hanging from a velvet band around Annelene's neck. An oval with tiny, grapelike clusters of jewels surrounded by gold filigree leaves, the piece is unmistakably the work of the Viennese art nouveau jewelry designer.

"It was a gift from my cousin," Annelene says, barely able to reply as she looks up at Quappi. "Marie-Louise von Motesiczky," she adds.

With squeals of delight and a sudden warm embrace, Quappi takes her into the circle. "Max, Max," she cries, and there are introductions, names exchanged, relationships sorted out. The famous artist takes Annelene's delicate hand in his large one. She feels faint but manages to steady herself.

"I am an ardent admirer of your work," she whispers, but before she can say more, the remaining Dubrovskys, alerted to Annelene's whereabouts by Hans Erich, catch up with her. Further introductions are made and before long, the artist and his wife have been invited to the home of Alfred Dubrovsky. Perhaps, Mutti is thinking, she will have her portrait painted. Perhaps, Alfred is thinking, Beckmann will view the family's collection of nineteenth-century masterpieces.

"Perhaps," Alfred says, "you would enjoy seeing the work of Annelene, our family's holiday painter." There is talk of Beckmann's new teaching position at the Academy in Frankfurt, Quappi says Annelene must join them there. Yes, Annelene is thinking, Yes, she will. Yes!

Hans Erich stands apart from the group. He considers the last time he saw Beckmann, ten years earlier, just before the artist was discharged from the medical corps, the wild, nervous look in his eye, his body thin, bent, exhausted. Tonight Beckmann stands before them, cool and self-assured in a black tuxedo, starched white collar, black cravat, a beautiful young wife on his arm. The war lies there in the gravity of his mouth, that thin line, almost a child's drawing of a downturned mouth, and the war's in every painting he's done since 1915. But Beckmann's won his internal war, Hans Erich is sure of that. As Alfred extends the invitation to the artist, Hans Erich, feeling himself forgotten and, more important, recognizing that Annelene is of a world very different than his, turns to go. A light touch restrains him. Bertha Dubrovsky. Shy, hesitant. "Please come as well," she says.

A Masked Ball

• • •

Three years following The New Objectivity exhibit and her first encounter with Beckmann, Annelene arrives in Frankfurt to attend his class at the Academy. Her father had objected. It was one thing to take pride in a talented daughter's watercolor landscapes, holiday mementos framed and hung in the family's vestibule. And it was quite another to send a beautiful, unmarried daughter in her early twenties to the metropolis of Frankfurt, alone, unchaperoned, exposed to the libertine atmosphere of art school, the proximity of male students, nude-God-help-us models. During those three years, Annelene turned the top floor of the house into an atelier, experimenting with oil paint and pastel, commandeering the servants to sit for portraits, missing meals, refusing the attention of more than one suitor sent up to the attic by Mutti. While Bertha interrupted her practicing, closed the lid of the Bechstein to receive the courtship of Dr. Hans Erich Silberstein in the drawing room, and Hilde took over the rosewood secretary in Alfred's study to write her first poems, Annelene made periodic attempts to break her father's resistance. My three Muses, he would say, how can I part with any of them, but Annelene would not be charmed. She cited the example of her cousin, Marie-Louise, who'd attended the Academy the previous year. Finally, Mutti intervened. The von Motesiczkys, she argued, belonged to Vienna's Jewish aristocracy, they were the vanguard of all that was worth aspiring to in terms of culture and assimilation. What was good for a von Motesiczky would be good for a Dubrovsky.

Annelene leaves for Frankfurt in the fall of 1928, and settles into the room recently occupied by Marie-Louise at Number 3 Untermainkai, the home of the editor of the *Frankfurter Zeitung*, Heinrich Simon. Anyone of importance in the cultural, intellectual, and progressive political life of Frankfurt attends the newspaper editor's weekly salon. Fridays, four PM, Annelene sits, tea cup in hand, surrounded by famous poets, composers, members of the City Council, journalists. And famous poets, composers, members of the City Council, journalists gladly—in some cases ardently—sit and drink tea with Annelene Dubrovsky. When there are no vacant seats in the circle, famous men hover at its edge. One gray afternoon in October, Emil Wunderreich finds a place next to Annelene. His latest drama, *Leid*, a work of suffering and torment, he tells her, a pacifist plea inspired by his time in the infantry, will soon be coming to the West End Theater. She must come to the premier, he would be honored. She might, she just might, but Annelene is distracted at that moment. She turns from the playwright because there, entering the salon, is a tall, broad figure, handing his overcoat to a uniformed maid who waits while he unwraps a woolen shawl from his neck. The woman takes that as well, and curtsies before leaving the room. Beckmann. Conversation stops as the guests register the newcomer's presence, silently acknowledge his grandeur, then turn and resume speaking. Annelene, however, cannot resume listening. She's been studying with Beckmann since September, and so disturbed is she by his strange, provocative demands, she's found herself increasingly less capable as the weeks progress of rendering even a line in charcoal. Find your Self, Beckmann tells them, the young men and women who stand in front of their easels under the skylight as the model removes her kimono and settles into a chair. Be truthful to all parts of your

Self, those that are most hidden, those that are least socially acceptable. Pay attention to your dreams, he says, your nightmares, your desires, that is what is of interest. All else is simply making marks on paper. Annelene would be grateful now to be able to make simple marks on paper, so unsettling are these instructions. Even more unsettling is Beckmann's own work. What does it mean, she asks herself, desperate to understand it, to understand him. All those buildings and streets at odd angles, now seen from above, now from below, as if he suffers from a sort of vertigo of the soul. What is he saying with his world of symbols, the fish, the horn, the agave? And the self-portraits, one after another, what is he looking for behind the impassive features of his face? As if he were as incapable as his students, she sometimes thinks, of finding himself and, not knowing what lies behind his own mask, he is compelled to paint Beckmann again and yet again. But most disturbing to Annelene is one particular painting, the one of torture, rape, murder, whatever does that mean?

"Marie-Louise," she writes to her cousin shortly after arriving in Frankfurt. "I have seen *The Night* and I cannot reconcile the bestiality of this painting with what I know of B, his kindness and nobility. I feel quite faint in his presence. Can so many parts of the Self exist in one person? Do they exist in you and me as well? Stripped of our civility, would we find in our Selves the will to bestiality and carnage? Please tell me what you think."

"Dear Cousin," she writes in her next letter, in the early morning hours following the November Masked Ball, "I have danced with him. My mind is feverish, my body as well. I cannot sleep. He came to the Ball as Harlequin, Quappi his Columbine. I, a simple shepherdess. As Harlequin bowed deeply before me, I lay my crook aside and stepped into his arms. Marie-Louise, I don't know how I was able to move to the music, so out of breath was I, feeling his hand on my back. I'm sure I did not say a word as we swayed to the music. And as he returned me to my seat, he bowed deeply again and smiled before returning to his Columbine, a smile that went from his eyes—you know how blue they are—to the corners of his mouth. I shall never feel for another man what I felt for B last night, I'm quite certain of it."

A week later: "Dissatisfied with my work, I stayed at the Academy last night after all had gone home, sifting through the pile of mediocre drawings and paintings that I've turned out since my first day here. Perhaps I could salvage something, I hoped, perhaps I could get beyond the maze of blocked feeling and create something I'd be proud to show him. I began to sketch in a background of tumbling clowns behind the least unpromising of my paintings, the one of the tattooed model, you know the model I mean, he was here in your time as well. As I became absorbed in the work, I did not hear B until he stood directly behind me. I don't know why he returned to the studio just then, but as I turned, I came face to face with his eyes, and again that smile as on the evening of the Masked Ball. My breath caught in my throat, the charcoal dropped from my hand. He bent, retrieved it, and as he gave it to me, his fingers rested just that moment lightly on mine. 'Please forgive me, Annelene,' he said. 'I didn't mean to startle you. Continue working.' Oh, Marie-Louise, I have always been for him Fraülein Dubrovsky. It was only that word, just my name, that opened the flood gates, and all the pent up feeling of these last months, the longing and despair, burst forth. I felt him hesitate. He took a step towards me and, just as suddenly, stepped back and waited silently. As he made no move to comfort me, I slowed my sobs, taking deep breaths, commanding myself to be quiet. I know with what contempt he regards excess but, dear cousin, had he taken me in his arms then. . . . Instead, he backed away, and just as he left, he said, 'You have a great wealth of feeling, Fraülein Dubrovsky. You must put that into your work.' And when I could not respond, he added, 'Tears, they are meaningless. Wiped away, out of existence, they are not worth the time it takes to dry them. Be strong. Tears are not for you. Tears are for slaves.' And then he was gone. Marie-Louise, I will not go back to The Academy. I cannot."

And she does not. Pleading indisposition, Annelene avoids the Friday salons as well. She stays on at Number 3 Untermainkai, however, until December, unwilling to go home, uncertain what to do next. Perhaps she will ask her father to allow her to join Marie-Louise in Paris. But before she can send another letter to her cousin, three things occur that determine her course. The first: she accepts an invitation to the premiere of *Leid* at the West End Theater and, catching sight of Beckmann and his wife in the front row, the second: she accepts the invitation of the playwright to meet the following afternoon at his home for a first encounter with meaningless intimacy. And, later that week, the third: she is called home, suddenly and unexpectedly, to attend the funeral of her father. Annelene takes two of her unfinished paintings from their stretcher bars, rolls them up, packs them with her other possessions, and boards the train to Mannheim. She does not return to Frankfurt. A letter arrives later that week: "With sincerest condolences, Max and Quappi Beckmann."

The Rabbi

• • •

"Three thousand five hundred Reichsmarks," a man to her left is saying. "Weimar filth, it's an outrage."

"Heino can paint better than that," a woman adds, indicating a small boy tugging at her hand. "Not that he'd paint a rabbi. Or any other Jew."

Annelene has made her way through the crowd standing at the corner of Breite Strasse in front of Lotterhos Jewelry. Among the gold watches and pearl necklaces in the shop window stands a large copy of Chagall's *Rabbi*. Next to it is a photo of Gustav Friedrich Hartlaub and a handwritten sign: "3500 RM. Taxpayers! Here is where your money has gone!" Hartlaub's no longer the director of Mannheim's art museum, he's been dismissed.

"What I could do with three thousand five hundred Reichsmarks," another man is saying, "t'hell with Hartlaub, burn the goddamn picture. Hartlaub too."

"Hartlaub too," a man next to him says and several people in the crowd begin to speak. Filth . . .irresponsible . . . unpatriotic. Hartlaub too.

As Lotterhos, apparently fearful for his window, appears, Annelene slips back through the crowd and quickly crosses the street. The mood of the people standing there has caught her off guard, the rapid shift from curiosity to anger, things getting out of control. Hartlaub dismissed, Hans Erich now working at the Jewish Old Age Home, the city hospital no longer requires his services, her teaching contract canceled, best to apply to the Froebel School, the Jewish school, she's been told, it's 1933, things seem to be getting out of control.

Annelene pulls her coat around her, closes the top button, it's cool for April. She's on her way to the art museum. She begins to walk quickly, then breaks into a run. There is a connection between art and outrage which, at another time, she thinks, might have amused her, considering the reaction to Chagall's unappealing painting of a religious fanatic from the east about to put snuff into his nostril, sidelocks ridiculously curled—she'd seen some of them that autumn in Frankfurt, their long black coats. Galizianer, people said. The weather had been warm, their clothing smelled of sweat and garlic. At the time, they interested her, she found them exotic and would have liked to draw them, but when she approached, they turned away. She suspected they were arrogant, they lost their appeal as subjects for her work, certainly she felt no connection to them. What had the woman said, *any other Jew*, but the Dubrovskys are German, this is clear, and Annelene, running up the stairs, enters the museum. The new director has taken Hartlaub's acquisitions of the last ten years, paintings by Ensor, Munch, Nolde, Chagall, Beckmann, and hung them in an adults-only show, "Cultural Bolshevistic Art." Still running, Annelene ascends the marble staircase and enters the exhibition hall. In an obvious attempt to devalue them, the paintings have been taken from their frames and hung close together. Below each is a card with the date and cost of purchase. She thinks of prisoners, unjustly sentenced, awaiting execution. Her visit is a leave-taking, a final word with the condemned. Huddled together, the pictures look naked, vulnerable, and at the same time, extraordinary. This attempt to ridicule them has done the opposite of what had been intended, it has enhanced their dignity, and she stays by *Christ and the Adulteress* till the museum closes.

Hilde and the Herweck Pool

• • •

Hilde changes into a bathing suit and stores her summer dress and purse in a locker at the Rheinbad Herweck Pool. She slips the bracelet with the key over her wrist and tightens the chain. It's the twenty-second of July, the year is 1935, and Hilde has just turned twenty-three. *Dew lingers on a grassy knoll . . .* , *Dew hovers o'er the grassy knoll . . .* , a line of a poem she began this morning goes through her head as she walks by bathers lounging on a patio. Still in their swimsuits, some wearing beach robes, they're drinking coffee, eating cake and croissants, playing cards, flirting. Hilde spreads her blanket on the grass between the pool and a rocky beach leading down to the Rhine River. Herweck's is the only bathing area left. The city pools have been closed to Jews, and all the private pool owners, with the exception of Herweck, have complied with a new nationwide ordinance, they've posted a sign at the entrance to their premises: *Juden hier unerwünscht.* Jews are not welcome here. Herweck is holding out. He despises the thugs who've sent threats to him, "to the owner of the Jewish aquarium."

Dewbeads cling to blades of grass . . . , it's no use. It won't come right. It doesn't sing, it doesn't lift effortlessly, it's not at all like the poems Immanuel Häring read earlier that week at Oppenheimer's soirée. Originally in Polish, he'd translated them into Yiddish, the language of the proletariat, he told her, as they balanced hors d'oeuvres on their plates after the reading. "Then translated again," he'd said, "into the language of Goethe and Schiller," and he told her of his childhood on the estate his father had managed in Podliszki and the hours spent with a Prussian tutor. Seeking a wider public, Immanuel Häring's come west. Given the political climate, it's ill-timed, he knows, but he's no longer young, time is of the essence, and his reception, so far, has been excellent. Jewish bankers, doctors, lawyers, owners of factories and property have welcomed him to their homes, sponsored readings. In the tradition of Amos and Isaiah, Häring rails against their worship of Ba'al. His hosts counter with foundations, food kitchens, the Mannheim Philharmonic, the Indigent Women and Children's Beneficent Society, the Max and Thea Rabinowicz Orphanage, they plead for absolution, hoping the poet can supply them with an amulet in these difficult times.

"I swim," he'd said to her as Oppenheimer's companion, the opera singer Viktor Bloch, passed by carrying a tray and filled their plates with Roquefort, caviar, anchovies smeared on little triangles of toast. Balancing her plate in one hand, Hilde sipped Riesling from a delicately tapered glass, and looked up into the eyes of the Communist poet.

"I swim," she'd said, and there it was, agreed upon, the following Thursday, the 22nd, a grassy knoll at Herweck's, half past three.

Half past three, Hilde's dropped her towel on the blanket and, turning, sees Immanuel Häring treading water in the middle of the Rhine, waving to her, pulling her in, enchanting her. Enchanted, she leaves the grass, crosses the pebbly beach and, ignoring the river's cold, she plunges in. "*Ikh hob dikh azoy lieb*," he murmurs as she comes up to him, her last stroke suddenly bringing her up against his bare chest. Small black hairs lie wet and curled around the pink of his nipples, along the muscles of his broad shoulders, and Hilde quickly backpaddles, startled by this pink, this black, the nakedness of it all. "I swim, you swim," he says, "*ikh hob dikh azoy lieb*," I like you so very much, as they tread water. Hilde comes closer and their feet touch as she leans in, trying to make out his words, but there's a sound coming from the shore and it's louder now than these strange words in this coarse, primitive cousin of German. The sound from the shore is coarse as well but without warmth, it's a noise that's been gaining in force from the time she entered the water, and they turn now in the direction of its source, young men in ties and brown shirts, they're carrying clubs and their faces are like masks at Carnival, loutish, bizarre, macabre, terrifying. Look: they're kicking over tables and chairs on the patio, smashing them, smashing beer glasses, cups, swinging their clubs at men and women in bathing suits who run screaming from their path. Two of the men have gotten hold of a large iron coffee percolator and they're hurling scalding liquid at the people who'd been playing cards, and she hears him now, Immanuel Häring shouting to her: "Swim!" With all of her strength, Hilde follows him downstream and, as they reach the pebbly undertow at a hidden cove, he holds out his hand and pulls her to safety.

The First Crate

• • •

The striped velvet wallpaper is a darker red, the original maroon, in the rectangles where the paintings had been. The Feuerbach had occupied the largest of these, just above the wingback chair. Frank Morav had had difficulty taking the painting down from the wall, it is a meter and a half wide, more than a meter high, mounted in a heavy gilded frame. Mutti had stood ready to catch it as he lowered it from the wall. She'd asked him to come alone. At a time when it seems impossible to count on anyone, Mutti counts on Frank Morav. There is no other employee from Hohenemser's whom she trusts as much. He'd been their chauffeur, his father the chauffeur for her father from the time before the Benz when the family rode in a horse-drawn fiacre imported from France. There'd been a little chestnut-colored pony with an Italian name, something with B, Christmas they'd hung bells on her harness and, *soft in the head*, she thinks, I'm going soft in the head, there's still so much to do, the crate with the Feuerbach, Spitzweg, and Menzel is standing in the hallway, the latest ordinance would have her register the paintings along with all the remaining so-called luxury items, their "assets." She won't do it, it's robbery they're planning, she's certain of that. Morav will come for the crate tonight, two AM, they've made out, he and Hans Erich will have to get it down the stairs without waking the neighbors. She needs to write instructions to their Dutch art dealer, Gronewicz. Insert the papers, seal the crate, Morav would find a way to get the paintings over the border. And if he's unable to get to Holland, Morav's promised to store the crate for them until they return. Surely we won't be in China more than a few months, she thinks, and should we settle elsewhere, Morav will find a way, what's taking her so long to send the papers. The American cousin, second cousin Alfred's family. *Beeidigte Erklärungen.* Affidavits. If they don't come through, Mutti's learned another useless language after three false starts, Swedish, Danish, Spanish, applications for visas, each requiring days of standing on line, and in the end, a clerk's indifference, a wordless gesture, dismissed. And the latest humiliation, the American Embassy in Stuttgart, where she's no longer Liselotte Augusta Hohenemser Dubrovsky, she's Number 18,455. 18,454 ahead of her in the quota. Whoever would have thought to leave, the absurdity of it all, but it's been eight months since the city evicted the Karminskis from their villa, an SS guard leading them up the stairs, barking orders as if the Karminskis were common criminals, all five of them suddenly here one afternoon in the Dubrovsky living room, set down like discarded baggage, she hardly knows them and here they are sharing the kitchen, sharing the toilets, Gertrud Karminski depressed and unable to do even the simplest tasks, her husband red-faced, angry. In the not too distant past he'd won all his cases in court with that anger, now here he is with his useless anger, his useless wife, useless children, it's intimidation tactics, that's what it is, up until the Karminskis she'd held out, there was no way she'd allow the city to "Aryanize" Hohenemser's. Aryanize. A meaningless but clever word, even a distinguished word, when all it is, in effect, is another word for robbery. Krauss had come along and offered a pittance, not ten percent of the worth of all three stores, not ten percent of the worth of one them. She'd refused, refused again, each time he offered less, not more, and as they'd gone from one office to the next, passport, emigration, police, Gestapo, internal revenue, and paid the assets tax, the export tax, the emigration tax, she knew he'd won. "Take it!" she'd said, throwing down the deed to ownership. He renamed the stores Krauss the same day, what else, and fired the employees, among them Morav, who'd been loyal to her. And that had been last Christmas, a fine Christmas for loyal employees. No baskets with food and toys. Instead, a slip of paper, . . . *service no longer required*, Bella was her name. When she walked, she pranced, her hoofs *klak klak klak* on the cobblestones and, as a small child then, Mutti had watched from the carriage as the pony's rump cantered left right left right through the snow. She dug her hands down into the little fur muff, it had been white and gray, rabbit fur perhaps, a gift from Tante Margrit, she warmed her hands in its silk lining as they rode to Hohenemser's to pick out Christmas gifts for friends and neighbors, and to distribute the baskets of food and toys to the workers and their families. On the way home, they'd chosen a tree, one of the finest from the lot behind the main store. Her father, the holiday spirit dispelling his usual reserve, had helped Morav's father load it onto the roof of the fiacre, they decorated the boughs of the tree with *stop. Just stop.* Mutti goes to the rosewood secretary, one of the only pieces that have been spared the auctioneer's hammer. She takes out a sheet of vellum from the top drawer, dips her pen in the inkwell, and begins: "To Josef Gronewicz & Sons, Fine Art, Amsterdam."

An Antique Armoire

• • •

It is 1938, the ninth of November, shortly before midnight. Hans Erich steps down from a streetcar at the last stop in Ilvesheim. He is on his way to a farmhouse, to the home of their housekeeper, Antje Schmidt. Earlier that day, Antje's nephew had gotten his hand caught in a thresher. As Hans Erich walks along a country lane to the house, he considers. For three years now, it has been illegal for a Jewish doctor to do what he is about to do. Antje had barely retained her job after the same set of laws prohibited young Aryan women, as they were called, from working in Jewish households. She'd lied about her age, and remained with them. So here is Hans Erich on a farm in Ilvesheim. He stays through the night, the young man's fever subsides towards dawn. At five AM, the morning of the tenth, there is a knock at the door, a whispered conversation followed by sounds of a gate closing, an automobile starting up, young men in high spirits. Later, Hans Erich will know they'd been on their way to Mannheim, to the main synagogue, they'd gone without Antje's nephew. He changes the dressing on the wound, packs his bag, and boards the streetcar for home around nine AM. A half hour later, he steps down at his station. Worn out from the night before, he doesn't immediately notice the smell of smoke. Black ash floats through the air and swings slowly to the pavement, but before he is able to make anything of it, a boy runs towards him and begins pulling him in the direction of the main street. "Come," he shouts. The boy is Siegfried Oppenheimer's neighbor. He runs ahead of Hans Erich through streets littered with cracked ceramic, paintings slashed and lying face down in the gutter, pages ripped from books, scattered, tumbling in the wind. Store windows have been broken, and slices of splintered glass in the grooves between cobblestones reflect the morning light. Arriving at the building where Oppenheimer lives, the boy stops. Jagged-edged shards of seventh-century Chinese porcelain line the curb in front of the entrance. A number of fine Persian rugs lie there as well, heaped on the street, strewn with irregular black pieces of shellack phonograph records. Hans Erich looks up. The windows of the living room on the third floor are open. A curtain moves in the wind. The boy takes off up the winding staircase and Hans Erich follows. They come to an open door. As they enter, he sees Oppenheimer and Viktor Bloch sitting on a sofa, its stuffing torn and lying at their feet. A cello, its wood splintered, strings snapped from the tuning pegs, leans against a grand piano whose ivory keys have been split. An autographed copy of *Die Meistersinger* lies open on the floor. In that moment before he unpacks his bag and draws forth what is needed to clean the gash in Oppenheimer's forehead, Hans Erich recalls a literary soirée some years earlier. Caviar on toast. A collection of Chinese vases. He and Bertha sitting on a sofa, this sofa, Bertha turning the pages of an opera score. She touches his arm, calls his attention to the flyleaf. A hand-written dedication to the original owner, a signature. Richard Wagner. A cellist playing softly, a servant with a tray of, Hans Erich shakes himself and quickly opens his satchel. Oppenheimer and Bloch are barely following his movements, their eyes are dull, their mouths hang open. He gets to work, cleans and bandages Oppenheimer's wound, and just as he is washing the bloody rags, he hears voices of men ascending the stairs. Grabbing his bag and coat, he runs to the bedroom, pushes open the door of an antique oak armoire, and climbs in. That the men who have come to take Oppenheimer and Bloch to police headquarters and, later, to Dachau, are not immediately interested in Siegfried's tuxedos, his camel's hair coat, furs, silk scarves, and woolen suits, is the saving of Hans Erich. He crouches there in the dark and listens to the men's voices as they descend and then, from the street, the sound of a car taking off. Hiding in the softness and perfumed smells of Oppenheimer's wardrobe, now dozing, now suddenly awake and alert as a hunted fox, Hans Erich listens, muscles taut, and when daylight no longer comes through the decorative slots carved in the door of the armoire, he steps out. Slowly feeling his way down the unlit stairwell, he comes to an inner courtyard and opens the door to the street. He looks out. Glass slivers between cobblestones reflect the light of the moon. The air is bitter with the smell of smoke. Hans Erich covers his nose and mouth with a scarf and, avoiding the light from the street lamps, he makes his way home.

Shanghai: January 18, 1939

• • •

Beriberi, smallpox, typhus, dengue fever, dysentery, cholera. Hans Erich makes a list of tropical diseases and finds, to his despair, that he is unable to come up with a cure for any of them. If only their crate with his medical books would arrive, but there seems to be something or someone holding it up at Whangpoo Harbor, and after the interview, he'll go to the customs house and pay the necessary *kumsha*, his first word in Chinese, to release the crate.

Beriberi, small pox, dysentery. Dysentery: Emitin. That's it! Emitin. Do they even have Emitin in this godforsaken corner of the world, he thinks as he walks along Avenue Joffre, passing a Chinese beggar baring an arm amputated at the elbow. The man holds out the hand of his other arm to Hans Erich who is obviously European in his gray worsted three-piece double-breasted suit and Homburg. Hans Erich quickly finds a coin in his trouser pocket and flees to the bus waiting at the corner, drawing from his briefcase the address with directions to the hospital in Washing Road.

Dengue fever, cholera . . . what else had the young doctor said as he'd waited to inoculate those who'd just arrived on the *SS Gneisenau*. Nurses had been standing by with needles, disinfectant, and smallpox vaccine as members of the Refugee Relief Committee welcomed the passengers with warnings about food and drink. When it was Hans Erich's turn to be inoculated, he'd rolled up his sleeve and clicked his heels (now why had he done that, never having been in Prussia, in fact loathing all that was Prussian). Dr. Hans Erich Silberstein, he said, and the young doctor had looked up from his work table. Dr. Sam Didner, he replied, and held out his hand. There were outpatient clinics in some of the refugee quarters, they could use doctors, here was the address of the Emigrant's Hospital. Didner wrote it down with the number of the bus to Washing Road and the date, a week hence, January 18th. Hans Erich would be expected at four PM.

Scarlet fever, typhus, cholera . . . damn the customs officials, pretending they had no idea what was holding up the crate marked Silberstein, and Hans Erich returning each day, inquiring politely, until Ostropovich set him straight. Kumsha. Bribery. The only way anything gets done here in Shanghai, their new landlord had said, baring his gold-capped teeth, the smile of a wolf. Ostropovich, here since the Revolution, pillar of the Russian Jewish community, owner of The Black Cat Night Club and the room Hans Erich has found for the four of them on the Avenue du Roi Albert. That first morning in Shanghai, after a sleepless night on cots in the Hongkew refugee quarters, they'd stood in line among the other new arrivals. Teachers, tailors, doctors, lawyers, hairdressers, professors, shop owners, indigents, after almost three weeks at sea their suits and white shirts creased and no longer clean.

Silent, stunned, uncertain, they stood there holding tin trays, waiting for weak coffee, bread, margarine. Bertha barely holding back tears, bedbugs, she'd said, pulling back her sleeve, showing him the bites just above her elbow. Streaks of blood on the wall, filthy gray flannel blankets, a thick layer of dust on every surface, she said. Frenchtown, Mutti said, she'd heard the other women talking, and that morning, Annelene accompanying him while Mutti and Bertha sat at the refugee center guarding the suitcases, Hans Erich had taken a streetcar to The Black Cat. Inquiring in Yiddish, he found Ostropovich and the room on the Avenue du Roi Albert. With cash from the Leica he'd sold while the ship docked in Port Said, Hans Erich paid a deposit and the first month's rent. He posted the address to Frank Morav and Antje Schmidt, and they'd moved in that day. There's a sink in the room, water red-brown with rust comes from the faucet, and a toilet down one flight of stairs in the corridor. Hans Erich waits outside the room each evening as the women wash and change into their night clothes. He averts his eyes when Annelene brushes her hair. *Wa-shee Ro*, the bus driver calls now, and Hans Erich steps down.

Beriberi, smallpox, it might all vanish were people simply taught to wash their hands, were people simply taught to use soap, to boil water. And not to defecate in the Whangpoo River for godsake, he thinks, remembering the man Mutti had nearly collided with just after they'd disembarked at Hongkew Wharf. Coolies wearing bamboo hats and patched and torn pants had run up to them, wildly pointing to the customs shed, offering to carry their luggage for pennies. They stank. With the exception of his brief alliance with the Communists, Hans Erich had been a Social Democrat his whole life, he thought of himself as progressive, tolerant, and not at all unfamiliar with bodies and their odors. Still he could not help noting: they stank. And where there was stink, there was disease, of that he was certain.

Shanghai: June 29, 1939

• • •

It's four PM, and Bertha's radio dial is set at 600 kilocycles. She's listening to XMHA, Horst Levin's program, "From Burned Books." Following the opening measures of the "Soldier's Chorus" from *Faust*, Levin's voice is heard announcing the schedule of ships arriving from Europe today, and news of the buildup of German troops along the Polish border. Then, "Thomas Mann, *Tonio Kröger*," Levin says, and begins: "*Die Wintersonne stand nur als armer Schein* . . . ," enunciating each word with reverence and longing. Bertha lies back in bed to listen. She's thrown off the cover, her fever's gone but she's no cooler now, summer's begun. Hardly a breeze comes through the open window, but it would be intolerable to keep it shut. Those who've been here since last June have already warned them of the humidity of Shanghai's long tropical summers. Bertha has yet to experience the flying cockroaches that will swarm through the window later that evening. For now, it's the noise that disturbs her, the streetcar as it passes, the driver evidently cannot stop ringing its bell. Car horns honking at the intersection. The click of mahjong tiles, Chinese neighbors have set up tables in front of the house. They play all afternoon and into the evening, hollering at each other at frequent intervals, while vendors carrying long bamboo poles on their shoulders march along the street, shouting to the players. At each end of their poles hang wooden tubs filled with rice curry or steamed buns filled with pork and blue beans. This afternoon, a cobbler enterprising enough to have learned the name of his trade in German, is calling "*Shoo-ma-keh, shoo-ma-keh.*" "*. . . und manchmal fiel eine Art von weichem Hagel, nicht Eis, nicht Schnee,*" Horst Levin is reading, and Bertha strains to block out the noise of the street. Must they shout everything? Are they incapable of living quietly? Have they no human sense of privacy?

Bertha's down with dysentery. Aside from trips to the toilet one floor below, she's not left this room since the third of June when, longing for the taste of fresh fruit, she'd eaten an orange from one of the outdoor stands on Seward Road. Golden it had been, tart and round and, as she later learned, fat with water injected just under the rind from the cesspool known as Soochow Creek, how could she have been so stupid. Hadn't they been warned the very first day not to drink the water, not to eat fresh vegetables, to wash fruit in disinfectant, they kept a bottle of potassium permanganate on the sink just for that purpose. Stupid she'd been. Greedy. Desperate for some semblance of normal living. Hans Erich recognized the symptoms immediately and, using his privilege as Medical Director of the Chaoufoong Road Clinic, he'd brought home enough Emitin to head off a major illness. Since last week's outbreak of scarlet fever, he's ordered Bertha, in her weakened condition, to remain at home. Ostropovich has reassured her that when she's well, she can resume playing at The Black Cat. Bertha, however, is despondent. She's longing to feel the keys of the piano, even that piano, to practice for her next concert at the refugee home in the hours before the nightclub opens and, when the patrons are there, to play Russian classics. Rachmaninoff, Tchaikovsky. "Bei mir bistu scheyn," someone calls from the dance floor, and she plays that too. Despondent she is, remembering the quiet of their home on Elisabethstrasse and the keys of the Bechstein, each in perfect tune, with perfect action, the whispered purity of her most subtle pianissimo, the magnificence of her most powerful forte. The Ullmans have the Bechstein now, it's improbable that their hopelessly untalented daughter will ever learn to play more than "Bruder Jakob." Bertha's certain they bought it only for the ebony shine of the wood, which is exquisite and will set off their large collection of imitation Meissen dwarves.

But what else was she to do, they couldn't have transported the piano to Shanghai, and almost everything else had had to be sold or auctioned for a fraction of its worth in that frantic month between the time they'd finally gotten their exit visas and the day they boarded the train to Rotterdam. One month to pack what remained into two crates. And now it's been six months since they'd sealed the crates in the presence of an SA man, a foolish young man, more naïve than evil, who'd been sent to see that nothing essential to the Reich was taken from the country. One crate to Rotterdam, one to Ilvesheim. The first destined for the *SS Gneisenau*, the ship from Holland to Shanghai, with clothing, featherbeds, pillows, sheets, the good cutlery, a dinner set for eight, Beckmann's charcoal drawing of Mutti, the two-volume Peters' Edition of *Mozart Piano Sonatas*, Hans Erich's medical books. The other, larger crate destined for the basement of Antje Schmidt's farmhouse, sent there for safekeeping with a promise of return. It held the rest of her music, the books that remained after most of their library had been auctioned, Mutti's collection of Meissen porcelain figurines carefully wrapped in one blanket, the cut crystal vase from the Mayor's wife wrapped in another, the phonograph, sixty-four invaluable recordings, and the remaining paintings from Hans Erich's collection, including the Adler.

Nice pictures, the SA man had said, eyeing a barometer on the wall. I painted them on holiday at the North Sea, Annelene said. We'll have to part with the barometer, she added, taking it down and placing it on a table. A family heirloom and quite valuable. On that morning, it was the 17th of December, Hans Erich emptied the secret drawer of the rosewood secretary, quickly removing the Leica camera and the pouch containing Alfred Ludwig Dubrovsky's gold watch and chain, a Josef Hoffmann pendant, the Swarovski brooch, Mutti's diamond ring, her diamond earrings. And while the young man examined the barometer and its ornate brass setting, Hans Erich slid the Leica into his valise and passed the pouch to Annelene who slipped off to the bathroom to hide it among the thick coils of her hair, sweeping everything together into a chignon, and binding it to her head with metal clasps. This was the way she carried the jewels to the police station in Mannheim before boarding the train to Rotterdam, past customs, and finally, over the border. Antje, moving between the crates, had inserted whatever fit in the crevices, making no distinction between what was valuable, what was ordinary. Who knew, anyway, a spoon, a cup might turn out to be worth more than a set of Furtwängler recordings. At the last moment, Bertha ran her fingers lightly over the keys of the Bechstein and closed the lid. The Ullmanns would have it carried up to their apartment the next day.

And then it had been time to go. Weeping into the hem of her apron, Antje received a last handshake from Hans Erich, a first and last embrace from Bertha, then she'd closed the door of their home on Elisabethstrasse, promising to look after Hans Erich's father and his sister, Ruth, and to send on the crates, God willing, with utmost speed and care. The SA man, barometer tucked in a pocket of his coat, had escorted Annelene, Mutti, Hans Erich, and Bertha to police headquarters, then to the railroad station, and from there, they boarded the train to Rotterdam.

Shanghai: July 30, 1939

• • •

What she will remember most, Mutti thinks, as she makes her way to the jewelry store in Bubbling Well Road, is the inescapable olfactory assault of the street, raw garlic and ginger, fried dough, fried tofu, fried bok choy and fish, all cooking and crackling in rancid oil, and wafting through it all, the unmistakable smell of raw sewage. The heat and humidity of summer have intensified the smell. She's waited till late afternoon to avoid the hottest part of the day but there'd been no use putting it off any longer, it had to be done, it is expensive to file applications for visas and send letters and documents, photographs, telegraphs to their sponsor, the American cousin. Second cousin, Alfred's family, Herschel's granddaughter, how was it? There were Isaac's sons, Leml and Chaim. They stayed. And a third son, Herschel, who left, set himself up in the brass trade in America, and his son was Aron and his granddaughter was this, what is her name, Gertrud something, Cantor, Gertrud Cantor. Who knows if she's reliable, this is Alfred's second cousin, and it costs money to live with any standard of decency in this purgatory of exile, in this "Venice of the Orient" as *The Shanghai Jewish Chronicle* calls it, Jewish humor, she's never cared for it, hardly ever sees the point of it. Mutti closes her parasol and enters the little store through its red and gold pagoda exterior. One of the lesser Sassoons is standing behind the counter, a minor relative in a wealthy Sephardic clan, not one of those with a hotel, a bank, not a philanthropist, thank goodness she hasn't had to resort to that. Mutti removes her white cotton gloves. She wears them, despite the heat, because she is a lady, a German lady, she does not leave the house, in this case, the room, without gloves. In addition, she wears them because when she returns to the room at night, she is able to remove the soiled evidence of what her hands have mercifully avoided. This Sassoon knows her by now and he bows graciously, even respectfully, although she suspects his family's picked up wily ways in the Orient, there's something inauthentic in all this seemingly respectful bowing and obsequious scraping. Mutti doesn't intend to make an afternoon of it, won't haggle or smile and pretend friendship, here is the gold chain, what is he willing to pay, that's it, finished. She deposits the ludicrously colorful Shanghai dollars in her pocketbook and pulls on her gloves. Sassoon, sweating through thin strands of hair combed sideways over the top of his head, rushes to open the door for her, and bows again as she exits. It's behind her, this indignity, she's free.

As she walks east on Bubbling Well Road, a Sikh traffic guard stops her at the corner. Double decker buses, streetcars, limousines go by and, racing between them on foot, coolies pulling carts and rickshaws. Mutti catches sight of herself in the window of Weinberg's Cigars. A European lady, solidly built, standing erect at a corner waiting to cross the street. She's wearing a feathered hat, white linen suit and a patterned silk blouse. She's carrying a parasol in one hand, a pocketbook in the other, she is dressed as she was a year ago in the city of Mannheim, this is what she wears in summer, she will not fall to the level of personal neglect to which some of her compatriots, in imitation apparently of coolies, washwomen, and fruit stand vendors, have fallen. She will dress as she always has, as Liselotte Augusta Hohenemser Dubrovsky, widow of one of Germany's most prominent bankers and mother to three of the most beautiful women of Mannheim (oh where is Hilde, surely if she'd written, Antje would have forwarded the post, it's so like her not to get in touch), and as the Sikh waves his white gloved hand, she crosses the street, walks one block west, and enters the Café Louis for afternoon coffee, Black Forest Cake, and a few words with the owners, Herr and Frau Eisfelder, formerly of Berlin.

Shanghai, November 3, 1939

• • •

The remaining floodwater from October's typhoons has barely begun to recede from the street. It mingles with the overflow from the Whangpoo River, and Annelene, descending the steps of the Consulate, considers the fastest way back to the Avenue du Roi Albert. Holding the precious papers to her chest, she wades through the water, then decides to hail a rickshaw. She's anxious to get home with the news: their visas have arrived! America!

Annelene settles back in the little cab now and watches the boy, the cuffs of his torn pants rolled up, struggling to pull her along Broadway, passing the other consulates. A flag with a swastika waves above the roof of one, a hammer and sickle above another. At Nanking Road, the boy takes a right and runs past the race course, carrying her on to Bubbling Well Road, past the Café Louis, Weinberg's Cigars, the Metropole Hotel, the offices of Radio Station XMHA and *The Shanghai Jewish Chronicle*, past the Wayside Theater now showing *Gone With the Wind*, past the Viennese restaurant called, inexplicably, The Barcelona, and The European Hair Salon where Mutti gets a wash and set every now and then and a touch of red for the roots. Bertha will be home now, fighting with the gas burner. Remembering the tilt of the *SS Gneisenau* almost a full year earlier, she'll greet the news with hesitation, reluctant to move again, might it not be better to wait out the crisis here, it can't last much longer. Exactly that tilt and the ship's fierce courage, daring the sea to tear it to bits, had drawn Annelene out of their cabin. She'd stood on deck sketching the receding cliffs of Dover and, as the sea opened out before them, she'd drawn masts and rigging, foghorns, sailors, refugees bundled in deck chairs, others playing skat in the card room. Coming through the Suez Canal, Annelene added Arabs and camels to her sketchbook; in Singapore, monkeys running wild between the trees of the Botanical Gardens. Passing the Straits of Gibraltar on New Year's Eve, the *SS Gneisenau* had been battered by rain and wind, its bulk leaned at a forty-five-degree angle to the water, and when it came upright again, the only passenger left standing had been Annelene. The ship's commanding officer requested the pleasure of her company that evening to share a glass of champagne. Shortly before midnight, Captain Heinrich von Emmindingen smoothed the ends of his thin mustache, straightened the collar of his uniform bearing the Nazi insignia and, upon hearing a gentle knock, he'd opened the door of his cabin to the tall, young guest. Annelene entered, dressed in an emerald gown, her hair piled high on her head, Mutti's diamond earrings reflecting the light of the cabin's chandelier. As the chimes of the ship's clock rang twelve times, she'd raised her glass to the captain's and, quickly draining it, gracefully declined his next request.

And now, almost a year later, they will pack another crate and arrange to have it shipped, this time to Brooklyn, America. She will buy a silk kimono, silk shirts with lovely Mandarin collars, she'll buy them with what she's saved from selling her pictures to the Kadoories and Sassoons, the sketches she'd drawn waiting to disembark, her first view of Shanghai with its gold, silver, copper and glass office buildings, hotels, and banks lining the Bund, the wealth of the old established Sephardic families greeting and misleading the refugees, the massive skyscrapers blocking the view of hovels and streets of misery that awaited the newcomers in the interior. Sketches of wealth that brought a good sum, and Annelene will buy a silk dress, embroidered red and gold with a slit at the side. She'll buy papier-mâché animals, the ones the Chinese bury with their dead, perhaps a tortoise, a frog, she'll pack them all in the crate along with her paintings of Shanghai's street vendors with their carts and large umbrellas, the Chinese families camped along Soochow Creek, the women fanning hibachis, preparing food, drying cotton shirts on bamboo poles. She'll pack Leopold's gift, his painting of sampans on the Whangpoo River.

Leopold.

Annelene consults her heart. No. It won't be difficult. Leopold will stay on at *The Shanghai Jewish Chronicle* where they've both worked these past nine months doing layout and drawings for the newspaper's advertising department. At night, they lay together in the only private place in Shanghai, a tiny dark corner behind the desk in the office of the *Chronicle*'s editor-in-chief. No. A box of cigars from Weinberg's to break the news, a promise to write, but Annelene's already gone, she's left Shanghai, the wheels of the rickshaw are turning, turning, the boy's powerful legs are picking up speed and, if Annelene promises to tip him well, he'll keep running, she's sure of it, he'll keep running till they reach . . . America!

The House on Marlboro Road

• • •

Those houses got fourteen rooms, an' on the outside none a them looks the same . . . trees, flowers . . . It's a summer evening, Louie's out for a walk. Since the arrival of Gertie's Shanghai cousins, he excuses himself after supper, goes out, crosses to Rugby Road, stays out, time alone, time to think . . . *a reg'la botanic garden . . . lawyers an' teachers . . . doctors . . . a judge in that house* . . . Families are sitting in white wicker chairs on front porches . . . *castles*, Louie smiles, he's proud to be here, never envied the neighbors. The last of nine children, one of three born in America, his father a baker, his brothers bakers, before the accident Louie was a baker. They lived in a tenement in the Bronx, a railroad flat, three rooms, he shared a bed with Irwin and Morrie. When the cousins came from Plotsk, his mother put two chairs together for him at night, and when the cousins moved on, he was glad to share the bed again. And now? The house. The house on Marlboro Road . . . *jus' the next block . . . an' we worked hard t' get here, Gertie the ILGWU, an' we got the liquor store, made a down payment. House needs paint. Floor in the living room sags. There's half a porch, no botanic garden, but we got a house, never been late on a mortgage. Couple months later, Gertie's mother moves in. She got a room. Harvey an' Neil got a room, me an' Gertie got a room, not like my father an' mother, how the hell d'ya make nine kids like that. . . . So when Gertie says the Shanghai cousins are comin', y' could say I wasn' delighted. An' y'd be right. But I didn' say no. I'm proud a Gertie. Gertie's smart, a fighter. The country don' wan' no more Jews, she gets 'em here anyways . . .* The day they came, Gertie waited at the subway and walked in front of them to the house. They carried big leather suitcases . . . *even the ol' lady, an' the doctor, he's carryin' two, an' their faces they was thin like they was worn out, no smilin', no one sayin' nothin'. Trouble* . . . Louie couldn't help thinking it. "Sholom aleichem," he'd called to them, but they looked at him like they didn't understand. Then the doctor put down his suitcases and held out his hand. He sighed. "Gut morneeg," he said. *Trouble.*

Begat; or, Ten PM, Marlboro Road, February 4, 1940

And Isaac begat Leml, then Chaim, then Herschel,

And Leml went west, Chaim followed and settled,

And Herschel went west, and went west again,

And Chaim begat Alfred, who then married Mutti,

And they begat Bertha, Annelene, and Hilde,

And Herschel begat Aron, and Aron begat Gertie,

And Gertie's lying in bed now with Louie in the house on Marlboro Road, it's the 4th of February, the year is 1940, and it's ten PM:

"So I say 'Sholom Aleichem,' y' know what y' say, I know what y' say, y'say 'Aleichem sholom,' y're a Jew, he's a Jew, y' know what y' say, y'know where y' stand. Instead, he says, 'Gut morneeg,' like he's in the Luftwaffe. An' it ain' even morning."

"Shh, Louie, you'll wake the kids."

Louie moves closer and turns on his side. He puts his arm around Gertie, his chest pressed to her back. He pulls the cover up around them, feeling the curve of her body.

"What kinda Jew don' say 'Aleichem sholom' y'say 'Sholom aleichem.'"

"Pop."

"OK Harvey, sorry. Just get to sleep. This don' concern you."

Gertie's body is warm and soft, and if the kids wasn't there. Louie moves away, turns onto his back.

"I wouldn'a been surprised he clicked his heels, y'know. Erich von Stroheim." He snorts.

"Shh."

Louie puffs his pillow, turns on his other side. He flexes his bad hand, kneads at the stiffness.

"Hans Erich. How d'ya name a Jew Hans Erich."

Gertie turns around. She puts her hand on his arm.

"Louie, these are Isaac Dubrovsky's great-grandchildren. Think. If Zayde hadn't come to America, we'd be standing like beggars at someone's door. Herschel had the foresight to see what was good for his children while his meshuggeneh brother Chaim couldn't see he shouldn't stay where he wasn't wanted. And Chaim's son Alfred the Shlimazel goes through one war and still doesn't have the sense to leave. Excuse me for saying it but thank God he's dead, he doesn't have to see his wife and his children running for their lives."

"Mom."

"Harvey, go to sleep. Louie, they're worried about their family. Hans Erich, he's here, OK, but he's got a father, he's got a sister. He's gotta trust God they'll be all right, and Hilde, everyone's going crazy about Hilde. The last they hear from her she's in Podliszki. Where the hell's Podliszki no one even knows."

"Mom."

"'Trust God,' listen to me. You might as well trust Hitler."

Ten PM, Marlboro Road, March 4, 1940

• • •

"Two down, two to go."

"Louie."

"Pop."

"So what's the deal?"

"They gave her the job. Sales and some window dressing. At the interview, Annelene takes out her stage designs and someone must of figured Macy's windows could look like *The Flying Dutchman*, it wouldn't hurt. So she'll be earning, it's a good thing, Louie. And on the way from the subway, she sees this For Rent sign on one of those old buildings on Newkirk Avenue. She goes in and the super speaks Polish and she knows a little Polish. And that's it."

"Excep' what's she doin' for a deposit."

Gertie turns on her side and puts her arm around him. She finds the back of his knee with her knee. "It's a small place, a living room, a bedroom, she'll take her mother, they can eat in the kitchen."

"How much, Gertie."

"Louie, we got savings."

"We got savings so we can breathe a little easy, God forbid maybe somebody gets sick, maybe somebody can't work. Maybe we need a vacation."

"She'll pay it back, Louie, I swear.

Louie turns over onto his stomach. They can hear the ticking of the clock, and Harvey and Neil breathing.

"A Chevrolet."

"Harvey and Neil can move out of here the minute they leave."

The Green Border

• • •

"Heil Hitler!" he calls to the dispatching agent, thrusting his arm out in salute before climbing into the ambulance. Heil Katzenjammer! Heil Dubrovsky! he thinks as he starts the motor. It's late August, 1940, Holland's down, fallen like a tin soldier. Frank Morav, drafted into the Wehrmacht, is a driver for the medical corps. He's on his way to Amsterdam. Heil Gulaschsuppe! A good meal is what he'd like, not what's sure to be waiting at the caserne at the end of the journey, something gray on a tin tray covered with something brown, viscous, coagulated. Morav knows the route, the trick is to cross over at the fields, the green border near the farmhouse with the blue shutters, avoiding customs and the guards. There must have been an accident on the autobahn, he'd say if questioned, we were stalled behind a row of trucks, we took a detour. "You're crazy," his wife had said a few hours earlier, as he brought the crate up from the basement and loaded it into the ambulance. "Careful," he said, "you never know in these times what your last words will be." And then he was gone and, anxious though she was, she was glad to be rid of it after seventeen months in their basement. She'd send him down to bring up the wood, apples, cabbage, she wasn't going down there. The crate with the Jews' paintings frightened her.

A doctor and two orderlies are asleep now in the back of the ambulance, unaware of what is suspended above their heads between the stretchers and the roof. The crate's smaller now, and narrow. He'd taken the large painting, the Italian mountains, from that damned frame. The gold paint stank as it went up in smoke, the frame chopped up for firewood, what else was he to do, he couldn't sell it, he dared not keep it. Then he'd cut the picture from the stretcher bars, burned those too, rolled the canvas so that it fit on top of the lady playing the piano, and slipped the little country scene and the letter from Frau Dubrovsky in between. The original crate he pried apart, saved the nails, sawed the slats, hammered them together again and there it was now, compact, resting just under the roof of the ambulance. He'd stop by the art dealer, Gronewicz, make out a drop off point.

Northwest along the Rhine, Morav keeps an eye out for the crossing. Left, not straight ahead, he remembers the route from their last holiday in Holland. The doctor hadn't been along, just the ladies. Take country roads, they'd said, stop at that lovely farmhouse, the one with the blue shutters, we'll ask to picnic there. Beautiful daughters with red hair, the oldest the doctor's wife. The middle one asked if she might draw his face. It was a good likeness, she was clever. Later, she painted him on the roof of his house and filled in the homing pigeons, their shed, his best dove Anjuska taking off from his outstretched arm. The painting hung in the art show at the Jewish Center. His wife hadn't gone but he had, and when it was over, Fraülein Dubrovsky, Annelene was her name, said she'd give it to him. The doctor brought it by, he brought cough medicine, too, for their youngest. He sat on the child's bed, listened to her chest, dropped off something stronger that evening.

Morav makes a right at the next crossing, the road's narrowed now, another two, three kilometers, he's over the border. Sign's ahead. Achatwies, that's it, slow down now, country road, house ahead, field of corn, blue shutters, that's it, slow down, bear left, northwest, farmer's wife, gravel road, laundry line, barking dog, edge on by, pick up the tempo, speed it up, bear north, bear west, Kamp-Lintfort, speed it up, Sonsbeck, Kalkar, northwest, over the Rhine, Zevenaar, Oosterbeek, Amersfoort, speed it up, go, go, Spakenburg, sign's ahead, sign's ahead, sign's ahead . . . Amsterdam!

Newkirk Avenue

• • •

Hans Erich has found work in a lab at Downtown Medical. As soon as he's saved enough for a deposit and the first month's rent, he and Bertha move to the apartment house on Newkirk Avenue. Annelene's already living there on the floor above with Mutti. After almost four months of Louie's bruising hospitality, Hans Erich comes home to quiet and can study for the American medical exam. Bertha takes the linen tablecloth and embroidered napkins from her suitcase and sets up photos on the lowboy left behind by the last tenant. She makes an attempt to occupy this space, call it home, yet she feels they are only stopping here temporarily. This is where they are while they are waiting. Waiting for the war to be over, waiting to hear from Hans Erich's father, from his sister Ruth. Hilde. Shortly after they move in, Hans Erich makes the first of twelve payments on a used upright piano. When it arrives, Bertha takes it as a sign: Newkirk Avenue, this is where our lives are, this is where our lives will be. She begins to weep. The movers, three men unfit for military service, struggle to lift the piano from the trolley and center it against the wall. They avoid Hans Erich's eye as he extends two quarters to each and signs the receipt. Then they tip their caps and leave, closing the door to the apartment quietly behind them. Hans Erich waits silently at one end of the piano, Bertha at the other. His hands are at his sides. His wife is weeping, he cannot help her. Later that night, knowing he is suffering, she will put her hand on his arm and say, "I am very sorry." It is several weeks before she opens the lid of the piano and takes a seat at its yellowed ivory keys. Meanwhile, there is the work that Antje Schmidt once did for them. Bertha does it gratefully now, aware that dull work dulls her longing. She dusts and sweeps and launders, she does this for Annelene and Mutti as well. She pulls a cart along Newkirk Avenue to buy groceries, this is America, a market is not simply a market, Bertha shops at a supermarket. At the entrance to their building, she pulls the cart up the steps to the heavy glass door and crosses the lobby to the elevator. There is an inlaid herringbone pattern of colored stone covering the floor, brown, burnt sienna, ivory, a touching attempt at elegance, this is not lost on Bertha. It is, however, such a tiny fraction of elegance. Like the piano waiting for her in the living room, it reminds her of what she has lost.

The South of France

• • •

Aufbau, November 1, 1940: "According to a report in *The New York Times*, it is estimated that 9,000 Jews from Baden and the Pfalz were transported to southern France in the last weeks of October. The Hebrew Immigration Aid Society contacted its office in Zurich immediately for information. The report has been confirmed, although the number of those transported is uncertain."

Aufbau, the German-Jewish émigré weekly, is on the dining room table when Hans Erich returns from work. Mutti and Bertha hardly greet him. They are unable to speak, unable to understand what it might mean. Mannheim belongs to the district of Baden. Hans Erich's sister, his father. He sends a telegram to the house on Elisabethstrasse. It is returned: "Failed delivery. Departed. Forwarding address unknown."

Letter from Amsterdam, April 1941

• • •

Herr Doktor Hans Erich Silberstein
c/o Mister Louis Cantor
Marlboro Road
Brooklyn, New York
United States of America

Most esteemed Herr Doktor Silberstein:

We deeply regret to inform you that the paintings we received this past August have been sold under circumstances contrary to your wishes. The purchaser is Herr Doktor Hans Posse, an art dealer from Dresden. According to a reliable source, he is the principal agent for Special Assignment Linz, which is acquiring works of art from the Netherlands for the Third Reich. As Dr. Posse, accompanied by three uniformed representatives of the Reich, was especially emphatic in his request to purchase the paintings, and as he intimated the consequences of attempting to deny his request, we thought it best to accede to his terms.

An itemized list of the paintings, and the sales price of each, is appended below. We are living, as you can imagine, under extreme duress since the Occupation. As soon as it is feasible, we will transfer funds to your American account.

I remain, in good faith,

Josef Gronewicz

Gronewicz & Sons, Fine Art
Amsterdam

Anselm Feuerbach, *In the Mountains of Castel Montero*, 800 RM
Carl Spitzweg, *A Country Visit*, 400 RM
Adolph Menzel, *Clara Schumann in Concert*, 500 RM

Hans Erich stands with his back to Louie, reading, and as he finishes, he turns to him. His hands are shaking. Louie goes downstairs to the liquor cabinet and returns with two glasses and a bottle of whiskey. He leads Hans Erich to the table. They sit, they drink. The letter lies between them. His glass now empty, Hans Erich looks up. He shrugs. "Ve lose ze pentens," he says.

A Birthday Celebration

• • •

Hans Erich shrugs and, on the other side of the Atlantic, Heinz Seligmüller pulls his shoulders back and stands at attention. Two months short of his sixteenth birthday, he has been chosen from among twenty others in his division of the Hitler Youth Corps to serve at the Reich Chancellery in Berlin. Chosen, perhaps, because of his exemplary conduct and classic Aryan features. Or, more likely, because an uncle who already works at the Chancellery and appreciates the value, in exciting times, of a desk job, has put in a word with his superior. In any case, the young adjutant stands in line now, shoulders squared, as the most powerful man in Europe enters the room. It is the first time Seligmüller has seen him. He senses a weakening in his knees and, with feelings of shame and distress, a weakening in his bowel which he manages to control. Next to Seligmüller stands the principal agent for Special Assignment Linz, Herr Doktor Hans Posse, recently returned from Holland. Most of the paintings he has acquired have already been sent to Austria in anticipation of the construction of Hitler's museum there but, this being April 20th, Posse has withheld six of them, the artists are known to be among the Führer's favorite. The officers gathered at the Chancellery call "Heil Hitler!" and Seligmüller shoots out his right arm in salute as the great man strides down the long brown carpet. Although he is young and inexperienced, Seligmüller is, nevertheless, aware of the daring Posse has shown in deciding to keep these six paintings back. No one speaks as the Führer discovers them now on the wall to the right of his desk. His mouth, Seligmüller thinks, appears stern, disapproving. Afterward, he is unable to say how long he'd been standing at attention before he saw the Führer's lips begin to relax. A smile appears now beneath the great man's beautifully trimmed mustache, his lips part, his eyes grow moist. "With my very sincerest best wishes for your birthday, Heil unser Führer!" Seligmüller hears Posse say, and the art dealer bows, his right arm stretched towards the wall. There, in ornate, gold lacquered frames, hang six paintings. One is by Anselm Feuerbach, another by Carl Spitzweg, a third by Adolph Menzel.

Sergei Brodsky's Wartime Diary, 1941

• • •

Still further east and two months later, another young man, just a few years Heinz Seligmüller's senior, boards a train. Settling into his seat, he removes the cap from his pen, and opens a notebook to the next blank page. "Tsarskoe Selo, June 22, 1941," he writes, as the train pulls out of the station. "In desperation, we attempted to move the mosaics and carvings from the Amber Room to safety, but as I tried to lift the first panel from the wall, it crumbled in my hands. The other student interns have fled to their home towns. I cannot be the lone defender of Tsarskoe Selo. Catherine the Great's Summer Palace will be left to the advancing German Army. I cannot save it." Brokenhearted—and perhaps this is the beginning of his strange illness, a heart that has simply broken—Sergei Brodsky returns to his native city, Minsk. It too, he finds, has been decimated, the rich art collections that were its pride and heritage carted off to Germany. In November, as he waits for induction into the Russian army, reports come to him from those who live near the Summer Palace. The walls have been stripped of their Chinese silk panels and carved wood, the Amber Room dismantled, its gilt bronze candelabras and Florentine mosaics loaded onto military vehicles. A bomb set off beneath the Grand Gallery. It lies now in ruins, the mirrors framed in carved amber reduced to dust, and German soldiers are using the remains of the Chapel as a motorcycle garage. When Brodsky appears before the draft board, the commanding officer takes a look at the young art historian and knows what the physical subsequently confirms. Unfit for active duty, Sergei Brodsky will spend the next three years working in the Art Division of *The Extraordinary State Commission on the Registration and Investigation of the Crimes of the German-Fascist Occupiers and Their Accomplices and the Damage Done By Them to the Citizens, Collective Farms, Public Organizations, State Enterprises, and Institutions of the USSR.*

Shanghai: October 12, 1941

• • •

Immanuel Häring peddles up to the fried bread stand at the outdoor market on Chusan Road and parks his bicycle against an umbrella pole. The vendor, turning twirled yeast dough in boiling oil, spears a large strip with a wooden fork and hands it to him on a sheet of paper. "*Zhe zhe*," thank you, Immanuel's acquired a few words in Shanghainese in the last year and a half, some Japanese as well. He's got twenty minutes before he needs to type his column at the office of *The Shanghai Jewish Chronicle*. Time for fried bread, followed by a steamed bun. Maybe fried tofu. Last night's boxing match goes through his head, he's thinking of how to say knockout in Yiddish. Immanuel's fans love to read about Sam Lefko and Kid Ruckenstein, especially if one of them has defeated the latest Japanese champion. Boxing, soccer, concerts, an occasional film from MGM, Immanuel's reviews are read daily. It's better than the previous job, selling ad space in the *Chronicle* to restaurants and night clubs, cigarette companies, Coca Cola. *Koyf a Camel!*, he'd written, *Trink a Coke!* Immanuel's not an adman, he's a poet and a Communist. Still, selling ads had been a step up from that first job at Sassoon's Metropole Hotel and he's lucky to be here at all after Shanghai's Municipal Council had threatened to stop immigration, he and Hilde already on their way from Russia. Immanuel had been the guest speaker at the Moscow Soviet Jewish Writer's Union when they saw the headline, *Germany Invades Poland.* Hilde sold her grandmother's diamond ring, they bought tickets and boarded the Trans-Siberian Railroad that night, carrying little more than a suitcase apiece. At the first stop, Immanuel wired Cousin Oskar Häring who'd left for Shanghai eight months earlier. Arriving in Irkutsk, they received the reply: Come. Oskar met them at Whangpoo Harbor with landing permits, work permits, *kumsha*, uniforms: elevator operator, chambermaid, they slept in the hotel laundry room.

Immanuel moves to another stand, considers the steamed buns, one with pork? one with blue beans? and decides on one of each. Knockout in Yiddish. He'll knock off the article quickly, he's got a meeting with Ostropovich, then one with Levin at four. Ostropovich has been getting midnight visits from a couple of representatives of a local Japanese fancy food importer, Hayakawa is interested in Ostropovich's caviar connection. For *kumsha* and a cut in the business, the importer will see that there are no more visits. Immanuel will interpret and help with negotiations, he and Hilde can use the money. He might even place a bet at the races, the Manchurian ponies are scheduled to run today, Ostropovich might have a tip.

The rice curry at the stand across the road looks tempting. As he searches in his pocket for a coin, he's approached by a gaunt man with long, lice-ridden hair and skin like rice paper stretched across the bones of his face. Immanuel draws a pen and notebook from his satchel. "Skin like rice paper stretched across the bones of his face," he writes, and gives the beggar a coin.

Ostropovich will offer him good, strong tea from the samovar at The Black Cat and, if the cook's already come, borscht with black bread. But just in case she hasn't arrived by the time they're finished, Immanuel's taking no chance on being hungry because, from The Black Cat, he'll peddle over to XMHA, Levin's interviewing him. Rice curry, "*dzhin*." Immanuel will read his Trans-Siberian Railway poems, but he'll also talk about the Chinese hotel workers' union, they're on strike. Jewish refugees have been taken on as scabs, who can blame them, twenty-five cents an hour they get in the factories when they can get work at all, a hotel worker's thirty cents looks good to them, and this is what Immanuel will say on Levin's show: Stop taking crumbs of bread from each other's mouths! Sassoon gives you charity but does he pay you a fair wage, no! The roast chestnuts don't look half bad, "a three-cent bag, *dzhin*," workers of the world unite!

Aufbau, May 1944

How Good Is Your English: Here are seven statements and most common replies—listed in the wrong order—and you will have to determine which phrase is the correct reaction to each:

1) Today is my birthday	a) Don't mention it
2) I'm sorry I stepped on your toes	b) Many happy returns
3) Meet Mr. John Doe	c) I'm terribly sorry
4) You lost my fountain pen!	d) You're certainly welcome
5) Thank you for passing the salt	e) I beg your pardon
6) Abrakadabra . . .	f) How do you do?
7) It was awfully kind of you to help me out	g) That's quite all right

"You lost my fountain pen!" That might be "I beg your pardon," Bertha is thinking, but why is there an exclamation point, is it an accusation, perhaps it would be better to wish a happy return? Or simply to say how terribly sorry you are. As for "Abrakadabra," she can make nothing of it. Possibly it is a Turkish word strayed into the English language, but how would one respond? "That's quite all right"? "Don't mention it"? Bertha is aware that she must make an effort to improve her English, it will be an American baby and, although there are indications that the war is winding down, they will not be returning to Mannheim right away, that is certain. Bertha resolves to study. The weekly language column in *Aufbau* is a start, but it's not enough.

• • •

Annelene has looped her hand through a strap to steady herself as the train goes over the Manhattan Bridge. No seat today. She's folded a copy of *Aufbau* to the Arts and Culture section.

> The Metropolitan Museum of Art: the return of the Met's treasures which had been in protective, wartime storage these past two years, are now on exhibit.

The art treasures of this city she's been set down in remain distant, the week filled with Macy's, Sundays and evenings precious time for painting. She will be thirty-nine next month. She will visit the Metropolitan Museum.

• • •

> Independent businessman seeking partner who, like myself, is tired of being alone and wishes to land in the safe harbor of married life. In a position to make the woman I love happy." "Salesman with academic background, 51 years old, from upper-class milieu . . ." "Seeking sympathetic, cultured lady for matrimony and possible business partnership. My wealth is in cash and I possess first-class connections. Discretion guaranteed . . .

What's the use, Mutti is thinking. Annelene almost forty and determined not to be sensible, there's no point in trying again after the evening with the jeweler. She hadn't consulted her daughter first, this is true, but sometimes a mother needs to take the lead, and answering Mr. Loewy's ad, inviting him to dinner, had hardly been a crime.

• • •

The doors of the subway open at Canal Street and Chinese people crowd onto the train. Annelene, squeezed now between two other straphangers, folds the paper to the next section. The man to her left smiles. A suit, a tie. Clean shaven. Annelene returns the smile, and continues reading.

> On the 5th of March during the American invasion of Los Negros, an island in the Admiralty Group, Private Kurt Frankel was killed. He was born in 1921 in Hodonin in Czechoslovakia, and fled in 1940 with his parents, Daniel and Gusta Frankel, as well as his brother, Max. On the 10th of June, he left Petaluma, California where his family had settled, to join the Army. His brother is also serving in the US Army and is at this time stationed in England.

1921, twenty-three years old, comes all this way running, she is thinking, California, Petaluma, and leaves Paradise for a grave on the island of Los Negros.

• • •

Eliminate your German Accent!
by Lewis and Marguerite S. Herman
Here is a book that will explain and correct your
mistakes in English.
TALK AMERICAN

Perhaps she will order a copy. She'll speak with Hans Erich tonight.

• • •

Mocca torte—Sacher torte—
Napoleon—Cheesecake—Linzerschnitten
ECLAIR: THE VIENNESE KONDITOREI

Mutti will ask Annelene for directions. There must be a subway connection to West 72nd Street and the Eclair, maybe she will be able to convince Annelene to consent to a birthday celebration there. We cannot sit out the whole war on Newkirk Avenue.

• • •

Fur coat storage, tailoring, watch repair, jewelry. Jewelry: oh no, that awful evening when Mutti invited the jeweler from 47th Street, he'd come with a box of crème bonbons, wearing his loneliness like a shroud. A close call, pity-driven she just might have, and grateful that good sense had intervened, she turns the page to

Send Habana Cigars to Friends and Family in the Army

and remembers the farewell gift to her Shanghai lover, Leopold. It has been a while now, no lover, no love, the man who smiled exited two stops earlier, thirty-nine next month, and she steps out of the subway into the crowd making its way up the steps at 34th Street. The women are wearing felt hats and flowered dresses patterned with large camellias, tiny tea roses, asters, dahlias. Against the grays, blacks, beige browns of the subway walls and stairs and intersecting iron girders, the women are a garden emerging from the underground. Annelene arranges the colors on her palette as she makes her way through Macy's revolving door.

The Caves of Hohenwalde

• • •

Adjutant Heinz Seligmüller, re-assigned to active duty, is leaning against a truck, holding his belly. He can still feel the grainy texture on his tongue of the wurst they'd been given for lunch. Some were saying the sausage had been ground from the flesh of animals who were killed during the bombing of the Berlin Zoo. His stomach muscles begin to spasm. He looks for a latrine, it's to the left of the caves, and starts to run, deserting the crew who are unloading paintings from the truck. The bombings have increased this past year. All artwork is being removed from the city to a safe depot, it's become too risky to keep anything valuable at the Reich Chancellery. Three tunnels have been dug to a depth of forty-nine meters each in the caves of Hohenwalde, a village not far from Berlin. Military engines and equipment are already stored there. Seligmüller, now recovered, helps carry the crate with the Feuerbach, Spitzweg, and Menzel down into the last tunnel and deposits it between two other crates, one marked "Oriental Vases," the other, "Antique Arms."

Three Mothers

• • •

Bertha stops at the local library and checks out a copy of the Old Testament. She puts it on top of the groceries and, with difficulty, pushes the shopping cart along Newkirk Avenue. Her legs are swollen, it's the ninth month, soon she will be forty. Home now, she drops into an armchair, puts her feet up, and opens to Genesis.

In the beginning . . . evening and there was morning . . . dominion over the fish . . . evening . . . morning . . . took of the fruit, thereof . . . no . . . *Jared lived a hundred sixty and two years and begot Enoch . . .* Here it is: *The stranger said, 'About this time next year I will be sure to come back to you, and Sarah your wife shall have a son.' Sarah laughed and said to herself, 'Now that I am worn out and my husband is old, will I really know such happiness?'*

Bertha massages her legs and considers the groceries still in the cart. Now that I am worn out and Hans Erich already fifty, half as old as Abraham but still, not young, and that medical exam when will he. She turns the pages, skimming the text. There: *And God remembered Rachel, and God hearkened to her, and opened her womb. And she conceived, and bore a son, and said: "God hath taken away my disgrace."* Such happiness, such disgrace. Bertha rests, the weight of the book on her lap. Frozen spinach and broccoli are thawing, milk growing warm, she ought to get up. Instead, she shuts her eyes. Had the family even owned a Bible in Mannheim? She remembers the titles of so many of their books, packed hastily in boxes, auctioned, given away, sold, lost, gone, a Bible? She can't place it, but

Genesis belongs to a basic knowledge of western civilization, somehow she'd learned there were matriarchs, they were old, too old really, it wasn't quite decent. Sarah, Rachel. Bertha. A disgrace? No, certainly there'd been no disgrace in not having children, who thought of children in these years, there'd been only struggle and uncertainty that filled their days, such happiness, is that what this is? Bertha's pregnancy has been . . . unexpected. This seems to be the word most often used.

The following week, Hanna is born. The year is 1944. The baby is given the bedroom and Bertha has a convertible sofa installed in the living room for herself and Hans Erich. At night, she takes a chair and brings it close to Hanna's crib, pulls the blanket up around the sleepy child, and begins to sing softly, "*Guten abend, gute nacht. . . .*" As Hanna's eyes close, Bertha continues to sing. She sits, looking at Hanna's face in the moonlight. Sarah laughed, Rachel was no longer disgraced, and Bertha? Bertha is in love, for love it is for this child who has come into her life so . . . unexpectedly and, in addition to such happiness, she knows that she will never more live without fear.

Sergei Brodsky's Wartime Diary, 1945

• • •

Shortly after Hanna's birth, Sergei Brodsky and his colleagues from the Art Division of *The Extraordinary State Commission* are called to the Central Office of *The Committee of Arts of the Council of People's Commissars of the USSR*. They are a lean group, the Division's historians, restorers, painters, sculptors, these have been years of hunger, yet the officer explaining their next mission, Brodsky is thinking, has had no difficulty filling his uniform. Berlin, the officer says, and the Art Division becomes the newly created Trophy Brigade. Their orders are to find all artwork of value and have it sent to the Fatherland. Military uniforms are issued the next day, they will enter Germany disguised as officers of the Red Army. Recalling the destruction of Tsarskoe Selo and the plunder of Minsk, Brodsky puts on a captain's uniform, shoulders a heavy canvas bag, and sets off for the train station. Tucked in with his identifying documents is the wartime diary.

"*Berlin, May 6, 1945.* The Trophy Brigade is housed in a multiple dwelling on Drachenfelsstrasse in Karlshorst, the only suburb of Berlin that still has electricity. I know from my studies that *Drachen* means either kite or dragons, *Fels* is rock, yet this dreary suburb with its flat terrain suggests neither toys flown at leisure nor mythical creatures. White flags of surrender hang from the windows of the few buildings still standing, the black skeletal structure is all that is left of others. A wall here and there has survived, fleur de lis wallpaper intact. Piles of brick, stone, plaster lie in the street. People dig silently in the ruins, looking for something that once held meaning for them, unearthing now and then a hand, an arm, a body. We were driven from Karlshorst yesterday to the center of Berlin in a new Opel Admiral. Our German chauffeur takes great care to polish its surface. The metal shines. Perhaps this is a sign he longs for a mundane future. I carry the Baedeker that Mother's Great Uncle Fyodor Rostropovich brought back from his trip to Berlin in 1892. With its help, I was able to identify the Kaiser Wilhelm Memorial Church or, more accurately, the remains of this structure, which is now a pile of smoking rubble. Our chauffeur drives slowly through the city past burned out tanks, trucks, streetcars, fires still burning, buildings barely standing or in the process of collapsing. Drunken soldiers roam the streets, liberated Dutch and Polish slave laborers as well. I am barely able to concentrate on the task ahead but there is so little time. The Americans are eager to claim control of Berlin and all that is valuable."

"*Berlin, May 7, 1945.* I have been assigned to act as interpreter whenever necessary, and keep a record of all that is said and done by the two commanding officers of our unit, Major Serafim Druzhinin, curator of the Tretyakov Gallery, and Lt. Colonel Alexander Voloshin, stage director of the Moscow Circus. In our Red Army uniforms, it is as if we, the Trophy Brigade, are participants in a masquerade. I begin to feel as if I really were an officer. I fix my cap the requisite two finger widths above my eyebrows, and straighten my back. Tomorrow, we will begin our work in the anti-aircraft tower at the Zoo, the *Flakturm*, an enormous steel structure resembling a medieval fortress. Its walls are reinforced concrete, two and a half meters thick, the windows just slits protected by steel shutters, an ideal bomb shelter. Homeless refugees are living in its corridors, and hospital wards have been set up on the fourth level. We've been told that valuable works of art from museums and private collections have been hidden on the first and third levels."

"*Berlin, May 9, 1945.* Although Major Druzhinin is patient, he must see that I am having difficulty concentrating. It is hot, too hot for these absurd uniforms, the Red Army overcoat buttoned to the neck, it is simply too heavy for this time of year. Worse, in the heat, I can smell the blood in the pool where the lone surviving hippopotamus swims among the dead. Coming from beyond the anti-aircraft tower, there is a steady high-pitched shrieking. We have been told it is the trumpeting of the last elephant in Berlin's Zoological Garden, driven mad by the bombardments. Siam is his name. The remains of the other elephants have already been hacked to pieces and made into soap, our chauffeur tells us, and the starving populace of Berlin have taken to eating sausage ground from the flesh of crocodiles, monkeys, and brown bears."

"*Berlin, May 10, 1945.* The *Flakturm*, 6 AM [alone]: a small piece of gold, most likely a coin, in the palm of my hand. It is said to have belonged to King Priam of the *Iliad*, part of Schliemann's excavation, the treasures from Troy. I closed my fingers around it and felt for an empty pocket in my overcoat, then quickly opened my fist and dropped the piece into the chest waiting for transport. How easy it would have been. My heart . . ."

"*Berlin, May 11, 1945.* An old man wept as our soldiers took an axe to the last oak standing in the courtyard of the *Flakturm*. Can it be he is still able to mourn a tree? It hardly seems possible. The few left standing after the bombardment of the zoo have been sawn and hammered into crates for transporting artwork. Major Druzhinin has commandeered mattresses, blankets, and pillows from the hospital. The reliefs of the Pergamon Altar have been wrapped in bedding and lowered carefully through a hole in the wall of the *Flakturm*, then guided onto flat cars. I relay orders from Major Druzhinin to the old men, the women and the wounded German soldiers and young boys who are our work force. The day after tomorrow, we will leave for the village of Hohenwalde. Its caves are said to be a storage depot for some of the Reich's most precious artwork."

The Caves of Hohenwalde

• • •

Orders have been given to guard the area around the cave. It is rumored that military engines and equipment, and valuable art, are stored underground. However, there is no one to guard the Soviet 69th Army. Every man in his battalion, including Private First Class Yevgeny Mikhailov, has spent the last four years slaughtering and in fear of being slaughtered. Now that the war's over, those who've survived are no longer governable. Most are carrying whatever they've been able to walk away with, radios, watches, jewelry, furs. Mikhailov, too, has a watch in his bag, left on a table in a room where an old woman had stood shaking in a corner, guarding the trap door to a cellar, and he had known what was down there, a younger woman, maybe younger women, and he knew the watch had been an offering, a plea. He'd taken it and left. The boasting of the men in his unit disgusted him. Now, as the soldiers fall upon the treasures at Hohenwalde, crushing ancient vases and porcelain figures under their dancing feet, and gouging out the eyes of centuries old portraits, Mikhailov isn't surprised. He doesn't join them, he makes no move to stop them. He watches as a mad will to destroy the enemy all over again seizes the 69th Army. They cease only when Major General Vladimir Piankov, their commanding officer, arrives with a group of officers, a Trophy Brigade he calls them, and fires his gun into the air.

Sergei Brodsky's Wartime Diary, 1945

• • •

May 14,1945. We arrived in Hohenwalde early this morning and were met by the commander of the 69th Army, Major General Vladimir Piankov, who accompanied us to the underground shelters. What a terrible sight awaited us, a terrible tragedy. I could hardly bear to witness the destruction our own army has wrought, the loss of world treasures through ignorance and sheer willful lust for revenge. At the edge of the caves, where the soldiers have set up a fire for cooking, there is wood from crates that have been torn open, their contents strewn about. Precious paintings serve as fuel for heating water which is then stored in those ancient vases that have not yet been damaged beyond repair. I hardly had time to take in the full extent of the loss, I was urged to begin listing the salvageable art immediately as the area will soon be turned over to the Polish military administration. I made my way through ill-lit, crowded tunnels and gave orders to pry open the crates that were still intact. With the help of a carbide lamp and some candles, I attempted to view and record the contents of each. The crates were then nailed shut. Major General Piankov and several of his soldiers accompanied me. We hardly had time to linger, yet I could not help taking a second glance at the crate containing six paintings from the Reich Chancellery, nineteenth-century German art. I noticed they attracted the attention of the Major General as well. It is unlikely that he knows a great deal about art. I believe it was the note attached to the paintings that stirred his imagination. 'April 20, 1941, in celebration of the Führer's birthday, Heil Hitler!' The largest of the six is a landscape by Feuerbach. Anselm Feuerbach!, the subject of my dissertation in what seems a lifetime ago, to think I'd ever hold a work of his in my hands. Even under these circumstances, I can see it is a landscape from his time in Italy, an excellent example of his work, the density of color, the skillful rendering. It brought back the time I spent at the University Library researching my dissertation. How I long for the quiet of the stacks, the daily routine, the satisfaction and safety of an uneventful day. Reluctantly, I ordered the crate to be sealed and I moved on to other inventory. I would need at least six weeks to make a complete list of all that is here, but I will have only fourteen days at most.

The Caves of Hohenwalde

• • •

For two weeks, Private First Class Yevgeny Mikhailov accompanies Major General Piankov into the cave and assists in the opening and closing of wooden crates. He stands by as a young captain from the Trophy Brigade lists their contents. At the end of this time, on the evening of the day the Brigade concludes its work, Piankov summons Mikhailov to a hidden storage room. There is a particular painting, he says, not valuable, and assuredly of no interest to the Trophy Brigade. It would, he is certain, please his wife who has borne his absence these past four years with heroic stoicism, just a small memento it is, a testament to the victorious bravery of the Red Army. My wife plays the piano, he says, it is a portrait of just such a lady at a piano, and Piankov explains where it is to be found. Bring it here before dawn, he says, indicating a large chest, and he gives Mikhailov a knife to cut the painting from its stretcher, a key to the storage room, another to the chest, and a third to a jeep standing outside the Major General's quarters. When Mikhailov returns from Hohenwalde the next day, he opens the chest and finds it already filled to the top. Lighting a kerosene lamp, he discovers: rolled carpets, silverware, an accordion, a violin, jewelry, gold coins, several pairs of leather shoes, three cameras, a cuckoo clock, a typewriter, a set of gold-rimmed dishware including a porcelain teapot packed in soft furs, fox perhaps, and mink. He places Menzel's portrait of Clara Schumann on top and, as instructed, he locks the chest and hides the keys beneath a loose floorboard before returning to the barracks.

Things Disappear

• • •

Sergei Brodsky delivers his report to Major Druzhinin the day the artwork is moved from the caves of Hohenwalde to an empty slaughterhouse by the train station. Rain comes in through broken windows and holes in the roof, pelting cargo stored there for transport. From here, the crates will be loaded into boxcars and sent to Moscow's Kiev Station. Checking a copy of the cargo list for Train 176/1759, Brodsky has an impulse to see the Feuerbach once more. He is alone. He pries open the Chancellery crate, and as he draws forth the painting, an empty frame falls out. Brodsky breaks into a sweat. Removing his overcoat, he searches the crate. There'd been six paintings, now there are five. It is Menzel's *Portrait of Clara Schumann at the Piano* that is missing, he'll be held responsible, possibly accused of theft, denounced, it matters little that everyone is stealing, there are people who envy his appointment to the Trophy Brigade, they wouldn't hesitate, his only hope is that he might retrieve the original inventory list and somehow alter it. Brodsky returns to Drachenfelsstrasse, sick, he has only one plan, to throw himself on the mercy of his commanding officer. Major Druzhinin, however, is nowhere to be found. Frantic now, running through the corridor, he comes upon Druzhinin's superior, Lt Colonel Voloshin. "In my business," the circus director says as Brodsky breaks down and tells of the missing painting, "things disappear," and he sends the young man to the infirmary before boarding the train to Moscow.

Shanghai: July 17, 1945

"*Moo-dong . . . moo-dong . . . aya wei!*" The call of the honey cart driver awakened Hilde this morning as it did every morning before dawn. She heard the Chinese neighbor open the door to the privy and take out the wooden bucket they'd used the previous day and through the night, five Chinese families, four Jewish refugees including herself and Immanuel, all sharing the little house on Tongshan Road. "*Moo-dong . . . aya wei!*" The driver emptied the contents of the bucket into his cart. He'd sell it later for fertilizer. She listened to the neighbor scrubbing the bucket with a stiff bamboo brush and cold water, throwing pebbles in and rattling them around. This would go on for some time before the woman thrust the bucket back into a little roofless room behind the stairs, visible from each landing, didn't the word privy have some connection to private, but nothing was private here. In the meanwhile, the wheels of the cart set off again along the cobblestones. Hilde heard it stop at the next house, "*Moo-dong . . . moo-dong,*" and when she was dressed and on her way to work, her bicycle followed traces of the brown trail his cart had left behind.

It's noon now and Hilde is thinking of the peculiar poetry of his call as she rides home for lunch. It's the opening line of "The Honey Cart," the fifth in Immanuel's group of *Twelve Shanghai Poems*. Herr Loewenberg might be interested in a reading, she'll ask him this afternoon. Loewenberg is the owner of The Lion Bibliothek, Hilde his assistant. She's worked for him since the time when the bookstore was still in the International Settlement, before the Japanese ordered them to move to the Hongkew Ghetto. No longer able to import books from Europe, The Lion's become a lending library. Hilde veers sharply to avoid hitting a pothole in the street and puts her hand into the basket behind her. Lunch is still there, steamed pork buns. Tonight they'll eat at the Café Louis, Immanuel's helped the Eisfelders bypass restrictions on using wheat, they're sure to get a piece of Black Forest Chocolate Cake.

That sound again. The drone of US bombers flying overhead out of Okinawa. For the past two months, they've flown over the ghetto in the direction of Whangpoo Harbor and beyond, their destination, the factories in the suburbs. The children in the ghetto stop playing and cheer each time a plane flies by, its steel-gray underbelly just above the clouds. Today, it seems, more of the aircraft is visible and the noise it makes, that searing *shhhh*, is louder. Still, she can hear three students from the Mir Yeshiva talking as she approaches the corner of Ward Row Lane. Huddled together in long, belted black coats, white shirts, black hats, penguins stranded in Shanghai, identical triplets, arguing just as they had in Poland, some point of Talmud she supposes, but aren't they always arguing, she thinks, well-fed though they are, some special deal between the Orthodox in America and the Relief Committee, Immanuel cannot abide them, and just as she turns the corner, Hilde rides past a corpse lying in the road, it's not the first time. This one, though, is a baby. It's wrapped in rags. Only its little gray head is visible. The Blue Cross truck's missed it, perhaps it was set out after the collection, and the day's ease is abruptly shattered and becomes that day almost a year earlier when she'd gone to the room on Chusan Road, Ostropovich had given them the address. She'd had to plead with the doctor. You're married, Didner had said, please reconsider. One of the bar girls stumbled out of a back room as he spoke, her face white and anguished, but Hilde persisted, there was no way in this place, no way, and then it was over. He'd been kind but firm as he woke her later, she'd have to leave, this was his home as well as his office, she couldn't stay, and she edged her way slowly and in pain along Chusan Road, remembering the unexpected extremity of pain as the metal prong pulled at what would not easily let go, she cried out, *Aya!*, and heard Didner, *Shtill!*, angry now, angry certainly, she thought, to find himself here in one shabby room in Shanghai delivering up the unborn to Soochow Creek. *Shtill*, he said, he'd be thrown out if the other tenants complained, but he'd been kind afterwards, when? a half hour later? an hour? as he woke her from a deep sleep. Exhausted, she dressed slowly, and made her way along Chusan Road to the corner of Wayside. Lowering her body into a chair at the outdoor café, she sat, alone, under a large umbrella, and ordered hot tea though the temperature must have been close to a hundred, but she was shivering and the strips of cloth between her legs felt cold and wet. No other way, she thought, as she held the cup in her hands, no way, she moaned softly, today, too, she thinks, no way, as she pedals slowly home, but questions herself still if this is true, if what landed in Soochow Creek would not have had his brilliance, his strength, his, Hilde will not go through this again today, she will not think this, in fact cannot think this because, in the next moment, she's thrown from her bicycle as Allied bombs meant for the Japanese radio station next to the Hongkew Ghetto hit, instead, a row of houses and, in the ensuing fire and smoke, burning limbs and headless torsos rise into the air before falling onto the cobblestones of Tongshan Road.

Lost/Found/Lost

• • •

The response to Mutti's query in *Aufbau* comes from Melbourne in November of 1945. "I do recall Immanuel Häring's sports coverage for the *Jewish Chronicle* in the years I lived in Shanghai and, if I'm not mistaken, there was a lending library in the International Settlement where the shop assistant's name was also Häring. I'm almost certain I remember that because I asked if she were related to the journalist and . . . ," they are alive! She contacts the Shanghai division of the Red Cross, they are alive, only then does she allow herself to feel their absence. Mutti, who rarely cries, has begun to weep, and it is several days before she is able to stop. She sends a telegram and receives a letter from Hilde. "We posted letters to Elisabethstrasse, then to Antje Schmidt's family in Ilvesheim, but there was no response. We feared the worst. But you are alive! Alive and living in America! We will come to you as soon as we can. It is difficult for Eastern European nationals to get visas to the United States. I will remain in Shanghai with my husband until he has his papers, hopefully that will be before Christmas. How I long to hold you all in my arms, little Hanna too!" But it is two more years before Immanuel is cleared for emigration and these two, now that their survival is no longer uncertain, seem longer than the previous six years of separation. Only now do they allow themselves the hope that Hans Erich's sister and father have avoided the deportation to southern France, to the internment camp Gurs, that they've somehow survived, nothing is certain. Letters go from

Newkirk Avenue to Antje Schmidt, to Frank Morav, to the Red Cross and the French authorities. No one responds. It's too soon after the end of the war, they tell themselves, who knows if the postal system in Europe is even in operation. Hans Erich is despondent. In the evening, when the weekly edition of *Aufbau* arrives, the family gathers at the kitchen table. Bertha is reading tonight from the International Search column. There is someone in Brazil looking for someone from Belgrad, another in Toronto looking for family from Vienna, Los Angeles looking for Amsterdam. No one is where he or she should be and the amount of human misery condensed into each two-line classified is overwhelming. "If she is alive," Mutti says, "Ruth will find us." The women decide to place an ad, Mutti is a member of *Aufbau*'s New World Club, an ad is affordable. They receive a response from a survivor of Gurs, a former resident of Mannheim living in Chicago after her release from Bergen Belsen. Herr Silberstein did not survive their first month in the camp, she writes, she is quite certain of that, there was hunger, filth, cold, many of the oldest perished, and Fraülein Silberstein, who was known to many of the internees, "selflessly attending to those in the prison's hospital," followed her father shortly before the writer boarded the train to the east. She may be mistaken, they think, how can she be certain after all she's lived through. She might not be capable of recall. She might not be in her right mind, how can she. They will wait for confirmation from the Red Cross before giving up. After another five months, it comes.

A Dacha in Rublevo

• • •

It is the winter of 1946 and Railway Official Pjotr Khrapchenko is standing at Moscow's Kiev Station. Eight boxcars loaded with wooden crates have just arrived. They've made their way slowly from Berlin through Poland across White Russia, stopping, starting up, unable to move forward till repairs had been made to the tracks destroyed by the war. Sheets of ice cover the exterior. Inside the train it is cold and damp, the only cars that have heat are the officer's quarters. The contents of the crates, it is rumored, are valuable, although assuredly damaged. Snow and sleet have made their way through the ill-fitting window frames of the box cars. The crates' wooden slats are warped and buckling, sodden. A blizzard whirls around customs officials as they attempt to register the number of each crate against the few existing cargo lists, and as the temperature sinks again towards midnight, one after another they retreat to the warmth of the railway waiting room and fall asleep. Khrapchenko hardly feels the cold. It is the winter of his love for Praskovia Sokolova, first glimpsed at the railway station coming from her home in the city, her servant carrying hat boxes and instructing porters on the transport of luggage to the family dacha. Praskovia Sokolova, slim, tall, regal, she is Anna Karenina, and Khrapchenko, a man enflamed, the tips of his mustache give off sparks. Alone at midnight, he forces open one crate after another to find treasures worthy of his love. He will bring them to the dacha just outside Moscow in the village of Rublevo where Sokolova, the wife of a Red Army General said to be missing in action, is waiting. For the General, for Khrapchenko, it hardly seems to matter, she is waiting, her life suspended in unknowing, the days are long, the nights longer. Khrapchenko takes a crowbar and works quickly. Within an hour, he has found what he needs.

The next evening, he brushes his blue serge uniform and tightens a wide leather belt around his trim waist, straightens his cap with the red star, hammer, and sickle, and shoulders a railway postman's leather bag. With a last look in the mirror, he stiffens the wings of his mustache, and takes off for Rublevo. Sokolova receives him in the parlor. She dismisses the maid. He takes the bag from his shoulder, opens it, kneels, and one by one, lays the treasures on the sheepskin rug at her feet. A fox fur with tiny paws and a head. A necklace of amber with matching earrings. Two Meissen figurines, a Harlequin, a Columbine. And a small painting in a carved, gold lacquered wooden frame, a gentleman extending a bouquet to a country lass on the doorstep of her cottage. An arc of roses in bloom clings to the doorjamb, a rhomboid intersected with the letter S can be seen in the pastoral undergrowth. The rhomboid is the Spitzweg insignia, although Khrapchenko does not know this, and even if he did, he would not care. He is busy kissing the lady's shoe and, as there is no protest, he kisses her ankle and continues on past her calf. He hears a sigh, comes out from under her skirt, and pushing the fox fur to the side, he pulls Praskovia Sokolova gently to the floor.

Letter from Ilvesheim, September 9, 1946

• • •

Herr Doktor Hans Erich Silberstein
Newkirk Avenue
Brooklyn, New York
United States of America

Most esteemed Herr Doktor:

We deeply regret to inform you that our beloved aunt, Frau Antje Schmidt, was killed in March of 1945 in the Allied firebombing of the city of Mannheim. She was our strength in times of desolation. We feel her absence with great sorrow as we feel the absence of her nephew, my brother Alfons Schmidt, who sacrificed his young life at the Battle of Stalingrad. May they rest in the light of God's love for all eternity.

With regard to the fate of your father and sister, I regret to say that I can only confirm what you already know, that those Jewish families who remained in Mannheim and the surrounding area until 1940 were ordered to assemble at the freight depot on the 22nd of October. It is only now that we have become aware of their destination, an internment camp in France by the name of Gurs. Our aunt came to us in great distress that evening after seeing them off at the train station. She'd made sure that both your father and sister had taken along additional warm clothing and winter shoes. She was especially fond of Fraülein Silberstein, whose dignity and concern for her father were evident even in this time of extreme hardship. Of their fate, I can tell you, unfortunately, nothing more. I pray you will all be reunited in the future.

As for the wooden crate you inquired about in your letter, I am sorry to say we have found no sign of it or of the contents you have listed. Should it be found, we will be in touch with you immediately.

As we are living under circumstances of extreme deprivation, we would be grateful for the receipt of any provisions you can spare.

Respectfully yours,

Caroline Klein

Dielweg
Ilvesheim, Germany

The Travelers

• • •

Earlier that day, Annelene had been sketching in the studio that is now her home, a large room on the top floor of a Victorian single-family house, not far from the apartment she'd shared with Mutti. Abundant light comes through the windows. She's set up her easel, paint and brushes, there's a bed behind a screen in one corner and a small kitchen down the hall. It's quiet, a place to work undisturbed.

The letter that came this morning is in her pocket and a catalogue of the exhibition at the Czechoslovak Institute in London lies open in her lap. She's been looking at the photos of the paintings her cousin had shown there, and one in particular, *The Travelers*. "I am not without hope that this will find you. The official I spoke with at HIAS told me they have had some success in locating family," Marie-Louise had written in the letter that accompanied the catalogue. Bent and torn and sent a year earlier, October 1945, the package had arrived with news of her cousin's flight from Vienna to London, news of Beckmann and of her brother Karl who'd remained in Austria. Annelene is thinking now of the summer in Hinterbrühl, the von Motesiczky country estate near Vienna. There's a photo of the five cousins, perhaps Bertha saved it, 1913 it would have been, just before the first war. She was eight, Marie-Louise seven, Karl and Bertha both nine, Hilde just a baby, and she remembers now the excitement of playing with that cousin who climbed trees and walked on slippery stones across a stream, shouting to them all to come over. It was the first time she understood the difference, boys leapt and climbed, girls didn't. Or most girls didn't, she'd thought then, and, defiantly, she'd stepped out onto a stone to follow Karl across the stream, fell, the children's nanny scolded as she pulled Annelene out of her wet dress. After the war, they returned to Hinterbrühl and there he was again, he was tall, he played the cello and read Hermann Hesse, he was excitement, adventure and something else now, she was fourteen by then, something in her responded to his presence differently.

Annelene takes the letter from her pocket and unfolds the thin blue airmail paper. "Mother and I moved to Amersham outside of London in 1942 to escape the Blitz, and it was there that I learned of his work for the Resistance, the arrest by the Gestapo, his death in the prison hospital at Auschwitz. Before Karl became ill, I was told, he'd asked that his cello be sent to him. There seems to have been an orchestra in Auschwitz that might have saved his life had he been well enough to play in it. The night the war ended, Mother and I, Oskar Kokoschka and the Bulgarian writer, Elias Canetti, their wives, and a few others from the emigrant community sat by the wireless listening to Churchill's speech, holding the wine glasses and brandy snifters that Karl had sent along with our furniture and books and so many other things. With the soft light from the fireplace, our Biedermeier chairs and tables, the paintings in their gilded frames, we might have been back in our drawing room at Hinterbrühl so anxious had Karl been to settle us in the comfort we'd always known. And as Churchill's speech ended and voices of the crowd singing 'Land of Hope and Glory' came through the static, I wept to think he might have been here had I insisted that he join us. 'It's not the case that I am courageous,' he wrote in one of his last letters, 'it's just that I am not Jewish.' Mother's conversion, our baptism, he was not Jewish. Those in power disagreed. Karl had a wonderful intellect, but a wonderful capacity as well for denial. He was a dreamer. My only comfort is the thought that my poor brother was capable of believing in something greater than himself and that his belief sustained him to the end. As we sat by the fireplace that night, each of us thought of what we had gained but, more so, what and who had been lost. For me and for Mother, it was Karl. Family as well, friends. Language. Heimat. We will live as refugees from now on, outsiders all of us, occupying this piece of land or that, forever adrift."

Annelene turns back to the photo of *The Travelers*: "Four figures adrift in a small boat surrounded by a dark and threatening sea," Canetti had written in his foreword to the catalogue. Wearing only a necklace and a bracelet, a naked woman sits at the center of the painting clutching a long brown cylindrical object, her expression sad or, possibly, contemplative. In contrast, the clothed woman next to her looks cheerfully at herself in a large mirror. A young man with one leg overboard in the waves and a simple female figure huddled in the back complete the group. Painted, Marie-Louise had written, "in 1940 in London, just after we'd arrived from Zurich by way of Amsterdam. Worn out by the move from one country to the next, settling and resettling for short stays in the homes of relatives, in hotels, furnished flats, rented lodgings, I nevertheless set up my easel, feeling the urgency to begin again. Max had written from Amsterdam where he and Quappi now live—'Damn it, Pizchen, paint a few good pictures and the world will become beautiful again.' Had he written no more than my nickname, I'd have begun again. The last time I saw him, it was just after he was no longer allowed to teach in Frankfurt and his room in the National Gallery had been closed to the public. We met in Berlin for a New Year's celebration and I remember how he raised his champagne glass, 'Here we are all together again,—Frankfurt—Berlin—Paris—it's just a change of the stage set. Unimportant! Wherever I can work and find friends,' he said, 'I am at home.'

"So there it was, I set the canvas on the easel and all I desired was to paint and dream, and from the dream, came this tiny boat unmoored, unnavigable, filled with refugees not knowing where it would take them. Like most others in our circumstances, we couldn't know where the journey would end, onto which shore we'd be thrown, China, America. We brought just a few things with us, those that were most meaningful, hoping their weight would ground us as the ground disappeared and all that we knew receded in the distance. Amid the hectic craziness, there were times I felt we'd boarded a Ship of Fools, that we'd found ourselves in that Hieronymus Bosch painting. In order to counter Mother's lifelong tendency towards depression, I found myself possessed by a desperate cheerfulness and an uncharacteristic determination to go forward and escape the sounds of Sieg Heil! Sieg Heil! that surrounded us in '37.

"So that is the origin of *The Travelers*. A visitor to my studio the other day asked about the brown cylindrical object. I laugh to think of all the different interpretations. His: a Torah scroll. No, I told him, it is a Wurst, but the Wurst is a Torah scroll for this woman. Ever Max's students, we seek to be truthful. Max does not care for *The Travelers*, you know how he cautioned us against creating fantasy paintings. Kokoschka, although often my most severe critic, counters his argument, and Canetti is always ready with praise. He tells me that every picture I paint will enter the history of art. Such rubbish. Would that I had the faith in my ability that he has—but why not work as if this will be true. We shall see. When Mother and I moved to Amersham, he set up his study and his library in one of our rooms, and came every day to work. It is difficult, especially in exile, to believe in nothing, and Canetti certainly inspires belief. Like Max, he believes in the transcendence of death through art and I am pulled along, wanting to believe.

"Beloved cousin, I cannot be certain that this will reach you, but should we have the great good fortune to find one another, please write immediately to the address above, Maida Vale, where I now live with my life partner and soulmate, Elias Canetti. Let me know that you and the family are safe. And that you are painting."

Annelene folds the letter and puts it back into her pocket. It's dusk now, the day's disappeared, the branches of the oak outside her window a black silhouette against the sky. From her corner, she can make out the easel and the outline drawn earlier that day on the canvas. *Straphangers*, figures in a subway car crowded together reading the headline on the front page of *The World Telegram*: WAR IS OVER! Yes, she'll write, we are safe. And I am painting.

But no longer today.

Adrift? Annelene considers. There is Macy's, and when most of the men had been sent overseas, she'd been promoted, she supervises four other women doing layout for advertising. There is the daily commute, the daily routine, daily chores. There is necessity. And there is exhaustion and there is getting past the exhaustion to paint on weekends and holidays. And there is little time or inclination to consider her state, adrift or grounded, she will carry on and, yes, she will paint.

The room has grown dark now. And because she cannot bear to think about the fate of her cousin Karl, she thinks instead of the evening ahead. In another hour, the mathematician from Düsseldorf, not a life partner, hardly a soulmate, a man traveling as they'd been on the ocean liner from Shanghai, destination New York, he'll come with flowers, she'll cook, this time she'll agree, there will be some closeness, some comfort, no more than that but enough for both, and Annelene will get down to *Straphangers* tomorrow.

Plundered/Replundered

• • •

They are out for a walk, she and Hans Erich. Hanna is four. It's autumn and she stops to collect leaves that lie scattered along the pavement. She chooses carefully, only the brightest colors, avoiding torn leaves and ones with faded curled edges. She'll give the most beautiful ones to her mother and bring bouquets to Mutti and Annelene. Hanna and her father don't speak, she's already understood that a gentle silence is best in caring for Hans Erich. Just her presence, her step keeping pace with his, will do. They turn onto Coney Island Avenue now, the main thoroughfare. Her father is holding her hand as they pass the antique and secondhand stores, then he's not holding her hand, he's rushed to the door of one of the stores and left her standing on the sidewalk. He is calling to someone and his voice is loud and excited. Her father, who is usually quiet, is shouting now and pointing to a painting propped up against a pair of candlesticks in the window. The picture reminds Hanna of Prospect Park, the long expanse of grass, the trees. There's a tiny figure, a woman. Hanna edges closer to the doorway.

"Soldie' comes in," she hears the shopkeeper say. "Says he picked it up over there. Says he liked the pitcha, gave the owne' some cigarettes, y'know, y'could get anything f'cigarettes. Tells me I should see what I can get." Hans Erich asks to see the painting. He holds it carefully, turns it over. *Wiesengrund mit Obstbaümen*, *Field with Fruit Trees*, is written on the back of the canvas, and the words "*Louis pinxit quod tes-*

tat Hans Thoma Eysen." Barely able to speak now, he asks the price. Then adds hastily, in a rare moment of cunning, "My vife likes trees."

"Two bucks, it's yaws," the shopkeeper says, and as Hans Erich seems to hesitate, the man says, "Look at the frame—that alone's worth two bucks." Breathing with difficulty, Hans Erich goes through the pockets of his jacket and finds a dollar and twenty cents. "Here," he says, laying the money on the counter. "You vait. I come beck vith the money. Fifteen minutes, t-ten minutes, I come beck." Hans Erich is halfway down the street before he remembers her. He runs back and grabs Hanna's hand.

"Louis Eysen," he yells as he runs past Bertha through the door of the apartment. "Dieser Idiot hat ein Bild von Louis Eysen, er hat keine Ahnung. Zwei Dollar!" And he reaches up to the highest shelf at the back of the coat closet and draws out a small metal box. Undoing the latch, he removes a dollar bill and runs out the door.

Visitors

• • •

Three women are sitting on the living room sofa. One is her mother, the other Tante Leni. Hanna has just met the third woman and is sitting on her lap. This is Tante Hilde, and she is visiting. Tante Hilde has a sad, warm smile like her mother and Tante Leni, and her hair is the same color as theirs, although hers is braided and wrapped around her head like a crown. She has given Hanna a Chinese cloth doll with a shiny red and gold dress. Hanna holds on to the precious gift and Hilde holds on to her, resting her mouth in her hair, pressing her cheek to hers, stroking her knee. Hanna is enveloped, protected, and at the same time, aware of a struggle in the room. Mutti is saying, "Why not," and Tante Hilde, "Canada." Something is being disputed and, possibly, it has to do with the man sitting next to the piano in a large chair with wheels. Every now and then, she turns her head to look at him but when she sees he is smiling at her, she tucks her head into Tante Hilde's arm and holds the Chinese doll more tightly. This, she has been told, is her Onkel Immanuel. He wears black gloves and moves through the living room by turning the wheels on the chair with his hands. Towards the end of their visit, several days from now, she will let him lift her to his lap and, with Tante Hilde behind them pushing the chair, they will go for a picnic at the Parade Grounds. This is a fine way to travel. Her uncle and aunt are laughing, they teach her to say "*Tsu eyns, zwey, dray.*" These are words to a song, and they sing it as they roll home. Then they are gone, they have left for Canada to what remains of the Häring family, and Hanna will follow their lives through letters and an occasional visit, and when Louie sings in Yiddish, she remembers Hilde standing behind Immanuel's chair, leaning against it, her arms around her husband's chest, her cheek to his, smiling.

The Black Market

• • •

The dacha of Marshall Georgy Zhukov, deputy supreme commander of the Red Army, has been searched by Stalin's agents and found to contain treasures of enormous value originating in Germany. Zhukov is denounced and banished beyond the Urals. Yevgeny Mikhailov, formerly Private First Class Mikhailov, is once again summoned to his former commanding officer, Major General Vladimir Piankov. It is the beginning of 1948, there is a rumor that certain comrades from the former 69th Army are trading on the black market. They are doing well. Others, including Mikhailov and his rapidly growing family, barely have enough to eat. Piankov arranges to meet him one evening in a part of the city with shut down warehouses and dim lighting. Zhukov, he whispers, and he confesses his terror. He has enemies, he says, men who are jealous of his military success and of the few mementos he'd acquired for his wife. His enemies would fight for the honor of denouncing him to the MGB. Mikhailov is an honest man, he'll help him, he will have to help him, and Piankov makes a move as if to kneel there on the cobblestones. The following week, on three successive evenings shortly before midnight, Mikhailov arrives at the home of his former commanding officer with his daughter's wooden sled and a heavy sheet of black tarpaulin. Piankov tearfully divests himself of the carpets, the silverware, the gold-rimmed et cetera, and, weeping, Menzel's *Portrait of Clara Schumann at the Piano*. The black-market quicksand sucks in the treasures.

Mutti in the Heights

• • •

Mutti sits under a hair dryer reading this week's edition of *Aufbau*. Her meeting with the lawyer is at three o'clock, this appointment with the beautician has been well-timed. A dab of red, no one would guess she is seventy-two. She turns the page and there's the ad again. *United Restitution Organization: Legal Aid available free of charge to victims of the Nazi Persecution. Help in filing claims for indemnification. Restitution and compensation for loss of liberty, health, profession, property, employment, and the loss of parents and family.* Loss. Who'd ever heard of Gurs, who could have imagined such a place, murder is not loss, it's murder. And Hans Erich unable to study for. And because she is determined not to think of Gurs, Mutti thinks instead of the rosewood secretary. The Bechstein. The wingback chair with the embroidered footstool. The Feuerbach, Spitzweg, Menzel, last heard of nine years earlier in a letter from Gronewicz. Something about an art dealer from Dresden, something about the city of Linz. Something in *Aufbau* later about a storage depot in Austria, a saltwater mine, a cache of paintings, it might still be possible to recover, if only Hans Erich were more. "*Schon trocken?*" Already dry? the beautician asks Mutti, removing the metal helmet from her head and touching her hair. *Schon trocken? Ja! Jawohl!* All that Mutti has longed for in these ten years of exile, it's here, she's found it today, *Jawohl!*

Wearing a pink worsted suit, matching pumps, and white gloves, she'd gone down into the subway that morning, and surrounded by noise and people from every conceivable part of the world, guarding her purse, at one stop Chinese people had gotten on, she followed Annelene's directions carefully, transferring to another train after walking through a long filthy tunnel. And coming up from the subway at 167th Street, there they were, her people, there it was, *her* neighborhood. The *Metzger*, the *Bäckerei*, the *Friseur*, *Aufbau* sold at every newsstand, *Heimat!* these few blocks of upper Manhattan, Washington Heights. Mutti has come home. She will live here. If it's America at all where she must live, then it will be here. After her appointment with the lawyer, she decides, she'll take herself to the Cafe Berlin, it's at the corner, she passed it on the way to the beautician, they'll have good strong coffee. Black Forest Cake. Inquiring in German, how good it is to say the words, confident she'll be understood, she asks directions to the office for legal aid. It's not far, second street on the left, the beautician says, helping her into her coat, "*auf wiedersehen, auf wiedersehen.*" She will live here.

And now, as she's shown into the office of Herr Fleischmann, the legal representative for the United Restitution Organization, Mutti experiences a moment of grace. Standing before her is Friedrich Fleischmann, Fritz!, Fritz Fleischmann, Mannheim class of '96, and he will help her to the Heights. Later that day, over coffee and Black Forest Cake, it will be confirmed what she surmised in that first moment, Fritz is alone, widowed under terrible circumstances, emigrated to America with the first transport after the liberation of Dachau, and he's longing for the comfort of a home, a German home.

"Liselotte Augusta Hohenemser Dubrovsky," he reads from the card the secretary has handed him, and he raises his eyes, finds her extended hand with both of his. "Liselotte Augusta Hohenemser. Lotte? Is it you? Is it really you?"

Hanna and Theresa

• • •

Another snowflake lands on Hanna's mitten and disappears into the wool. Snow has been falling since early evening of the night before, it's the first snowfall of the season. The railing in front of Theresa's building is covered by a thin white layer. Hanna runs her finger along its loops, exposing the black wrought iron underneath. Her mittens are cold and damp. Neighbors going to work walk by as she waits for Theresa. The super hasn't cleared the steps or the pavement yet, and the neighbors' boots have left their shape on the walkway leading down from the front door. Hanna's thinking of the fresh tracks she and Theresa will make on the way to school. Theresa is her friend, they have secret talks. Hanna won't tell her, though, about the thick woolen homemade pants under her skirt, the leggings. Her mother's insisted she wear them. She'll burrow in behind the coats in the closet as soon as she gets to school and slip them off. As far as Hanna can tell, no other first grader wears this kind of leggings. Her coat is different from the other children's as well. It's a long, dark, worsted coat, and it's large, it will last more than one season. Annelene bought it with her employee discount at Macy's. It reaches to the top of Hanna's boots, covering the hated leggings and leaving room for a second wool cardigan. Despite the extra layers, she's starting to feel the cold in her thin arms and legs.

Theresa comes charging out of the building now, nearly slips coming down the stairs, grabs hold of the railing. "Snow!"

she yells, and she throws her sturdy body down on the sidewalk, opening and closing her legs and moving her arms up and down at her sides. She stands up slowly, and carefully steps out of the shape her body's left in the snow. "An angel," she says. "Like us." Theresa's family are angels, there's no doubt, it says it on their bell: D'Angelo. From her bedroom on the second floor, Hanna can look down over a narrow alleyway into the D'Angelo kitchen. She watches Theresa's mother chopping tomatoes and garlic at a counter, adding herbs, olive oil, never measuring, with a sure hand she throws everything into a pot on the stove. A nylon stocking twisted into a headband holds back Mrs. D'Angelo's black curls. Theresa often sits at the kitchen table doing homework and talking to her mother. Sometimes her older brother, Anthony, comes into the room. Towards evening, Theresa's father joins them. He is broad and muscular but not as tall as his wife. When he stands behind her, pressing closely up against her, Hanna sees his little mustache touching the back of Mrs. D'Angelo's neck. Sometimes Theresa's grandfather, Mr. Forte, is there for lunch. He's small and brown, his nose is long, his body straight. Forte, Theresa tells her, means strong. Mr. Forte is a tailor. He made Theresa's coat and her summer skirts and he will make the white frilled dress she will wear for Communion next year. The bridal dress. Mr. Forte wears three-piece suits, even in summer. He carries a cane and twirls it as he walks down Newkirk Avenue. At lunch, Mrs. D'Angelo sets a delicate glass at his place and fills it with red wine. From her window, Hanna watches the D'Angelos bow their heads before they begin to eat. "That's grace," Theresa's told her.

If she stands on the seat of the toilet in the bathroom and opens the window, Theresa can lean out and call up to Hanna across the alleyway. A spindly ailanthus grows there by metal garbage cans and weeds that flower in the spring. The super has parked his motor bike up against the brick wall.

"Pssst, Hanna," Theresa calls, "hey, wake up, you," and Hanna bounds out of bed and opens her window. She misses Theresa those two weeks in July when the D'Angelos stay with their family in the country. Last summer, Theresa says, her Uncle Vinnie, Aunt Fiona's husband, chopped off the head of a chicken and it ran around the barn without its head. When it stopped, Mrs. D'Angelo cooked it for supper. Hanna's decided that if she's asked to go with the D'Angelos to the country, she'll say she's busy.

New Year's Eve, 1950: Another Masked Ball

• • •

Annelene tightens the waist of her short black dress, little more than a chemise really, and adjusts the garters of her stockings, which are also black. Several inches of thigh are exposed. She picks up the pink clown's hat with red pompoms, puts it down again and takes a drag on her cigarette, then she wipes the tears from her eyes and begins to pull a black mask over them, but the tears come more quickly now, streaking her white makeup. This will not do. "Tears are for slaves," he'd said that night in Frankfurt, twenty-two years earlier. An artist puts his feelings on canvas, he told them, as his students stood at their easels listening, "only on canvas." And now Max Beckmann is dead, his heart suddenly given way four days earlier in Central Park, and not even now, she's sure of it, had he somehow been here at the Brooklyn Museum attending the New Year's Eve Ball, attending his own wake as it's come to be, not even now would he have condoned an elaborate expression of mourning. And so they're going ahead with it, honoring the man who'd loved masked balls, who'd maintained it was costume, not nudity, that revealed the Self. We are our fantasies, our dreams, he'd told them, his students at the Academy.

Annelene dries her tears, powders her face once more, and leaves the ceramics studio that is serving as a cloak room for this evening's ball. She fixes the mask in place and steps into the crowd. Some guests, out of misguided feelings of respect for the deceased, have ignored the invitation's request to come as a favorite painting, and are wearing black suits and formal dress. But others have taken the opportunity to transform themselves. There's Millet's sower, Manet's boy playing a fife, and his bartender at the Folies-Bergère. A group of women with good legs have come as Degas' dancers, and a colleague who'd always been loud and abrasive has come as the Mona Lisa. Annelene's appearance causes a disturbance, she is aware of it, you can't step out of a Max Beckmann painting under any circumstance and have it go unnoticed, but under these particular circumstances, there are some who will consider it poor taste. Others, homage. For Annelene, it is neither. She is grieving. She has not considered the implications of her costume. It is simply what she must wear. She might have come as any of his red-haired women, the fishwife holding a blue cod to her naked chest, the ballerina amazon. The mother in purple, large pink breasts exposed, holding the prodigal son, Beckmann, who else, in her arms. She'd chosen instead to come as Columbine, green, violet, and pink, masked and ready for Carnival, just as she'd come to him, of this she's certain, in the middle of the night, all these years since leaving Frankfurt, come to him just as he'd come to her. How vivid these dreams had been, how much more vivid they've become since the evening this past September when they'd stood opposite each other for the first time in twenty-two years at a faculty meeting of the Brooklyn Museum's art school. They were colleagues now, Annelene instructing a night school drawing class, Beckmann come just that autumn to teach a master class for advanced students.

"Annelene," he'd said. "Yes," she'd answered. "Annelene Dubrovsky," he'd said, no surprise in his voice or his face, she was certain he knew, had always known as she'd known, they would not leave this world without finding each other again. He leaned forward and put his cheek to hers and, as he lingered there, their tears held them together.

Jones Beach

• • •

The temperature's in the nineties, the forecast's a hundred. Bertha, remembering Dubrovsky summers at the North Sea, stands on the sidewalk in front of their building as Hanna takes off with the D'Angelos in their new Chevrolet. Mr. D'Angelo is the first on Newkirk Avenue to own an automobile. It's mustard colored with green plastic upholstery that smells like fish. Hanna, sitting between Theresa and Anthony in the back seat, waves till her mother disappears from sight.

The car windows are rolled down, the wind cools her neck and arms as they ride along Ocean Parkway. Underneath her T-shirt and shorts, she is wearing a swimsuit of Theresa's patterned with shells and a seahorse. Her bare thighs stick to the plastic. The bones of her knees are angular, white and exposed. Theresa's knees are soft and dimpled, brown from the previous weeks in the country. Anthony's are brown as well and there's something twitching just below the kneecap under his skin. It seems to be winking at her. Hanna looks away. Mr. D'Angelo drives with one hand on the steering wheel, singing along with the big band on the radio. "You and your glance—tada—make this romance—tada—too hot to ha-andle." His left elbow rests on the ledge of the open window and his fingers drum against the door as his head nods from side to side, keeping time. Seated next to him, Mrs. D'Angelo's hair blows loose in the breeze, it's no longer bound by a stocking. She sits with her elbow resting on the opposite window ledge. Hanna can see her face in profile. Mrs. D'Angelo is smiling. She's packed a wicker basket with a beach blanket, extra towels, a change of clothing for the children, and there's food. Sandwiches with peanut butter and jelly, ham and cheese. Pickles, potato chips, peaches from the country. A thermos with Kool-Aid. Paper cups, paper plates, paper napkins. Mercurochrome for cuts, band-aids. A baseball and a catcher's glove, the latest issue of *Life* magazine with Clark Gable on the cover.

Mr. D'Angelo steers the car into a lot now and with a single quick, one-handed right-left movement of the steering wheel, they're parked. Anthony and his father carry the wicker basket, the others trail behind, slipping off their shoes where the sidewalk ends and the beach begins. The sand is white, a mirror to the sun. It burns Hanna's feet as she tries to keep up, running after Theresa towards the ocean. They stand together at the water's edge. This, then, is the beach, and this is the Atlantic Ocean. Far away, her mother's told her, the Atlantic meets the North Sea. Cool water washes over Hanna's feet now, then retreats, leaving white suds between her toes as they sink into the spongy gray sand. Up ahead, bodies tumble and turn with the insistent motion of the water, an arm reaches out, then disappears behind a wave that's sprung up suddenly, roaring and terrible. Hanna sees a leg, then it's gone, yet more people rush past and dive under the next wave as it comes crashing down. Just as she fears they've been swallowed up, they appear again far out in the distance as tiny heads bobbing in the water. Hanna cannot swim. She retreats to Mrs. D'Angelo who's opened the wicker basket and spread the beach towel. There's no mercy here, however, as Theresa's mother pulls off Hanna's T-shirt and shorts and slips them into the basket. There she is: Theresa's suit sags, exposing Hanna's left nipple, she's naked among strangers, more naked in public than she's ever been, but she hardly has time to reflect on this, she's all of a sudden confronted with the hairy belly of Mr. D'Angelo, who picks her up, hoisting her onto his shoulders. She grabs his head and holds on, he's running with her towards the ocean, plunging in, her face is hit with salty spray, her teeth have begun to chatter, she can barely say it, Stop, stop, but Mr. D'Angelo can't hear her, he's dodging the waves, sprinting, leaping, thrusting his arms forward in wild circular motions until, finally, he comes to a stop. He and Hanna bob up and down among the other heads. The oily pomade on his hair is now mixed with saltwater. It feels slippery in Hanna's hands as she continues to hold on. Her body is shaking. From the shore, she sees Theresa waving at them. Hanna can barely make out what she's saying. Theresa's arms are extended above her head, she's jumping up and down, calling, calling, and Hanna thinks she can hear her now, she's calling, "Me, too! Me, too!"

Dealing

• • •

This time, instead of undoing the wrapping, Hans Erich puts the package behind the coats in the back of the closet when he gets home, and quickly closes the door. "N-nothing," he says when Bertha asks what he's bought, and she saves further inquiry for later that night. Hans Erich is an art dealer now, Louie's liquor store his gallery. After each purchase, he tells himself this will be the last. A month goes by, maybe two, once he'd held out for three before he began once again looking through the Yellow Pages, consulting a map of the city's five boroughs, locating areas with pawn shops, secondhand stores, antique stores, noting subway and bus connections. His heart racing, he sets out early, twenty maybe twenty-five dollars in the inside pocket of his coat. He descends the staircase at the Newkirk Avenue station and heads for the Bronx or Flushing or the Meat Packing District, wherever he'll try his luck that day. Once he's arrived, he strolls through shops where ex-soldiers, hard up for money and unaware of the value of what they're trading, had left paintings they'd picked up in Germany when the war ended. *F'cigarettes, f'stockings, sometimes f'nothin', jus' took it. Why not. Souvenir.* The secondhand dealers, ignorant of the value of the paintings as well, pile them on dusty floors and on shelves next to cracked ceramic candy dishes and cheap cutlery. Stealthy, poised as a thief, Hans Erich takes his time in the shops, feigning interest in an old phonograph, mildewed books, a piece of tarnished brass. After examining the painting in their midst, he moves on to a broken pair of binoculars, a chipped porcelain figurine. Coming back to the painting, his heart pounding, he asks the price. Then he turns away again, once more fingering the binoculars, glancing around, making his way to the exit. If the shopkeeper hasn't come up with a lower price by then, Hans Erich turns once more, picks up the painting and says, "I like ze frame. How much jus' ze frame?" After another few minutes of hesitation in which the price might be adjusted once more, he hands over six dollars, five, once it had been three, and receives in return a Max Klinger, a Friedrich von Amerling, a Paula Modersohn-Becker, wrapped in brown paper.

Arriving home, he sits on the couch, panting, holding his heart, excitedly relating the story of the purchase, and when he's calmed down, a painting is taken from its wrapper and hung on a nail in the living room. But not for long. The Silbersteins never hang on to these valuable paintings for long. Perhaps it was the memory of Oppenheimer, 1938, Hanna thought later, or perhaps they really were in need of money, Hans Erich didn't seem to be advancing from lab assistant to physician, Bertha's piano lessons often brought more frustration than income, Mutti and Onkel Fritz hadn't yet negotiated their relationship or the family's indemnification, Annelene's paintings weren't the success they would become, perhaps it was a matter of necessity. The painting would disappear from the living room one day and the next stop was the nail on the wall of Louie's liquor store. If its colors were bright and appealing, Louie would suspend the canvas from hooks he'd constructed for that purpose in the window, above the display of wine bottles and scotch. This arrangement had begun three years earlier, after the discovery of the first painting, the Louis Eysen. Louie had spent the last years of the war in Aruba as a cryptographer, deciphering codes for the Navy. Advancing to liaison officer between the Americans and the community, he'd rented a house, hired a laundress, a cook. Back behind the counter of the liquor store after the war, nothing held his interest for long. He was glad of Hans Erich's scheme, funny guy Hans Erich, but he knew his stuff, and word seemed to get around. A different kind of clientele started showing up at Louie's, men from Manhattan who had their driver wait outside while they examined the merchandise. Don't let it go for under two hundred, Hans Erich would say to him, try three hundred first, and d'ya know, they paid it. Cash. And sometimes, they bought a case of Johnny Walker, or his best Burgundy, and had their driver put that, too, in the back seat of the car. Now and then, a painting made a stop between the nail in the Silberstein living room and the one in Louie's store when Annelene took it to her studio to examine the colors, the composition, the brushwork, the wonder of a Modersohn-Becker, an August Macke, and sometimes she'd attempt a copy. When Louie offered to sell hers too, though, Annelene said no. There was the original owner somewhere, or maybe not, news of the destruction of the Jews was making headlines now, but no one wanted to talk about that or about the extra cash Hans Erich was putting into the metal box. Each time he went out, he would come back animated, unable to restrain his excitement, he'd describe each broken object he'd passed on his way to the prize. This was inevitably followed by days of self-reproach and depression as the disembodied voices of the dispossessed visited him at the lab and in the middle of the night. His stutter and his eczema grew worse, the old problem with acid reflux reappeared, he hardly slept. His symptoms were relieved only after the painting was taken from the nail in the living room and deposited with Louie. Hans Erich swore he'd stop. Two, three months. Then Bertha would find the Yellow Pages and the map spread on the kitchen table, and he'd be gone till evening.

Tonight he isn't talking about the painting still in its brown wrapper at the back of the closet, and he's unusually tense at dinner. Egon Schiele, he's thinking, who in his right mind could have resisted. It hadn't been out front with the radios and toasters. The owner had kept an eye on him as he'd gone through the motions of examining the junk. The paintings had been worthless as well, and Hans Erich had been ready to leave when the owner took a chance. "Got a pitcha in the back," he said. "Soldie' comes in, says the new wife don' wan' it aroun'." He motioned Hans Erich to follow him. Through a dusty curtain, along an ill-lit passageway, past a toilet with poor ventilation, they came to a room filled with broken furniture where the owner reached behind a wooden cabinet, and drew out a painting about a foot wide, sixteen inches long. A young girl, thin naked hairless body, the bones of her pelvis thrust forward, the long fingers of her right hand touching the pink and violet of her watercolor vulva. There was a signature, but even without it, it was unmistakably the work of Egon Schiele. Hans Erich had seen Schiele's paintings only once before. Oppenheimer had arranged an invitation to a private showing, and then, as now, the color had risen to his face, and he'd felt light-headed. Hans Erich held on to a table for support. Perverse and, yes, degenerate, Egon Schiele was fearless in exposing what lay hidden in our, and here something in an essay by Beckmann surfaced briefly in his thoughts, when he heard the shop owner say, "Twenty-five." Without a word, Hans Erich drew forth two ten-dollar bills and a five, and put them on the table, and now the painting is hidden in the closet, and Hans Erich is unable to understand the wild mix of feeling, the fear, horror, exhilaration, shame, pride, that has followed this purchase. An original Egon Schiele in his coat closet. He is unable as well to know what to do next, but he is sure he cannot tell Bertha. He is less sure he cannot tell Louie, and the only person he might be able to tell is Annelene although—dear God, no—what is he thinking. He imagines her sudden shocked withdrawal, her disgust, her suspicion that he is a pervert, a child molester, no, never will he tell Annelene. Egon Schiele has cut him off from all those he depends upon, Schiele has made a pariah of him, and suddenly he thinks of his first purchase, now missing, no doubt missing forever, Hermann Adler's still life, a porcelain pitcher with a chipped handle, a bowl, a spoon, an egg.

The Trinity

• • •

They are sitting on a long wooden bench at the back of the Church of the Holy Innocents, and Theresa is waiting to say confession. "If y' don' tell him all the bad things y' do," she tells Hanna, "y' go t' hell." According to Theresa, it's hot there, hotter than last summer, and if you get sent to hell, you can never go home again. Hanna's eight years old, she's never heard of hell, and she's never been in a church before now. For that matter, she's never been in a synagogue either. Earlier that year, Theresa had appeared on Newkirk Avenue carrying a long white candle and wearing a white frilled dress, a bride's dress, with white stockings, white shoes, white gloves, and when Hanna could bring herself to ask, Theresa had said, "Church, First Communion."

Sitting now in the largest room she's ever been in, Hanna cannot say for sure how she's gotten here. Unlike hell, it's very cold, she's shivering, she keeps her jacket on. They'd been playing jacks on the stoop when Mrs. D'Angelo called to Theresa from the window, then they were walking past blocks of single-family homes. It was a long walk and Hanna didn't know these streets. At the courtyard of the church, Theresa had said, "Come in," and when Hanna hesitated, Theresa said, "I dare y'," and Hanna followed her through the heavy wooden door. As her eyes adjusted to the light, she thought she saw Theresa touching her chest. "Cross y'self," Theresa whispered, and she took hold of Hanna's finger and guided it to Hanna's throat, then left-right along her chest, then to her belly. Apparently satisfied, Theresa led her down a long aisle between rows of wooden benches. Light came in through large colored windows high up on the walls. At the front of the church, there was a man, Hanna's heart started pounding, no, it was a statue of a man wearing only his underwear, and he seemed to be suspended above them. Someone had apparently hung him up there, and now her stomach began to heave and she kept swallowing, someone had hung him there with a nail through the open palm of each of his hands and a nail through both of his feet, one on top of the other. "Jesus," Theresa said, starting to walk to the back of the church. She held up three fingers of one hand and ticked them off with the index finger of the other. "The Father, the Son, an' the Holy Ghost, that's the Son." Hanna stumbled after her and sat down on one of the long wooden benches. "Y' don' wanna go t' hell," Theresa continues now, "so if y' didn' do nothin' bad one week, y' gotta make somethin' up." She indicates a curtain to her right. "There's two little rooms behind there," she says, "an' a man sits in one a them, that's the priest, y' can't see him, he sits behind a window, an' y' gotta whisper into the window an' say"—here she whispers into Hanna's ear—"'Bless me father, for I have sinned,' then y' cross y'self." She demonstrates this again and Hanna follows. "Then y' say, 'I didn' help my mother four times, an' I hit my little cousin two times an' I stole some chocolate from the Frigidaire before supper and I didn' tell my mother, y' know, y' make it up, then the priest says, 'Bless you,' an' he says y' have to say a Hail Mary, an' that goes 'Hail Mary full of grace'. . . ." Theresa hesitates. "I forget the rest." A woman comes from behind the curtain now, kneels on a wooden bar attached to the bench in front of them, and crosses herself before walking up the aisle towards the door. "See y'," Theresa says as she gets up.

Left alone, Hanna zips her jacket and rubs her arms for warmth. She watches the curtain for signs of movement. It's a heavy dark purple cloth stitched with golden birds, their wings spread wide. To the left of it, set in the stone wall, there's a small painting. Two men in sandals and skirts with helmets on their heads are carrying something large and colorful, red and yellow, it looks like a tablecloth, and between them, there's a man with a bare, pink chest, he's naked to his belly button and he's barefoot. A gold circle frames his face and something spiky rests on his head, it seems to be hurting his head, cutting it. Hanna can see what she thinks is blood coming from the spiky points running down his face. This might be that son, and her stomach begins to heave again but she doesn't look away. He seems to be waiting for something, she thinks. His face doesn't look frightened or angry, or even as if he's in pain, he just seems a bit sad, and he's waiting, and what interests Hanna is the color of his long hair and beard, it's orange-red, like the hair of the Dubrovsky sisters. Before she can think about this, Theresa is standing next to her and she's saying, "S'your turn," and as Hanna doesn't move, Theresa opens the curtain. "Jus' go in and stay till I count ten."

Hanna gets up from the bench and walks into a small dark room. She hears Theresa prompting her from the other side of the curtain, "Bless me father for I have," but she can't say the words and, from behind the small grated window of the room next to hers, she hears breathing and a snuffling noise. "One, two, three . . ." Theresa has begun to count, when a man's deep voice says, "Yes?" and Hanna rushes out. She runs for the exit, Theresa close behind her. As they reach the back of the church, Theresa dips her fingers in a marble fountain, crosses herself, dips again, and flicks water at Hanna. Outside in the courtyard, Hanna throws up, wipes her mouth with Theresa's handkerchief, and they walk home.

ALIU/OSS, MFA/A, JRSO, BEG

• • •

The painting by Anselm Feuerbach had been a wedding gift from his father-in-law. A large, gloomy landscape, *In the Mountains of Castel Montero*, it hung in their living room in Mannheim above the Bechstein and the wingback chair. Bertha's grandfather, Chaim, had purchased it at the turn of the century from the family's art dealer, Gronewicz & Sons. Hans Erich had never cared for it, he felt oppressed by the sheer size of it. He was aware that ownership automatically conferred status and inclusion in a conservative hierarchy to which he, by nature and conviction, did not belong. Putting aside the injustice of losing the painting, he was glad to be rid of it. Putting aside the injustice of losing it, however, did not seem to be an option as Mutti urged him to at least attempt to recover the Feuerbach. Wherever it was, she insisted, it still might be found. Henriette von Motesizcky had recovered their German Old Master painting of St. Christopher and the Devil. Hanging in plain sight in the Munich Art Museum, the outrageous lack of shame, the lack of decency. Henriette had persisted and it hung now in her home. Persistence, Hans Erich, do what's called for. And while you're at it, look for the other two as well. Carl Spitzweg's country lass with her well-to-do gentleman caller, and Adolph Menzel's portrait of Clara Schumann at the piano.

It is twenty-five years now since Alfred Dubrovsky had drawn the curtain from the Feuerbach and presented it to the newlyweds, fifteen years since Frank Morav, arriving at their home after midnight, had taken the crate with the three paintings and brought it to his home. Eighteen months later, he'd gotten it over the Dutch border, that much was known, Gronewicz received the paintings in the summer of 1940. How Morav had gotten them to Holland, this is a mystery, and more important, why. Smuggling was illegal, he'd risked his life, but why? Hans Erich has ruled out money. Gronewicz wouldn't have paid for receiving the paintings. Then what was left? Loyalty? Morav had been loyal to their family beyond reasonable standards of loyalty. Under the circumstances, he'd been courageous to the point of recklessness, and perhaps that was it, the gamble, the adventure of the enterprise. Unless there'd been a religious or political conviction that Hans Erich was unaware of, perhaps a hidden connection to a resistance movement, but that seems unlikely, and Hans Erich ultimately has no explanation for Frank Morav's daring, and no idea what happened to him following the summer of 1940. He's tried unsuccessfully to find him. Soldier, casualty, prisoner of war? Had he perished in one of the firebombings of Mannheim? Hans Erich feels a longing to speak to Morav once more. To Ruth, to his father. This is loss, he thinks, he cannot feel the other, the loss he will now try to reclaim.

Four envelopes, indemnification forms from Mutti and Fritz, are lying unopened on the kitchen table. Hans Erich cuts open the first and draws forth the papers. *The Art Looting Investigatory Unit of the United States Office of Strategic Studies.* Fritz, now Mutti's fiancé, had offered to help but, averse to the idea of it all, Hans Erich had declined and changed the subject. Now, as he sits at the kitchen table, he regrets his decision. *The Monuments, Fine Arts, and Archives Unit of the United States Army.* Mutti looks well, age is apparently no obstacle to romance, she and Fritz are suited to each other. Already they've sued the new Federal Republic of Germany for pensions, damages to health, loss of property. On that afternoon when they came from the Heights to tell the family of their engagement, Mutti and Fritz had urged him to apply, as well, for compensation. Veteran's benefits, pension, and of course, restitution of the paintings, assuming they could be found. But Hans Erich is a doctor now at Downtown Medical, and even if he weren't, he is certain, he would still be against taking money from Germany. There was a discussion the afternoon of Mutti's visit with arguments similar to those recently debated in the new Jewish state. In the end, he'd been outvoted. The injustice of the theft, as well as practical considerations, trumped aversion. Hans Erich had agreed to apply but the forms remained in the bureau drawer for several months until today. In the meanwhile, Fritz sent new ones. Hans Erich opens the third envelope. *The Jewish Restitution Successor Organization. Der Bundesentschädigungsgesetz.* He scratches the top of his head and the insides of his arms.

Eczema. He recalls a particularly bad case of it as he sat at the rosewood secretary that afternoon in 1933, Ruth sitting beside him. It had been the 19th of May. Five men, she'd said, students, had entered their grandfather's book store. Ruth had been the owner then. They cleared the sections marked Politics, she told him, and Judaica, and carried the books to a truck waiting at the corner. Before they left, they swept volumes of art onto the floor and looked through them for those with modern paintings and the New Objectivity catalogues. Degenerate art, they said, and carried those to the truck as well, climbed in, and took off for the banks of the Neckar River, this he'd read later in the paper. A pyre had been built, a crowd of more than a thousand gathered to watch and cheer. Annelene had stood by the door of his study as Ruth spoke. Now? she asked, and within a week, she'd gotten emigration forms, six of them. They lay in the rosewood secretary through the next year. Ruth had hesitated, their father was old, he wasn't well, surely things couldn't go on this way.

Then came the Röhm Purge, wasn't that a sign, the situation had to get better. "I served in the Army, I was honorably discharged, I have the citation. We are German citizens," he'd said, "it will all be over soon." "You're the man, make a decision." "It can't last much longer," he'd said. In the meanwhile, Annelene applied for visas to Switzerland, Denmark, Sweden, Panama, they studied Danish, Swedish, Spanish, Mutti found Gertie, they began to learn English. Bertha confronted the Tax Office, the Finance Office; Annelene, the Police; Mutti, Gestapo Headquarters, Emigration, the American Consulate. The drawers of the rosewood secretary filled with correspondence, passports, tax statements, exit fine certificates, permits, visas. Ruth said she'd stay. You're the man, make a decision.

Hans Erich rubs his heart. Lately he's had some shortness of breath. He removes the cover from his fountain pen, writes "Silberstein" where family name is indicated. His father's name, his sister's, this is loss, and of all they'd owned, it is really only his books he misses, the books and the Adler, the first painting, sent to Antje's family, gone. On that afternoon in December of 1938, standing among their suitcases and the two remaining crates, he'd thought to transfer the painting to the one accompanying them to Shanghai but, reluctant to arouse the guard's suspicion, he refrained. There hadn't been a way to know, in any case, which of the crates would arrive at its intended destination, which might be lost. He regretted not cutting the Adler from its frame a day earlier, rolling it up and putting it in his suitcase as Annelene had done with her most precious paintings, but then he'd never had her courage, nor her spontaneity. In America, when he visits the antique and secondhand stores, he imagines finding it, holding it in his arms like a dear friend thought lost forever. *Bundesergänzungsgesetz, Supplementary Law for the Compensation of Victims of National Socialist Persecution.* The new Federal Republic has agreed to attempt to locate and restore works of art to their owners. Adenauer, what had he done during the war. Resistance, it was said. He hardly looked the part. Resistance. Hans Erich replaces the cover on his fountain pen. He makes himself a cup of tea and considers going for a walk but he's promised Bertha he will have the forms ready to be mailed this evening. He looks through the instructions that accompany the application for the restitution of artworks.

Provide proof of ownership (invoice, inventory list, photograph, bill of sale). That will be difficult. Hans Erich goes to the closet and takes down a box with photographs Bertha had cut from family albums. How beautiful they looked, the Dubrovsky sisters, how untroubled, picnicking in Alsace, bathing at the North Sea, Annelene standing at an easel on holiday in the Italian Alps, her hair loose, the wind blowing through it, her hat lying in the meadow. Hans Erich sighs and continues shuffling the pictures, looking for an interior photo that might include the Feuerbach. There are two, both taken by Bertha in the early '30s. The first shows the Bechstein, the second, the wingback chair and, standing next to it, the cut crystal vase from the Mayor's wife. In both photos, a corner of the Feuerbach's gilded frame is visible. In the one with the Bechstein, there's even a thin slice of rocky terrain. Hans Erich puts the photos back in the box and returns it to a shelf in the closet. The Schiele lurks there behind the coats, still in its brown wrapper. He finishes his tea, puts on his hat, and leaves the apartment. There is no bill of sale for any of the paintings, he hadn't had the sense or the foresight to take Alfred's papers with them to Shanghai. Instead, the papers had disappeared with the crate sent to Antje Schmidt's farmhouse. The letter from Gronewicz, the inventory list, possibly Louie remembers it, and a walk will do him good, he's feeling hemmed in, overwhelmed by the effort to understand the application procedure.

It's a short walk to Louie's house. Hans Erich leaves their block of apartment buildings and small shops, walks to the streets with large single-family homes. Each house is different, some have stained glass windows, Doric or Ionic columns, porches, gables. Azalea and rhododendron on the front lawns, large shady maples and sycamore bordering the sidewalk. There might be a Feuerbach in one of these living rooms, a grand piano, a wingback chair. When he and Bertha are out for a walk, he notices she looks longingly at these houses, he senses an unspoken reproach. It has taken him too many years to pass the medical exam. He has failed her. Although she does not say this, he knows. Now that he is once again able to work as a doctor, he is an old man. They will remain where they are.

Gertie opens the door. Louie is making bread in the kitchen, kneading the dough with his good hand, throwing it on the counter, beating it with his fist. "Sholom aleichem," he says. "Aleichem sholom," Hans Erich says. "Could be," Louie says when Hans Erich tells him why he's come. Could be. Louie washes his hands, wipes them slowly on a towel, considering, goes into the room at the back of the house with the television set and shelves with stacks of board games, Monopoly, Backgammon, decks of cards, *Reader's Digests*. He gets a ladder and climbs up. Rummaging on a top shelf, he removes several boxes covered with dust, hands them to Hans Erich, points to the shelves below, Hans Erich should put them there, and Louie reaches further back, draws out a box containing Harvey's stamp collection. It seems there were two or three years, letters were coming from Germany, then Shanghai, Louie gave Harvey an album, they soaked the envelopes, separated the paper from the stamps, lifted them carefully with a tweezer, and placed them on the pages. Beautiful stamps, works of art, Louie said. Then Harvey joined the football team, started in with girls, stopped collecting stamps, but, maybe because he thought Harvey might get interested again some day, Louie had kept the album. Could be he tossed the letter from Gronewicz into the box on top of the letters Gertie saved from the time he was stationed in Aruba, Louie seems to remember that, could be. From the top of the ladder, he opens the box, and looks down at Hans Erich. He hands him an envelope. It is postmarked Amsterdam 1940, and in the envelope is the letter.

The Brighter Day

• • •

Swing and Sway with Sammy Kaye is winding down now and Hanna is watching Laverne closely, trying to gauge their chances of remaining in the kitchen for the Reverend Richard Dennis. "And so ladies," the radio announcer is saying, "when your housework is done, why stay at home within the confines of your four walls when the key to your freedom is close at hand, a deluxe Chrysler all your own." Half-singing, he draws out those last words, " a de . . . luxe . . . Chrys . . . ler . . . all . . . your . . . own," as Sammy Kaye's clarinet goes way up high and his band hits their final notes. They hold on before circling down. Laverne sways a bit and hums along, this is a good sign.

Hanna is sitting at the counter in Carol Levine's kitchen eating mallomars and drinking milk. Laverne seems to be in a good mood today. This is important, as she is the one who gives and withholds permission in those hours after school when Carol's mother is somewhere else. Laverne is large and dark brown except for the skin underneath her fingernails which is pink. Her palms, Hanna has noted, are pink as well. Laverne hugs Carol when she comes home from school, and since Hanna's been coming with her regularly for the past year, she hugs Hanna, too, but Hanna's alert to something else in Laverne, something that makes her careful. Some days, for instance, Laverne's not interested in talk and they'd better eat quietly all of whatever she's set in front of them, and go up to Carol's room without any extra discussion.

As they sit at the counter now, a man's voice comes over the radio. "Our years are as the falling leaves," he says, taking time with each word. "We live, we love, we dream, and then we go. But somehow we keep hoping, don't we, that our dreams come true on that brighter day." The music gets louder now, then softer, and the voice begins again. "When we last visited Reverend Richard Dennis, pastor of All Souls Parish in the town of Three Rivers . . ." Hanna listens intently, hoping Laverne will allow them to stay till the end. *The Brighter Day* seems to be about real Americans and what the man with the serious voice, the narrator, calls "the stirrings of the heart." She thinks of Anthony D'Angelo although she suspects he might not be what the Reverend Richard Dennis would have in mind for his daughters. There are four of them, Elizabeth is the oldest, then Althea, Barbara, Patsy. Elizabeth is called Liz, Barbara, Barby. The Reverend Richard Dennis is both father and mother to his children. Liz, Barby, there's something particularly American in this, and Hanna considers. Han. Hanny. Hans Erich, father and mother to Hanny.

This afternoon, there seems to be a problem on *The Brighter Day* but, then again, there always is. It's never a problem like her father's eczema or her mother's sudden tearful breakdowns on the couch. No one speaks excitedly in a language that isn't English. In fact, no one speaks excitedly at all, and when there is a problem, Liz or Barby go to the Reverend Richard Dennis. His voice is gentle, and he knows what to do. Today, Liz is unhappy because her fiancé, Dr. Jerry Forrester, seems to have more than a future brother-in-law-like interest in her sister, Althea. Althea, they already know, is beautiful and selfish, and consumed by theatrical ambition. It seems now, though, that her career plans do not keep her from seeking the attention of what the narrator calls her sister's fiancé, that's French, Carol says, and Hanna is anxious to know how they will resolve this. There doesn't seem to be enough of Dr. Jerry Forrester to go around.

Inspired by *The Brighter Day*, Hanna has constructed a Dubrovsky-Silberstein narrative, complete with Chrysler Deluxe sponsorship. She has included a minor role for herself, even one for Mutti and Onkel Fritz, but hasn't come up yet with a title. Something like "brighter" hardly seems fitting. The Dubrovsky sisters are the main players, and it occurs to Hanna that possibly one of them, Annelene, is not married because at one time she felt a stirring of the heart for Bertha's fiancé, namely, Hans Erich. And as Bertha has been the one to marry him, Annelene has remained single, consumed by artistic ambition. Bertha's marriage to Hans Erich, however, has not always made her happy, Hanna is aware of this. There is a photo on the lowboy of her mother seated at a grand piano in front of a row of footlights. She is wearing a long black dress, a concert gown, and a single strand of pearls hangs round her neck. Her hair is pulled back loosely from her face and bound with a ribbon. The cameras have caught Bertha with her eyes focused on her hands. Hanna cannot know if her mother has ever had theatrical ambition, but if she has, it might account for some of her unhappiness.

From her chair at the counter now, Hanna can see into the garden at the back of the Levines' house. There's a garden in front as well, a broad lawn, and bushes that flower in the spring. Tonight, she's been invited to sleep in this house with its upstairs and downstairs rooms, its attic and basement and large front porch with white wicker furniture and a swinging loveseat. There's a room called a den, and it's here that Carol sits at a piano and practices the pieces she's learned from Hanna's mother. Bertha teaches most afternoons now and when she does, Hanna goes to the library or visits Theresa. Though she senses this is disloyal and cowardly, Hanna sometimes feels ashamed of her mother. People who live in houses like the Levines' don't teach children to play the piano. They don't sit stiffly in a chair and use up the last of their patience,

Hanna knows this, would know it even if her mother didn't say it, as one classmate of Hanna's after another, ill-prepared, uninterested, fumbles his or her way through "Merry Tunes for Little Hands." Carol's mother doesn't take money from the mothers of classmates, and when they call to cancel, which they do with some frequency, Mrs. Levine wouldn't say, "*Um Gotteswillen!*" after she hangs up, and break into tears. On the other hand, although Mrs. Levine never cries, Hanna finds her smile cold and unappealing.

She thinks this again, tonight, as they sit at the dining room table. Mrs. Levine, her mouth pinched, her forehead creased, is at one end. Far away, at the other end, is Dr. Levine, home from the hospital. Carol's older brother, Arthur, sits opposite Hanna, and her teenage sister is next to him. The table is covered with a white cloth. There are cloth napkins, too, and on either side of each plate, there's a lineup of forks, knives, and spoons. Laverne comes from the kitchen carrying a tray with grapefruit halves. Something small, red and round, is in the middle of each. This turns out to be a maraschino cherry. Hanna looks down at the spoons and forks as Laverne slips a plate with half a grapefruit in front of her. The Levines don't move or talk until Laverne leaves, then Mrs. Levine takes her napkin, unfolds it, and puts it in her lap. Hanna is about to do the same when she catches Arthur looking at her. Somehow, she's understood, he knows this isn't the way she usually eats. He's daring her to get it wrong.

"Fulbright, Morse, the only ones who voted against it." Dr. Levine is talking and he seems to be angry. Mrs. Levine folds her hands in her lap. Hanna does the same. "Humphrey, Johnson, Kennedy," Dr. Levine is saying, "bunch of cowards. Two hundred and fourteen thousand dollars for McCarthy's thugs. Two hundred fourteen thousand." He shakes his head, picks up the outermost spoon and plunges it into the grapefruit. "For a goddamn witch hunt." Hanna has not understood any of this, but the important information, which spoon to use, has been communicated. Or maybe not. Mrs. Levine is glaring at Dr. Levine.

"A Communist witch hunt," Arthur says, drawing out the words and shaking his head, but Hanna thinks he's enjoying this, as he's got his eye on her again. Communist. That's Mrs. Levine. Carol's told her this, whispered it after making her promise not to tell. "It means you have to share," she said.

"Eli," Mrs. Levine says now, "Arthur!," and she glares at Hanna. Everyone gets to work on the grapefruit. Laverne comes in with roast beef and mashed potatoes, and leaves with the grapefruit dishes. Arthur, breaking the silence, begins. "We talked about the explosion on Bikini Atoll at school today. Mr. Kamnitzer said strontium 90 is all over the world by now. Everybody's got it in their body from the H-bomb tests." He grins at Hanna and passes her the bowl with mashed potatoes.

Later that night, Hanna lies on a cot in Carol's room. Moonlight comes through a window and she can make out the pattern of the wallpaper, something with flowers and each of them seems to have a face that's repeated in the next flower. She's thinking of her own room and the softness of her blanket, the smell of her pillow, and she regrets having agreed to sleep over. Just before getting into bed, while brushing her teeth, she'd examined herself in the bathroom mirror for signs of strontium 90. Arthur said, when you have it, your skin glows like a lightening bug. She thinks, then, that she hasn't gotten it yet, although she can't be certain. Carol is lying in the bed next to Hanna's cot. She's begun to talk about Dr. Jerry Forrester. Carol says he'll soon understand that Althea's only playing with him in order to make her sister angry. There'll soon be a wedding in Three Rivers Parish, she says. This line of thought is comforting to Hanna and she allows herself to speculate about bridal clothes and bridesmaids. Whether Althea will be chosen as one is problematic but they're not ruling it out if, as her father's told her, she reforms her ways. As for the ceremony, the Reverend Richard Dennis will surely conduct it, and Carol says she's been to a wedding, the bride and groom kiss at the end and then they make a baby. "They kiss and make a baby?" "No. You know what I mean."

But Hanna doesn't know and she'd rather leave it at that, but Carol's gotten out of bed, slipped under the blanket of Hanna's cot and is whispering in her ear, "You don't know?" And as Hanna is still quiet, Carol says, "He gets on top of her and sticks his thing into her coolie. Then he moves around a lot and they scream and make a baby. Like this." And Carol's rubbing her body against Hanna's thigh and she says, "Now scream. But not loud." Hanna imitates the sound Carol makes, a small high sound of despair, and when Carol goes back to her bed, Hanna turns away. She puts her hand on her thigh, warming it, and willing herself not to cry.

A Lady at a Piano

• • •

Some ten years after the war, former Private First Class Yevgeny Mikhailov is walking along a side street in Moscow towards the Church of the Nine Martyrs, holding the hand of his youngest child. In the window of a state-run antiquary, he spots a painting of a lady sitting at a piano, hands poised above the keys. She is wearing a long dark gown with a white collar, and her hair, parted in the middle, is drawn over her ears and gathered in a braided bun at the back of her head. The painting looks familiar. When he returns to the shop a week later, hoping to confirm his impression, it is no longer there, and the dealer can tell him only that it had been purchased by an older, distinguished gentleman.

War

• • •

Some are hot, some cold, but as far as Hanna knows, war is hearsay. Nevertheless, very frightening hearsay, and difficult not to think about. Sometimes, as she's falling asleep, Hanna can hear her parents talking about a war that ended just after she was born. Airplanes dropped fire onto cities. This has a connection to hell, also to Arthur's H-bomb, but what a bomb is and how it makes fire, Hanna doesn't know. She's heard that people were burned in the street during that war and, this can't be true yet she's heard this too, people were burned in ovens. These are cold war days now, that's what she's been told, but there is little comfort in this. It seems that cold can very suddenly go from cold to hot. At school there are practice drills for the day the Russians bomb Brooklyn. Sirens sound, she gets under her desk, the other children get under theirs, they crouch with their heads away from the windows until the sirens stop. Hanna can see the back of Theresa's skirt under the next desk. Sometimes Theresa wiggles it to tell Hanna she's not afraid. Carol's not afraid either. She says the Russians love peace, they would never bomb Brooklyn. Hanna isn't so sure.

Gardening

• • •

> "*March 31, 1955.* In the course of the Great Patriotic War, the Soviet Army saved, and removed to the Soviet Union, masterpieces of classical painting from the collection of the Dresden Gallery, which are of great international value. The Council of Ministers of the USSR has decided to return to the Government of the German Democratic Republic all paintings of the Dresden Gallery that are kept in the Soviet Union, for the purpose of further strengthening and developing friendly relations between the Soviet and German people, and because the Government of the German Democratic Republic is loyal to the policy of peace and friendship between our people."

Shortly after *The Declaration of the Council of Ministers* appears in *Novye izvestia*, Sergei Brodsky is denounced. Curious, he thinks, as two men from the KGB show up at his door. He'd been expecting them for ten years now, since the disappearance of the Menzel, but it is, rather, a party he attended some years ago at the home of the Minister of Culture, Georgy Alexandrov, not the missing painting, that brings about his downfall. Curious as well, he thinks, as they push him into the waiting van, that it's come just now after he'd survived the purges of '48, when charges of cosmopolitanism had been brought against anyone worth envying. Unlike many of his colleagues, he'd retained his teaching job at Moscow State

University, but the strengthening of ties to East Germany has precipitated what he always knew would happen. Finally, denounced. There is a strange sense of relief that it's over and done with. And after Brodsky settles into exile, he is first able to piece it together. The return of the paintings to Dresden had been initiated by his acquaintance, Alexandrov, a liberal, whose increasing popularity had caused concern among certain high officials at the Kremlin. A secret letter circulated, accusing Alexandrov of taking part in drunken orgies with artists, poets, actors, intellectuals. It implied that those who attended his parties were homosexuals. Alexandrov was exiled to Belarus, and Brodsky was allowed to resign from the university on the condition that he leave the city. He has taken refuge in the town of Belye Stolbi, and is now the curator of its Regional History and Folk Art Museum. He tends a large vegetable garden behind his modest bungalow, and plays chess twice a week with Professor Vladimir Blavatsky, formerly Lt. Colonel Blavatsky of the Red Army Trophy Brigade. The Professor, likewise fallen from grace and landed in Belya Stolbi, contributes archaeological findings to the Museum and has become an expert on composting. He and Brodsky follow, from a safe distance, official statements regarding art treasures that have been "*saved from the ruinous conditions of the abysmal German salt mine depositories by the humanitarian Red Army.*" Brodsky considers canceling his subscription to *Novye izvestia*, he rarely reads it, preferring *The Official Soviet Farm Collective Guide to Planting, Composting, Pruning, and Harvesting.* Now and then, but not very often, he gives a thought to Adolph Menzel's portrait of Clara Schumann. He is not aware that it has been sold by a state-run antiquary to the director of Moscow's Tchaikovsky Conservatory, and that it now hangs in the main recital hall, just above Marshall Zhukov's plundered, confiscated, and re-confiscated Bechstein grand piano. And now and then, Sergei Brodsky thinks of *The Mountains of Castel Montero* and the longing he felt the day he stood in a cave in Hohenwalde and held Anselm Feuerbach's painting up to the light.

Letter from 139 Maida Vale, London, May 15, 1955

• • •

You may have something there, Leni. All those self-portraits, one every year, the ubiquitous mirror, Max forever searching for an identity while never removing the stern mask he wore to hide his true warm nature. After reading your letter, I began to think of the impulse towards self-portraiture and why it is that we stand before the mirror taking note of each slow and inevitable change, arranging our palette according to the season. When we were young and thought of ourselves as beautiful, I think there was a desire to record that moment, especially when we became aware that it would not last. And now that we will soon be fifty and need other colors, grays and white for the strands of hair that have begun to overtake the auburn, sketching in softer lines around cheeks and chin that were once taut, we feel a need to be truthful to the passage of time. It's not something I dwell on. Although I am aware that I am no longer young, I hardly feel old. Perhaps as long as Mother lives, I will never be truly old. She has remained in Amersham while Canetti and I live together here in London. He will not separate from Veza, he is living a kind of double marriage, yet I feel we have made progress. There is something solid in the sharing of our daily lives although, as I write this, I must add that he is anything but easy. He writes late into the night, sleeps well into the morning. I mustn't be heard then or receive phone calls. And when I meet with friends or greet acquaintances, he reacts as a jealous child. Still, he is a most ardent supporter of my work. He likes me best not in my elegant suits and dresses but, rather, in my painter's smock. He tells me that when I am wearing it, I am most myself. Perhaps he is right, although the question is, Are you ever truly yourself when you allow someone else to define that for you. And I do confess, I rather enjoy the coming alive of elegance, the women walking through Regent's Park in their best clothing. Here in London, bombed out buildings and craters in the streets are everywhere—now that I've begun to drive, I am most aware of it—and the women's sense of style forms a sharp contrast to the misery of what the war destroyed.

Strange as it seems, London will be my home now, I no longer think of returning to Vienna. And although I may never truly feel a sense of belonging here, England gave us refuge, and I will always be grateful for that. Unfortunately, the results of my erratic attempts to learn the language are pitifully unsuccessful, and the London art world is hardly welcoming. The continent a bit more so. Two of my Regent's Park paintings were exhibited in Amsterdam and The Hague recently, and the Stedelijk Museum has agreed to purchase *Finchley Road at Night*. Quappi wrote from New York that Max would have been delighted with the sale, which pleased me very much, of course. Any recognition of German and Austrian artists is worth celebrating. In England, we are largely ignored. The American abstract expressionists, with their "patterns for neckties and carpets," as Max used to say, have invaded London.

For myself, I have resolved to ignore the latest popular trends. They come and go. Instead, I work on what interests me most, what is most true for me, particularly now the wonderful raw, stoical faces of the British. Mother sometimes agrees to sit for me, although her 'sitting' involves, as always, lying in bed smoking her pipe. She is very sad these days, as we've had to sell Hinterbrühl. It will become an orphanage.

I believe this would have very much pleased my brother. "It was the last really grand thing I possessed," Mother wrote to me after the sale became final, adding, "Sometimes it seems like I have lost a leg and will have to stand on one foot in the future." As I, too, often feel I am standing on one foot, perhaps in holding on to each other, Mother and I will retain our balance.

Affectionately, your cousin,
Marie-Louise

Camp New World

• • •

Hilde is sitting on the step leading to the back porch. She moves her bare feet on the lawn, feeling the wet grass between her toes. Women's voices come from inside the cabin, they're in the kitchen. She hears the clatter of pans, the door of the refrigerator opening, closing. The women are frying eggs and setting large pots of oatmeal on the stove. With herself and Immanuel, there'll be seven for breakfast. Tonight's the folk song concert, mandolin and banjo players, protest songs. The Travelers are performing at Camp Naivelt, Immanuel's here for the *Vochenblatt*, they're spending a few days in the country. "I dreamed I saw Joe Hill last night, alive as you and me. . . ." The sound of a record comes from the living room, Ana Yanofsky's deep voice joins Paul Robeson's, ". . . I never died says he, I never died says he." "Put out all the jams and the honey, no, not that one, the other," that would be Eva Kovno.

Hilde tells herself she ought to get up and help the women in the kitchen, this is communal living, but she needs a minute more. For the sun making its way up from the horizon, the bees already at work on the marigolds. Children's voices come from the camp in the distance singing "Zu eyns, zwey, dray" as they march to the dining hall. Perhaps her niece Hanna will come to camp next summer. The United Jewish People's Order keeps the cost down, a Communist camp isn't expensive, maybe Bertha will bring Hanna to Toronto. Bertha, Annelene, Mutti. Bertha's husband, Hans Erich. Hanna. For almost twenty years now, Immanuel has been her only family. New, old, he is her world, he and, now that they've settled in Toronto, the Yanofskys and Gershons, the Finkelmanns by way of Shanghai, Joe Salsberg, Eva Kovno. Comrades. Although sometimes it comes to her, she'd like to feel a circle of Dubrovskys surrounding her, shielding and cushioning her life, far from the struggle. She dwells awhile in their midst, curled up small and quiet and loved. Her father's there as well, smelling of cigars and Cologne. *Kölnisches Wasser.* "Hildy," he says, "my littlest Muse," and just as she's climbed into his lap, she jumps off and runs for her life. The Dubrovskys come too close. In her last letter, Mutti wrote again, Why not. Very simple, why not, because the American consulate in Shanghai had refused to give them visas. Immanuel's political past, they'd said, the time he was arrested in the hotel workers' strike. So it was Canada, he had a cousin in Montreal who'd sponsored them and, you see, it's all worked out, Hilde's found a job with the United Restitution Organization, Immanuel's writing for two newspapers, his poems are published, they've got two rooms on the first floor of a house, no steps, he can manage the entrance himself. They have friends or are they, rather, comrades, she's not certain, and now Hilde hears the voices of men in the kitchen, they're continuing where they left off the night before, "bourgeois nationalism," "democratic socialism," "proletarian internationalism," "the reactionary press." "The Jewish question." "Lies." Their voices are already strident, filling the kitchen with the hairsplitting contentiousness of their fathers arguing Talmud, and it's only eight AM. She listens for Immanuel's voice but he doesn't seem to be joining in. Immanuel's quieter now, less inclined to debate after that day in Shanghai when they'd pulled him out from under the collapsed roof of the house on Tongshan Road. She's quieter as well. Once she'd been able to say *Tovarich* easily, it's more difficult now. Is it possible, she'd like to say, we might also see it this way and leave it at that, but there's Eva Kovno, hands on hips, mouth twitching, Eva's been waiting for someone to say that. Hilde would have to retreat, she suspects, she'd offer her bourgeois background, it reasserts itself when she's tired.

Lately she suspects Immanuel is tired as well. It seems Aron Shtern, too, longs for a simpler time. This is the name Immanuel uses when he writes for *Der Yiddischer Zshurnal.* His first job in Canada had been with the Communist paper, the *Vochenblatt*, but after a year, he'd met secretly with the editor of the *Zshurnal* and Shmuel had hired him. "You'll translate a little, cover the culture, we'll print some of your poems, not the commy stuff, some of your real poems, the ones with Yid-dishkayt, but we gotta get you another name. Y'can't use your *Vochenblatt* byline, we're a family paper, how's Aron Shtern. I went to cheder with Aron Shtern in Swidnik, his family owned the brewery. Probably dead." Shtern, they've decided, is a bourgeois philistine going soft in the belly, yet Hilde always finds his poems moving, their longing for another time, an estate in Podliszki, a cook who turns beets just pulled from the field into borscht. A brass samovar, polished, reflecting the sun.

"Hilde." Ana Yanofsky's calling her. Not yet. Not yet, just a minute more. She's tired. It's not the wheelchair, not the day-to-day care, she thinks, it's the doubt that's begun to grow, for her, for him, worse for him, it's been his life. It began with the doctors, so many of them Jews. Rounded up, charged with plotting against the Kremlin, put on trial, how could this be happening. Anti-Soviet propaganda, the others said. Maybe he believed that as well, but when Leib Kvitko disappeared, that was when things changed. She'd find him looking out the window like an old man with nothing to do. Leib had been a friend, no comrade this and comrade that. Immanuel had written to him c/o the Anti-Fascist Committee, Moscow, after the war, and Leib had written back to their address in Shanghai, he was alive! They celebrated that evening. How did the Soviet Army make a captain out of a Yiddish poet, Immanuel asked when he wrote again, but this time Immanuel's letter came back, addressee unknown, and there was no longer a way to reach Leib Kvitko or to find out what had happened to him until they heard Khruschchev's voice on the radio one night. Crimes of Stalin, the interpreter said, The Night of the Murdered Poets. Children's books he was writing, books for children in Yiddish, how do you murder a man for that, and now, although Immanuel's here and they'll go to The Travellers' concert tonight, something's gone from him, and Hilde's tired. She stands now, turns towards the kitchen, and as she leaves the lawn, it comes to her, she hadn't thought of it all these years, "Dew lingers on a grassy knoll."

Let's Rock!

• • •

It's 1956, the D'Angelos are the first on Newkirk Avenue with a television set. It stands on four short sturdy legs opposite a large comfortable couch in what used to be Mrs. D'Angelo's sewing room. Colorful balls of hard candy lie in little dishes on either side of the couch. It is here that Hanna and Theresa sit, waiting for Bobby Blaine's teenage dance program, *Let's Rock!* to begin. Hanna comes to watch the older girls, the fifteen- and sixteen-year-olds who are on the program every day. The regulars, as they're called. They wear tight skirts and tight sweaters. Delicate crosses, worn as necklaces, lie just above their breasts. During the slow dances, they press up against the boys. They don't talk, the boys don't either, they don't smile, this seems to be the way to do it. Hanna's learned their names. Francine Sullivan, Mary Catherine Giordano, Doreen Gibson, she watches them to understand what it is to be a teenager. The boys are less interesting. Most of them wear suits and ties, their faces indistinguishable beneath neatly cropped crewcuts. Some of the more daring have long, pomaded Elvis hair like Anthony D'Angelo. Sometimes a boy raises half his upper lip in an imitation Elvis sneer. Hanna knows it's only imitation, it's the girls who are women already, the boys are just boys. Before *Let's Rock!* begins, Hanna and Theresa look through *Life Magazine* for photos of celebrities. They discuss hairdos, bodies, dating. Hanna finds it difficult to align this information with the lives of the Dubrovsky-Silbersteins. She senses her family would not approve of people called "stars" and it is only here in the D'Angelo television room that she allows herself to share Theresa's enthusiasm. This week, *Life*'s featuring the actress Jayne Mansfield in her wedding gown. Twelve yards of pink Brussels lace, so tight, they read, the bride hobbled to the altar, where she needed help mounting the steps. Jayne's smile is radiant, her back straight, her large breasts swell the bodice of the gown. Her buttocks are tightly wrapped as well, and her stomach is flat. "An hourglass figure," Theresa says, but Hanna, although she doesn't say it, thinks there's something oddly misshapen about Jayne's body.

Glancing at the clock now, Theresa puts the magazine aside and turns on the TV just as a man's voice announces, "Live from Newark!" Credits roll up the screen and the camera focuses on a group of girls sitting in the bleachers. They're wearing Catholic school uniforms like Theresa's, pleated skirts, smocks, white blouses, and saddle shoes, and they're watching couples glide by on the dance floor.

"I'll be there next week," Theresa says then, not looking at Hanna. The girls in her class at Holy Innocents have written to Bobby Blaine, he's answered their letter with an invitation to appear on the program. "You can come over and watch." Aware that she ought to express enthusiasm for Theresa's terrific good luck, Hanna's throat suddenly feels tight, and she concentrates on holding back tears. She focuses on Bobby Blaine. "Get ready girls," he's saying, "it's Ladies' Choice," and the dancers begin crowding the floor, most of them hardly able to keep time with the music as they knock against each other, stumbling, looking, Hanna sees now, overheated and dull.

When the song is over, Bobby Blaine announces the next one, "a very special song now by The Platters," he croons, drawing out the words, "'The Gr-r-reat Pretender,'" and suddenly it's clear to her, this is Bobby Blaine himself, only then does she discover it, his sly insincerity as he holds a microphone to the mouth of a girl from South High. He is listening, pretending interest in the boring photos she's brought of her school's cheerleaders. Hanna knows it now, why hadn't she known it before, she swallows hard, Theresa won't catch her crying. Bobby Blaine with his brylcreamed hair and boyish smile, he's no boy, he's probably twenty-five, he's probably twenty-nine already, he'd have everyone think he's a nice guy, he might fool them all, but he isn't fooling her, so that when Theresa stands up and begins swaying to "Love Me Tender," Hanna remains sitting, she doesn't join her this time, this is all too boring, she'd rather be home reading. As the program ends, credits rolling up the screen, Bobby Blaine urges viewers to send a dollar for a CARE package to feed a hungry family overseas, but Hanna sees through this too now, sees what's obvious, his lack of real feeling, she knows more about overseas than Bobby Blaine ever will, Bobby Blaine and the crowd of emptyheaded bodies moving pitifully out of step behind him on the dance floor.

The Self I

• • •

Following Bobby Blaine, there is a time of experimentation which Hanna will later associate with Max Beckmann and the search for an authentic Self. A Self, however, proves elusive. Something not entirely under her control seems to determine her behavior in these next years. There are, for example, her feelings for Anthony D'Angelo. Shortly before Hanna turns thirteen, she waits on the landing inside her building each afternoon to catch sight of him as he walks home from the local candy store. From the third-floor window, she's discovered, she can see Newkirk Avenue without being seen. Sometime between 4:35 and 4:50, Anthony appears wearing a leather jacket, his long black hair pomaded and slicked back. His walk is predatory, he is Elvis. Hanna waits to see him flick the butt of his cigarette into the gutter and disappear from sight, then she goes to her room, makes an entry in her diary, and finishes her homework. Anthony hangs out at the candy store, a place that sells, in addition to candy, magazines, comic books, cigarettes, sandwiches, and Coca Cola. It's the territory of older boys, and girls who tease their hair, back comb it so that it lays high and stiff around their faces. Like the boys, the girls wear black leather jackets. Hanna studies the ones who stand outside the store when she goes by. They chew gum, and now and then, one of them puts her thumb and forefinger to the tip of her tongue to remove a bit of tobacco. Watching herself in the bathroom mirror, Hanna practices this, observing the effect from the front, then in profile.

After several weeks of waiting on the landing, she devises a plan. She visits Annelene, and while her aunt is painting, Hanna removes three cigarettes from a small wooden box that has been set out for guests and quickly hides them in her pocket. The following day, she back combs her hair on the landing, and leaves the house at 4:30. In the alleyway, she strikes a match, holds it to the cigarette, and inhales. Its taste is bitter. She feels it in her throat and swallows to keep from coughing. The tip of the cigarette glows orange surrounded by gray ash. Holding it in her right hand, she walks along Newkirk Avenue in the direction of the candy store. A figure, black leather jacket, pomaded hair, steps from the store, and begins walking in her direction. Hanna feels an uneasiness in her stomach and a shortness of breath, but she keeps walking. As she passes Anthony D'Angelo, she puts the cigarette to her lips, walks to the end of the block, then turns the corner, and quickly rubs the tip against a wall to save it for the next day. And the next. Sometimes, if Anthony is late, or if she's approaching the candy store too quickly, she'll bend down and stall for time by pretending to tie her shoelace. After Hanna has passed him four times, Anthony notices her. He nods and continues stalking his way home. Then one day, he says, "You're Theresa's friend," and Hanna says, "Yes." She rushes home to record this in her diary. "You're that Germany girl," he says on another day. Elvis has been drafted and sent to the army installation in Hanau, and Anthony has become aware of a world beyond Brooklyn. "Yes," she says, but she's thinking, first of all, it's German girl not Germany girl, and second of all, she isn't. She answered too quickly. She might have said, "I was born here. I'm American." She might have said, "You know, like Mr. Forte is Italian and you're American." She might have said, oh what she might've said, she records all she might've said in her diary later but omits her new doubt. This is love, isn't it supposed to weather doubt. And yet. Germany girl.

Hanna stays home the next day, and the rest of the week, then finds herself once again on the landing of the building, backcombing her hair. There is the thrill of adoration, and it is far more powerful than doubt. She lights the stub of the last cigarette and begins the walk down Newkirk Avenue. Anthony's not yet visible, so she stops, bends down, unties, then ties her laces, when suddenly she becomes aware of a pair of shoes that have stopped in front of her and, looking up, she sees her father, home early from work. "Hanna?" he says. "Papa?" she says, the color coming to her face, and as she rises, she slides the burning stub under her shoe and crushes it. (Has he seen it? He has. Does he mention it? No, he doesn't.) They walk silently home and, as they ride together in the elevator, Hans Erich takes a quick look at his daughter's hair and looks down at the floor. In the days that follow, Bertha and Hans Erich are quieter than usual. Hanna catches them looking at her then looking at each other. She knows they are puzzled and more than a little fearful. It is with some relief that she renounces Anthony D'Angelo and volunteers after school at the library.

Macy's, Adieu

• • •

Hanna has just left with three of her cigarettes and Annelene stops to consider this before turning back to the easel. No longer a child, not yet a woman, there's a touching awkwardness to Hanna's movements, like a fawn whose limbs are long and thin and not yet in rhythm with its body. Hanna's face is round, her cheekbones high, this she has from the Dubrovskys, but she hasn't their coloring. Hers is dark, olive-toned, and from Hans Erich as well, her nose is long and thin, her eyes brown and flecked with gold. Burnt umber, perhaps, if Hanna will consent to sit for her. Her niece has no idea that she is beautiful, she may never know. Annelene will have to alert Bertha to her daughter's new body, her sister will not see it. When she's finished this last painting for the exhibit, she will take Hanna to the Metropolitan Museum. Or *The Threepenny Opera*. Perhaps Emil will go with them. He knows Lotte Lenya, loves Brecht and Weill. Emil.

"I powdered my face once more, pulled on my mask and, leaving the ceramics room, walked boldly into the crowd at the Brooklyn Museum in the direction of the bar," she'd written to Marie-Louise, seven years earlier, following the evening of the Masked Ball. "A man with a gray trimmed mustache and goatee stood there, a drink in his hand. Beckmann's age, I estimated. European, of course. Portly, wearing a tuxedo, not tall, the top of his head came to just below mine. He turned to me and noticed the unlit cigarette in my hand. 'Feuer?' he said, taking a lighter from his pocket and cupping my hand in his. This is Emil Franz Bauer, formerly of Leipzig, now an art dealer and gallery owner on Madison Avenue in New York. Emil is a great admirer of Max, whom he met briefly in Amsterdam. 'Columbine,' he said, bowing to me and smiling, and he asked me to turn so that he might see the full effect of my costume. Together, we toasted the New Year, and drank to Max. We will meet again."

"Emil has organized an exhibit of Beckmann's students, there are a number of us here in New York," Annelene wrote to her cousin a year later. "I gave him five of my paintings, the tattooed model from Frankfurt, a Shanghai prostitute, a self-portrait, a still life with pears, and *Mutti on the Gangplank of the SS Gneisenau*. With the exception of the pears, he will show them all. Dear Marie-Louise, I know you would like Emil. He's got the courage to go against the current trend, all those drips and splotches, the so-called abstract expressionists that Max so disdained. A classical idealist, Emil reassures me that figurative art is not dead. After meeting him, I began again to paint in the evening after work and not just on weekends and holidays. Sometimes, if I've had a particularly vivid dream, I'll do a sketch before getting ready for work. The other night, I dreamt of a two headed horse. The mouth of one of the heads was tightly set in a proud, grim, thin line, the mouth of the other was full lipped and smiling. This second head sported a goatee. The horse was frisky, it ran around my room clicking its heels and neighing. I laughed and stroked both heads, pressed them to my breast in an attempt to calm the animal. A horse, two heads, what might it mean? Tomorrow is Saturday. I'll lay out the sketch of my dream on canvas, decide on the colors, I already have an idea what they will be, my head is bursting with ideas. If the exhibit at the Galerie Bauer is a success, I will bid Macy's adieu."

In the years that follow, letters come and go more frequently between Brooklyn and London. "Marie-Louise, I am delighted to hear of the invitation you've received to exhibit in Munich. How I'd love to be there, to see Munich once more, to share in your victory! Which paintings will you give them? Following your exhibit in Amsterdam, I feel certain you will soon be recognized as one of the outstanding artists of our time. And Canetti? Does he encourage you, does he celebrate your success? He is undoubtedly a genius," Annelene adds, "but you, you must continue to paint, and put all thoughts of a future together far from your mind. Gain a 'new objectivity.' From your letters, I gather his wife will never grant him the freedom to follow his heart. Work, dear Marie-Louise, and continue to travel, and to visit your good friends."

This last letter is sent at a time when Annelene is reviewing the state of her own heart. Emil Franz Bauer is married to a Hungarian actress with an American passport who'd helped him, at a critical moment, to escape from Europe. Although he has become a frequent visitor to her studio in the years following the Masked Ball, and although he will succeed in helping to free Annelene from Macy's, Emil Franz Bauer is apparently unable to free himself from his Hungarian wife. Instead, he organizes a number of group exhibits featuring Annelene's work. "Jewish Refugees and the Artists of Shanghai" travels to progressive synagogues in and around the city. At Temple Shaare Zedek on Long Island, *Mutti on the Gangplank of the SS Gneisenau* is placed in the middle of the wedding and bar mitzvah hall where the lighting is best. Annelene stands in front of her work at the opening, wearing the red and gold silk dress she bought in 1939, the one with the Mandarin collar and the slit at the side. A member of Shaare Zedek, a manufacturer of hula hoops and other plastic sports equipment, approaches and remains at her side throughout the evening. He buys two of her paintings. This is Howard Epstein.

Annelene is considering. Will she invite Emil Franz Bauer to come with her and Hanna to *The Threepenny Opera*? Or will she invite Howard Epstein, and she picks up a brush, takes another look in the mirror, and adds more gray to the hair of the self-portrait she's just begun.

Soviet/German Democratic Republic Friendship

• • •

Natalia Seminova releases the pedal of the piano and waits till the last chord no longer sounds before standing. She has played well, she can feel that now. Her teacher at the Tchaikovsky Conservatory, Elena Siroko, is sitting in the first row, clapping and smiling. Next to Siroko sits the mayor of Moscow and, to his left, the mayor of the East German city of Dresden. Members of the City Council are there as well, this is the closing ceremony of a week-long celebration of Soviet/German Democratic Republic Friendship. It is a great honor to have been chosen to perform this evening. Natalia Seminova is torn between feelings of humility and pride as she lowers her head to receive the applause. She is dressed modestly in a long dark gown with a tight bodice and ruffled white collar, and her hair, parted in the middle and drawn over her ears, comes together in a braided bun at the back of her head. The critic for *Novye izvestia* will write, "*Young Natalia Seminova might have been the lady in the portrait above the piano, Clara Schumann, stepped forth and wondrously alive, playing with the dramatic intensity and technical expertise required for the execution of Beethoven's Piano Sonata Number 5.*" As she reads this the next day, she recalls the face of the director of the Conservatory, a distinguished older gentleman, his head bowed, his expression grim as he listened to the mayor of Moscow's speech. She, too, knows she will miss Adolph Menzel's portrait, taken from the wall that night and restored to the Dresden Gallery in compliance with the Council of Ministers' effort to further Soviet/German Democratic Republic Friendship.

The Self II

• • •

Searching for the Self in these first teenage years, Hanna assumes several exploratory identities. She arrives early at school, smuggling in makeup, a comb, and a tight black skirt that matches her leather jacket. The jacket had belonged to a cousin of Theresa who'd outgrown it. And although Theresa had made an effort to diet, it soon became clear that she would never be thin enough to wear it, so that when her mother suggested she give it to Hanna, she reluctantly agreed. Bertha, on the other hand, is uncertain. Although she is unaware of the significance of a black leather jacket for Hanna and her peers, she associates this type of garment with young men and motorcycles. Certainly it has nothing in common with the clothing Mutti brought from Hohenemser's the year Bertha turned fourteen. In consultation with Annelene, she is willing to be convinced that her daughter looks chic, modern, and, hopefully, Hanna is just going through what is called, in America, a phase. And so, Bertha tells Hanna she is only concerned, as the season advances, that it might not be warm enough. Hanna promises to wear several layers of cardigans and long underwear this winter. In the school washroom now, she teases her hair into a beehive, changes into a tight black skirt, and pats her lips with white powder before setting her mouth in an expression of boredom. Next, she draws black lines with a soft pencil around her eyes and pats purple mascara on her lids before joining the flow of junior high school students drifting through the hallways, unsmiling, self-absorbed and remote, like dancers on *Let's Rock!* She's almost one of them, but not quite. Rather, Hanna drifts at the edge of their flow, avoiding the colorless, insipid students in her honors classes. She chews gum. After school, she returns to the washroom, combs out her hair, rinses her face, and changes her skirt. At the library, Hanna is a young adult, shelving books, helping Miss Bildersee, the librarian, at the checkout and information desk. She and Miss Bildersee discuss *Jane Eyre* and *Wuthering Heights*, and Hanna reads everything in the Classics section. After work, she sometimes visits Gertie and Louie, the house on Marlboro Road is near the library. Harvey and Neil are young men now, they're rarely at home. Gertie is happy to see her. On Marlboro Road, she is a well-adjusted American teenager. Gertie buys Hanna her first pair of high heeled shoes and a skirt with a crinoline. Louie's caught the spirit of the '50s, he's bought a TV console and a stereo FM set, he's evened out the living room floor with vinyl tiles, finished the basement with knotty pine walls and furnished it with a ping pong table. He's bought Gertie an electric can opener and a washer-dryer, all on credit, and he'll pay for his latest purchase, a four door Chevrolet, in twenty-four monthly installments. Louie is fearless in creating abundance. Hanna returns at times to the D'Angelos, their warmth and familiarity is a powerful draw, and here she is Theresa's oldest friend, a good listener, she gets along and fits in. Anthony's usually out with friends, but when he's there, Hanna notes with some sadness the effortless passing of love. If she visits the family towards evening, Mrs. D'Angelo will set an extra plate at the table. Hanna will say the food is delicious, and it is. After dinner, they'll sit together in the television room. Mr. D'Angelo puts his arm around Mrs. D'Angelo, they snuggle on the couch, Theresa and Hanna wedged in close beside them, and they watch *Father Knows Best*, *December Bride*, and *Divorce Court*. They watch Liberace at the piano and, one evening, they witness the wedding of Grace Kelly to the Prince of Monaco. "Je veux," Grace says, and the D'Angelos and Hanna cheer. And she visits Carol, where Hanna is a political idealist, she believes in sharing. She observes Carol's sister who wears a black leotard. She is a beatnik. Her boyfriend is as well. He has a beard, he never talks. Hanna observes Carol's brother, Arthur, who talks a lot. "'I saw the best minds of my generation destroyed by madness, starving hysterical naked,'" he says to Hanna on the day he invites her into his room to see his science project. Arthur's walls are painted black. The only decoration is a poster of a balding, bearded man sitting cross-legged on the floor. There is a sign in front of him with the words "Smoke Pot." Arthur has constructed a model of an Intercontinental Ballistic Missile for the science fair. Hanna watches television at Carol's house as well. This is how she learns about disarmament, Richard Nixon, Martin Luther King.

Each of these visits requires advanced planning with regard to costuming. For example, whereas visiting Gertie and the D'Angelos might require high-heeled shoes and a skirt with a crinoline on special occasions, or a modest blouse and plaid jumper for everyday wear, this will not do at Carol's, where a leotard, black sweater, and skirt are more appropriate, which, on the other hand, would shock Miss Bildersee and undermine her image at the junior high. These years require a lot of time in washrooms.

Letter from Toronto, January 14, 1958

• • •

Dear Leni,

Four PM is hardest, the time of day when the sun begins to retreat. Till then, I walk. I leave the house just after dawn, wearing all of my sweaters and a long-sleeved thermal undershirt that was his. I wrap the woolen shawl, the one you sent, around my neck and shoulders. Hat, gloves, my warmest coat, I walk till the sun turns blue with cold, then clouds over, then gives up. Toronto this winter is a city of ice, I still don't know how the gravediggers opened the ground. I have a memory of wondering How did they do that, as we stood there. Clumps of frozen snow stuck to the black earth lining the rectangular emptiness and I found myself wondering however were they able to do that, to dig through the ice, and I thought, I'll ask Immanuel. I think at that moment the terrible pain, more profound than anything I'd ever felt, perhaps even more profound than what I'd called love, took me. I seem to remember one of Immanuel's colleagues lifting me from the ground and drawing me back through the gates of the cemetery. Someone brought me home and offered to stay the night. I think I said no. And now, I walk the streets of this city till I reach the far western fringe which is High Park. I walk alone. You mustn't worry, I prefer to be alone. The cold, clear air, the outline of winter trees against the sky and my exhaustion, this is my comfort. You asked how I am managing, dear Leni, this is how. I will return to work, but not just yet. And I will come to you, thank you dear heart, but not just yet.

Your loving sister,
Hilde

Satyagraha

• • •

Shelving books one day at the library, Hanna finds *The Diary of Anne Frank* and, for a short but intense period of time, becomes convinced she is the reincarnation of its author. Even after calculating, soberly, the date of her birth, the date of Anne's death, it is impossible, yet the certainty persists, it is unavoidable, this is her history. Before falling asleep, as if taking part in a ritual, she imagines herself seated at the table in the attic of the *Achterhuis* next to Hans Erich, whose sensitive and intelligent face, long nose, and receding hairline bear a strong resemblance to the photo of Otto Frank. They wait. There is a knock at the door and, each time, her wild sobs bring release. Hanna discovers, along with this new Self, the attractions of morbidity. Hunter, a high school for girls, saves her. There is an entrance exam and the academic standards are high. Carol Levine's already there. She helps Hanna enroll. For now, the dilemma of The Self has been solved. There is no longer a necessity to have one. Hanna spends all of her time commuting to Hunter by subway and studying. One day, reading Goethe's *Faust* for Advanced German, she fails to notice the man sitting next to her in the train. His hand's on her knee, working its way up her thigh before she's aware of him, and she quickly leaves her seat and walks to the far end of the car. Holding onto a pole, she stands close to the door, her face hot with shame as she waits to get off at the next stop. Focused on nineteenth-century Germany, Hanna has failed to see twentieth-century America. This is, of course, the new dilemma, although Hanna ignores the warning. Like her shtetl ancestors, Hanna experiences the transcendence of study, the escape into learning, the high and protective walls of routine. She is only marginally aware of those around her. Her father has borrowed *The Rise and Fall of the Third Reich* from the library and reads aloud after dinner. Theresa's discovered The Pill although she and Joey Franco are still using the rhythm method. Carol's discovered *Peyton Place*. Arthur's discovered tranquility. A strange smell comes from behind the closed door of his bedroom, and when he infrequently emerges, his eyes are hooded and his smile unusually benevolent. Carol's sister and her Negro boyfriend have gone south to Alabama to help integrate Woolworth's. Nonviolent, passive resistance, this is Satyagraha. Hanna thinks there is an element of Satyagraha in her immersion in books. She no longer waits in the *Achterhuis*, she's found a place of refuge. She hardly takes in the wall going up in Berlin, dividing east from west, and she ignores the handsome new president urging Americans to build bomb shelters. Where would they put one on Newkirk Avenue anyway.

Poetry at the Lion

• • •

A flash of white-bellied geese caught her eye one morning as they flew over Grenadier Pond, and Hilde searched her bag for a pen and a scrap of paper, ". . . white-bellied flocks of geese in flight . . . ," she wrote. Sometime later, ". . . the spiky plumed grandeur of bare-limbed black oaks . . . ," and, another day, ". . . the waves of the Humber River caught mid-plunge, frozen. . . ." Some twenty-five years earlier, it seems, without ever having consciously decided, she'd decided, it's enough that he writes. It was shortly before their wedding on the way to Podliszki. They set their suitcases down on the floor of an ornate chamber in Krakow's City Hall, it had been just the two of them and a witness, a thin man from one of the clerical offices in the building, who'd rubbed his eyes and yawned as the presiding official read a long paragraph in Polish, and she'd said, as instructed, *Tak*. After that, she helped translate Immanuel's poems into German, and she took on the business of living, doing what needed to be done for the two of them. A sealed envelope at the bottom of her suitcase held the poems she'd written at the rosewood secretary in her father's home, and that was the way they traveled from Mannheim to Podliszki to Moscow; they rode the Trans-Siberian Railroad to Shanghai, docked there unread, half forgotten, left China for Canada, the sheets of paper they were written on turned yellow and brown at the edges, spotted with a kind of mold, tiny holes replaced a word here, a word there. They were fragments now, as she removed the pages from the envelope some eighteen months after Immanuel was gone. The paper broke in her hands. Gently, she eased the pages on to the table and pieced what was left of them together. *This is who I was.*

The following week, Hilde stopped in at Papyrus, the foreign language bookstore near the university, and, shortly after that, she left her job at the United Restitution Organization and began working for the owner of the store, Britta Steinmetz. It was because she'd begun to write again, she thought, confiding only to Annelene, "perhaps it's given me courage, my poetry. I'd become so cautious. Do you remember, Leni, how Papa used to call us his Three Muses? It would surprise him to see how practical his youngest Muse has become. Now that Britta's retiring, I've decided to buy Papyrus. Perhaps renaming it 'The Lion Bibliothek' will give me a lucky start." She keeps Britta's specialty, foreign language books, and adds poetry.

There's a reading at The Lion tonight. Hanna, who is eighteen, is visiting this summer, she and Hilde are putting out chairs, twenty, maybe twenty-five, the poet is well-known locally. A graduate student is helping them. His name is Pavel Varschau. He's just completed the dissertation he'd begun during the months he worked with the poet: "Immanuel Häring and the Soviet Jewish Writer's Union." Immanuel had looked forward to Pavel's visits. They'd taken his mind, briefly, from what was now and what was to come. Hilde had been grateful. She made coffee for the young man, sat with him by the bed. Pavel had grown up speaking Polish with his mother, Yiddish with his father, English from the time he entered first grade in Toronto. He studied German at McGill, they laughed, it was only Shanghainese and Japanese that were missing. And afterward, Hilde and Pavel had worked together editing the first volume of the posthumous collection, *The Complete Works: Youth in Podliszki/Moscow Nights.*

On a day soon after they finished the work, Pavel had rung the doorbell, and when no one answered, he let himself into the house. He found Hilde in the living room, a pair of scissors in her hand. Two long red braids lay coiled at her feet. Her mouth open, hardly breathing, she stared down at them. "Without a king," she said, "I do not need a crown." He came to her, lay the scissors aside, smoothed her hair, and took her in his arms. Only then did she weep, loud wordless sounds, keening. It's been four years now, Hilde owns a bookstore, Pavel's teaching at the university. He comes by The Lion regularly, she makes coffee, they don't mention the day he held her in his arms. Maybe she notices how bright his eyes are when he looks at her, how attentive he is as he sits there, maybe she doesn't. Pavel is twenty-four years younger, she inquires about his mother. This summer, she leaves him talking with Hanna at the coffee table, she finds that work needs to be done in the storeroom, excuses herself, and Hanna is aware that Pavel's eyes become less bright when she leaves, he is only as attentive as he needs to be, he is waiting for Hilde to return.

A Table for Twelve

• • •

It was Louie's idea, the birthday celebration, and here they are, table for twelve at DeNiro's. The waiters have just brought bread and antipasto, and Louie has risen, holding a glass of wine and calling out, "Toast. A toast!" Over the hum of noise in the restaurant, he begins, "To Hans Erich, our birthday boy, seventy years, three continents, a long life of hard work and hard times, but here we are. I remember . . ." and now Louie is telling how he watched the Dubrovsky-Silbersteins approach the house on Marlboro Road twenty-five years earlier. Gertie and Harvey are smiling, enjoying Louie's speech, although Gertie has heard it earlier that day. Mutti and Fritz are smiling as well, politely, they're hard of hearing, they're sitting closest to the kitchen, the noise of waiters coming through swinging doors and calling to the chef is louder than Louie's voice. Bertha is looking anxious. She'd urged Hans Erich to accept the invitation, Gertie and Louie had, after all, taken them in, but she's aware of her husband's discomfort in groups, his aversion to being the center of attention. Hilde is here for a visit. It would help, Bertha had said to him, to have something to celebrate, family, a restaurant, wine. Although a toast, she's thinking now, is it really necessary. And that story again, *um Gotteswillen*. Annelene sits between Emil Franz Bauer and Howard Epstein. She's considering Howard's recent proposal. She's not ready. Will she ever be. On the other hand. Emil Franz Bauer is thinking he's seen this man somewhere, the one who's standing now and talking, holding a glass of wine. . . .

Burgundy . . . a liquor store, 1950? '51? A tip from another art dealer, a call to a livery service, the ride into Brooklyn, and there in the window, above a display of bourbon and scotch, a painting by Max Klinger, and one by Friedrich Amerling on the wall behind the cash register. They'd bargained awhile, not that it wasn't underpriced already, the man owned a liquor store, he obviously didn't know what he had. This was the man, he's certain now. Emil Franz Bauer is glad he's sitting in the corner and in shadow.

And the birthday boy? Hans Erich loosens his tie and attempts to breathe deeply. His chest feels tight. Since retiring from Downtown Medical, he's noticed an increase in pressure, sometimes pain in his shoulder, he should know the signs, he's a doctor, yet he usually puts it down to retirement, too little to do, at times he tells himself he's had enough, why not now. He looks over at Hanna. Hannale. A college girl. Why do they say girl in this country, at twenty she's a woman, a beautiful young woman, and he's seen this young woman before, Hanna, she reminds him, ah. Hard to believe he'd been a little brother once, their mother hadn't been well, Ruth had taken him to school, to the park, taught him to read, protected him from the older children, and when she was twenty, she told him, I am in love. And when she was twenty-three, her lover was dead, killed in the Great War, and here Hans Erich looks up, Louie is saying, "'Gut morneeg,' like he don' know Yiddish, an' it's four o'clock in the afternoon!" Louie's grinning; he's come to the end of his speech. The others clap politely as he raises his glass. "To Hans Erich! L'chaim!" "L'chaim!" says Howard Epstein and the rest raise their glasses, drink, and note with relief that Louie has taken his seat.

The waiters are passing around platters with antipasto when a young man approaches the table and goes to Hans Erich. "Mazel tov!" he says and claps him on the back. This is Neil, Gertie and Louie's other son. He appears unexpectedly, he's driven in from Queens to surprise his Uncle Hans Erich, there was a lot of traffic, he explains, pardon the delay. A thirteenth chair is drawn to the table, and Bertha will remember this later, thirteen, an unlucky number.

Death at the Armory

• • •

It was Emil Franz Bauer who alerted him to the International Art Show at the Armory. There it was in *The New York Times*, with a listing of the dealers, and there was the name, Hans Erich saw it was his fate, Gronewicz & Sons. Following the night at DeNiro's, Bauer had sent him a ticket to the show, a dealer's ticket to view the paintings a day before the general admission. The Armory would be quiet, he'd imagined, a place to transact business. Hans Erich slowly climbs the stairs now from the subway. Rubbing his chest, he waits till his breathing returns to normal, then shifts the parcel containing Egon Schiele's painting to his left arm and withdraws a pocket handkerchief from his overcoat. A cold wind from the East River comes towards him. It ruffles his thin hair as he removes his hat. He mops the sweat from his forehead and the back of his neck, and considers. This makes no sense. He doesn't even have a bill of sale. It is not too late to turn back. He replaces his hat. And heads for Park Avenue. Inside the Armory, the guard suggests he check his overcoat but Hans Erich is chilled now and he continues to wear it. Although it is one of the pre-viewing days, the hall is crowded. There is a map at the entrance indicating the location of each of the galleries. Durand et fils: French Impressionists; Feigenbaum: German Contemporary; Gladwell Gallery: Joshua Reynolds. Gronewicz & Sons: 19th and 20th Century European Fine Art. Booth 27. Down the second aisle, at the end and to the right. The aisle is long, dealers have set up paintings in booths like wares in an Oriental bazaar. Hans Erich walks slowly. With luck, there'll be a booth with early-twentieth-century European art before he reaches Gronewicz, he'll unwrap the Schiele, take whatever is offered, walk away. But Hans Erich is feeling anything but lucky. The aisle is long, too long, too many people block his way, and he's starting to sweat again in the heat of the crowd, the glare of the lights, his throat is dry, his tongue feels heavy, every step is an effort. It occurs to him he might put the painting down somewhere, prop it up against a wall, walk out, return home, but he has arrived now at Booth 27. Beneath the sign, Gronewicz & Sons, a young man is standing at a desk, smiling, shaking the hand of another. Both are elegantly dressed, something has been exchanged, an address, a promise, perhaps a painting. He cannot. This has been ridiculous, absurd, this has been shameful, the idea of selling a Schiele at an Oriental bazaar, particularly this Schiele, what had he been thinking, is this a pre-view of senility, this, and Hans Erich's eyes come to rest on a large nineteenth-century landscape in a gilded frame hanging on the wall behind the young man. A gloomy landscape, a rocky terrain. Feuerbach. Undoubtedly Anselm Feuerbach. *In the Mountains of Castel Montero*, it is, it is (it isn't. *In the Mountains of Castel Montero* is lying in a storage room in the basement of the Pushkin Museum in Moscow), "it is, Gronewicz, you," Hans Erich struggles with the weight of his tongue, "cheat! You thief! Gronewicz, you scoundrel, liar, *goniff*!" Hans Erich is holding his chest and he sinks to his knees, he collapses on the floor of the Armory and by the time the medics have arrived, there is nothing they can do. In the overcoat pocket of the deceased, they find a card with the name Emil Franz Bauer, Fine Art. Called to identify the body, Emil collects a few dollars, a subway token, and a soiled handkerchief from Hans Erich's pocket, and a parcel wrapped in brown paper. Later that week, the birthday party reassembles for a funeral.

Stunned, there are no speeches. Harvey says *Kaddish.* Consulting with Annelene, Bauer quietly sells the Schiele and gives the proceeds of the sale to Bertha. Funerals are expensive. The little painting that her husband had been carrying at the time of his death, he tells her, had brought in more than enough to cover the cost. "A . . . a Spitzweg," he replies.

Quite Well

"Quite well," Bertha says when asked, not certain that these English words convey what she means to say. But what is the correct answer to the question "How are you," she certainly isn't used to sharing her feelings with strangers. And it never would have occurred to her to receive guests, but after the funeral Mrs. D'Angelo had appeared with a kind of cake, panettone, she said, and her pregnant daughter stopped in later that day carrying a little girl no more than a year old in her arms. The Polish Jews who lived down the hall had come with a box of cookies. They seemed to be in shock, although death was no stranger to them, the wife wore a long-sleeved shirt even in summer to cover the tattooed number on her arm. Hans Erich had spoken Yiddish with the husband. Louie, shocked as well, and deeply saddened, brought bread and a bottle of brandy. He came often that week, sometimes with Gertie, sometimes alone. "That was some birthday party," he'd say, trying for lightness, "It's good memories y'gotta have, Hans Erich, he was a mensch." "And boy, was he clever," he'd add, remembering the days of dealing. Gertie brought a casserole. Harvey came and ate most of it, and Gertie told Bertha she needed to keep up her strength. Neil drove in from Queens one night and that's when Bertha remembered he'd been the thirteenth, the angel of death, and scolded herself for morbid superstition. On the third day, colleagues from Downtown Medical showed up, a Negro doctor and his wife, two male nurses, the retired head of Internal Medicine and the department secretary. They came with flowers, and she sent Hanna to Annelene for vases. Bertha was surprised by these people who'd known Hans Erich, who seemed to have liked and respected him. But after a handshake and a few words of condolence, there didn't seem to be anything more to say. On the fourth day, two women who taught piano with her at the Brooklyn Conservatory came. The director came as well. Each of them brought flowers, and Annelene, out of vases, called Louie and asked him to come by with extras and another bottle of brandy. Doctor and Mrs. Levine came with their daughter, Hanna's friend, and their son, a quiet young man. Bertha liked that he didn't talk. They finished half the second bottle of brandy and Mrs. D'Angelo's panettone and Bertha was aware of how small the apartment was and how unsuited for guests. All who came were kind. It occurred to her how much easier it is to be kind than to receive kindness. She hadn't meant to sit shiva, a Jewish custom that, like most Jewish customs, was alien to her. They hadn't sat shiva for her father. Grief, it seemed to her, and she realized she was tired, and irritated by the outpouring of kindness from people she hardly knew, their cakes and cookies and flowers, grief would have been company enough for her. But the Polish Jews kept coming, they were evidently marking off seven days on the calendar, and she didn't want to hurt the feelings of these people towards whom her own feelings, considering the extent of their suffering, were awkward enough. The truth was, she'd have gladly been by herself. Alone, she might have begun to accept that he was gone, too suddenly gone, as if he'd taken his hat from the closet and simply walked off. Alone, she might have been able to understand what she was feeling. It had been a cruelty, having to respond to all of the well-meaning visitors, to smile graciously at the crowds in her living room and thank them for coming.

"Quite well," she still says, a year later. Bertha has returned to teaching, the director of the Conservatory has asked her to consider conducting the school's chorus, Voices for Peace, they're discussing an Asian tour. Hanna's back at college, they've found a daily life for two. She feels the missing third most intensely in the evening when he'd read aloud to them or sat listening to her play the piano. She misses Hans Erich at breakfast drinking coffee, and she misses him when she opens the convertible sofa. This is what happens, she thinks, we select from the past what gives us least pain, "good memories y'gotta have," but Bertha is averse to falsifying the past, and since he's gone, she's been trying to understand what was true and separate it from what wasn't. This first occurred to her when the Negro doctor and his wife walked through the door. Who were they, and more important, who was Hans Erich? What had he thought, what had he felt, thirty-six years together and she cannot say. It had all gone so quickly. There'd been so little time for reflection. It occurs to her again, as she is cleaning the coat closet. There'd been a package wrapped in brown paper, she remembers now, she never opened it, he'd asked her not to. She recalls the day he brought it home. He'd been agitated, but this was not unusual, Hans Erich was often nervous. He was sensitive. Hardworking, conscientious, a good doctor. Difficult. Sometimes.

Bertha looks for the package at the back of the closet but it is no longer there. When had he removed it? She assumes it had been a painting, one of those he'd bought secondhand. Gone, as he was gone. And what had he been doing with a Spitzweg painting at the Armory? Emil Bauer said that her husband had bought it, he told her there'd been a bill of sale from one of the dealers. He and Annelene had decided to resell the painting right away to cover the cost of the funeral. They hadn't consulted her, she'd been too distraught, Annelene said, and the Spitzweg had been slightly damaged. It had been necessary to sell it quickly while the show at the Armory was still on. It wouldn't have interested her anyway. Yet, Bertha thinks, the time of trading at Louie's had been over for many years already, had he meant to bring the painting home? Had it been, and here she breaks down again, had it been a gift for her, to replace the Spitzweg they never recovered? Because she knows there was, despite how rarely it was expressed, affection, and a deep concern for her happiness. And she knows this too, that Hans Erich, who'd loved Annelene, had loved her as well.

Coming of Age at Luchow's

• • •

"'. . . Wherever I encounter a feeling—whether it be beautiful or ugly—I grab hold of it and drain the cup to its dregs without considering how it will turn out. And each time, I find that even the bitter aftertaste of a meaningless, unpleasant experience is worth more than the flat taste of indifference.'" Annelene removes her reading glasses and raises her wine goblet. "To Hanna," she says, "may she drain the cup of life to its dregs," and the guests, following her example, turn to Hanna and salute.

This is unbearable, Hanna is thinking, close to tears. She looks around the table. Emil and Annelene, Bertha, Mutti, Fritz. "Thank you," she manages to say, and as if she's released them, they tip their glasses, drink, and begin to recall their own coming of age parties. It had been Emil's idea, a celebratory dinner at Luchow's. Emil is her employer now. Hanna had begun working at the gallery while finishing her final year at Barnard. She has a Bachelor's Degree, a thesis, "Max Beckmann: Work and Exile in Amsterdam," and she's ready to go out into the world, to drain the cup of life to its dregs. It's her twenty-first birthday, and her launching is here, tonight, at this opulent, old-fashioned German restaurant on 14th Street. Annelene, quoting Kurt Weill, has just counseled her publicly against timidity. This is timely, for Hanna has been making secret plans to move to Manhattan, to the City, as they've always called it. Just today, before coming to the restaurant, she'd answered an ad in the paper, spoken with the landlord, made an appointment to see the room. Now, as she looks around at the faces of those who love and depend upon her, she cannot imagine betraying their trust. The idea of Bertha coming home to an empty, what had she been thinking. Bertha, unsuspecting, and still somewhat fragile in widowhood, nods as a waiter puts sauerbraten and dumplings on her plate.

"Sehr schön," she whispers to Hanna, indicating Luchow's décor, beautiful, the heavy brocade curtains hung with braided gold tassels, the chiseled oak chairs, and tables set with white linen. They've re-entered the Dubrovsky dining room, Mannheim, 1928, and despite whatever is already threatening in the streets below, the lights in this room, flickering, illuminating warm shades of brown and maroon, promise years of unending, uneventful prosperity.

"Beautiful," Bertha whispers again, and sighs. Emil's chosen The Nibelungen Room, their table is in a corner by a mural of the lovers, Brunnhilde and Siegfried, and under the lovers, Mutti and Fritz are pouring gravy on their Wienerschnitzel. Mutti, likewise unsuspecting, looks up and smiles at Hanna. She's given her granddaughter the Swarovski brooch tonight, the one Annelene smuggled out of Mannheim hidden in her chignon. It had been an anniversary present from Alfred in 1914 on their holiday in Vienna. "This is moonstone," Mutti said to Hanna before dinner, pointing to each of the tiny inlaid jewels on the surface of the brooch, "and this is malachite, and mother of pearl, opal, and turquoise, and it's yours, darling. Wear it in good health." And Mutti helped pin the brooch to Hanna's blouse where the breast pocket now sags under the weight of it. "Yes. Beautiful," she says to her mother, and she smiles at Mutti.

Unbearable. But what exactly is unbearable? Her grandmother's smile, her bright red lipstick extending into the tiny vertical lines around her mouth, this is unbearable, and Mutti dabbing with a linen napkin at the saliva dripping from Onkel

Fritz's lower lip, Onkel Fritz asking "Whose birthday?" and, later, "Birthday?" Emil, a widower now, his paunch pressed against the table, ignoring his doctor's warning, ordering a second stein of beer, this is unbearable, and Annelene, presenting her with *A Maiden and a Fawn*, the portrait of Hanna as a young girl, then setting reading glasses on her nose before reciting Weill's text, and Bertha, sighing, remembering who is not here in the Dubrovsky dining room tonight, and, most of all, their unquestioning trust in her, Hanna, their traitorous American child.

Unbearable?

Yes. Hanna would spread her arms and gather all of them in, lifting them up and out of time and carrying them far from all that is threatening outside The Nibelungen Room. This is what is unbearable, that she cannot. And something else. That her body aches with carrying them, she cannot. She will not. Hanna leans back in her chair now and extends her arms, resting her hands lightly on Bertha's shoulder on one side, Annelene's on the other. Bertha inclines her head so that it rests on Hanna's hand. Tomorrow morning, Hanna will call and cancel.

Hanna in Babylon

• • •

"Come. It's not that far," Theresa says later that month, calling to congratulate her, and Hanna boards the Long Island Rail Road for the town of Babylon, where Theresa and her husband, Joey Franco, now live. Theresa is standing next to a parked station wagon when the train pulls in. She runs to embrace Hanna, and Hanna can feel the weight in Theresa's body where the next child lies waiting to be born. "Say hello to Aunt Hanna," Theresa says to a small child sitting in the back seat of the car. The little girl keeps her thumb in her mouth and slowly twirls a lock of hair, looking away. A younger child is sleeping next to her. Theresa looks different. Older, heavier, she seems part of their mothers' generation. And she's done something to her hair. "'If I have only one life,'" she says, "'let me live it as a blonde.' Clairol." Then she eases her body behind the steering wheel, Hanna gets into the passenger seat, and they drive to a small house, identical to the other houses on the block, with grass in front and a driveway to the left. "We'll have peaches next year," she says, indicating a sapling propped up by two long poles in the middle of the lawn. "Joey's into gardening."

It's as if Theresa had been playing house, Hanna thinks, and then it was no longer a game, it had become her life, permanent and irrevocable and somehow programmed, the babies tumbling out one after the other, *Good Housekeeping* and *Reader's Digest* on the TV console, the finished basement with a new washer-dryer, the prizewinning recipe cookies from Betty

Crocker's Annual Bake-Off. And Theresa in the middle of it, her sense of purpose, her obvious contentment. If she looks older, Hanna decides, it's because Theresa's no longer a child, she's become a woman, a grownup, she's started life. A life that Hanna does not want, although here in Babylon, her own life suddenly feels weightless and unnaturally thin, as if she were still standing at the edge of the ocean in an ill-fitting, hand-me-down bathing suit while others plunged in.

When she gets home that evening, Annelene and her mother are reading a letter from Marie-Louise. ". . . We have just returned from the Retrospective at the Vienna Secession. I managed to give them fifty-three paintings, and the Austrian critics were appreciative. They referred to the influence of Beckmann and Kokoschka, of course, but granted I'd found my own 'voice.' My suspicion is I represent Austria before the war and those who would return to that time are most enthusiastic. One critic wrote that I was a 'piece of Austrian culture, my aristocratic bearing straight from the pages of an album of old Viennese society.' I had to laugh. In light of all the hoop-la coming now that I'm already sixty, I must work harder to maintain my aristocratic bearing. Especially since it is truly exhausting, the business side of art, the hours of tedious preparation, the exposure—ever a mixture of pride and humiliation—the effort to maintain a sense of dignity. And the anxiety that someone will walk off with a painting that is particularly dear to me in exchange for some Deutsch Marks or Austrian Schillings. I think, Leni, you would understand my reluctance to part with my work. Canetti certainly doesn't. We argue, but less often now that we are no longer living together and his work has gained the recognition it deserves, the publication of *Crowds and Power*, literary awards, constant requests for interviews, lectures, readings. 'I am truly famous in Germany,' he wrote to me recently. With all of the international attention, he accuses me of insufficient attention, of not making an effort to understand his work. Possibly he is right. His work is difficult to understand, and I have never considered myself an intellectual. He keeps a large part of his library in his study, one of the rooms in the house Mother and I have bought in Chesterford Gardens. He comes often to work and dine. Our new Austrian housekeeper, Bauzen, turns out the most extraordinary Viennese dishes and Canetti is always glad of an invitation to lunch, but he does take considerable time, as well, to look at my newest paintings. In his absence, I confess, I hardly ever finish one without thinking, I will show it to him. The other day, as he left with my latest self-portrait, Mother complained that whenever there is something beautiful, Canetti gets it. These days, she is quite disgusted with him. It's been three years now, she complains, Veza is dead, he's free to marry again, what's stopping him. I have difficulty restraining her. You know how Mother is when she gets an idea in her head (do you remember my portrait of her in the boat holding a rifle and waiting for the ducks? I fear she'll take up hunting again the next time she sees him).

"For my part, I will not say anything. He's a free man, I'm a free woman, we are modern people. Yet, and Leni I confess this only to you, I do wait for clarity, for resolution. We sit together in my recently completed *Self-Portrait with Canetti*, he and I at the dining room table. I am at the far end, my brushes have been cleaned and stand in their jars on the table, my work is finished for the day, and I am looking at a large and imposing man in the middle of the canvas who is smoking, holding a newspaper, reading, aware of nothing but the text. And I am waiting. This is what is difficult. You mustn't think, though, that I am unhappy. I enjoy so many things, particularly our garden, but small things as well—Bauzen's Apfelstrudel—the city with all its lights—the exotic English faces, marvelous eccentric old ladies and a whole race of quixotic gentlemen, a veritable sanctuary of human individuality, intricate and inexhaustible. And my painting, of course, although between the demands of these two grand figures, it is a wonder that I'm able to paint at all. Still, the decision to bring Mother back to London and buy the house together has been the right one, as she had become increasingly frail and lonely, unable and unwilling to live apart from me."

"I must confess, I feel spared all that," Annelene is saying. "If Mutti hadn't moved to the Heights . . ." Hanna makes a phone call that evening to the landlord in the City.

Saving Arthur?

• • •

Hanna sets a bag of groceries down in the kitchen and changes out of her good shoes. She fills the kettle with water and puts it on the stove to boil, then removes the florist's paper from twelve roses, a gift from one of their oldest customers. It's Valentine's Day.

". . . Approaching the Viet Cong base near the Cambodian border . . ." she becomes aware of the sound now coming from the living room, the news, ". . . forty-five thousand American troops . . . Operation Junction City. . . ." This means he's home. Or maybe not. He sometimes leaves the television on when he goes out. She puts a can of carrots and peas on the counter and takes a box of rice from the top shelf. Arthur might be home for dinner. Or he might not, he might have to work late at Steinway's. They've been married for eight months now and their lives still have very little routine. Hanna makes herself a cup of tea and carries it to the living room. She turns off the television and goes to sit at the table, and there's the note "gonetocana da." Suddenly dizzy, Hanna catches hold of a chair and sits. She breathes deeply, inhaling the sweet smell of his last joint and something else, smoke, and now she sees, in the ashtray, the charred remains of Arthur's draft card, and she begins to cry. Why she is crying, however, she cannot say. That it's come to an end is not a surprise, that it ever began is something she's never understood. It all had to do with saving Arthur, didn't it? Or did it? She sees him pleading, she sees herself all no saying yes. There'd been Babylon, then Arthur and his plan for her life, and here she was. She'd understood there'd never be a washer-dryer or a tract house in the suburbs, she didn't want that anyway. She'd hardly considered whether she wanted Arthur, but Arthur, it had seemed to her, was real life, possibly life's dregs, she sometimes thought, but real life nonetheless, so that perhaps there had been something in it for her, perhaps it hadn't all been about saving Arthur.

Hanna looks around the room now. His guitar's gone from its stand in the corner. Otherwise, it seems, he's taken nothing. Three black socks lie drying on the radiator. This ground floor apartment near the university has been her home for two years now. There's a kitchen alcove and a small, paved backyard. Her job at Emil's pays the rent. "You're young, you're working, go, enjoy life," Annelene had said when Hanna tentatively mentioned the ad in the classified. Bertha didn't say anything at first, and Hanna didn't look at her mother as she mentioned the long commute from Brooklyn to her job in the City, the proximity of concerts and lectures and museums in Manhattan, and just as Annelene began to talk of her time in Frankfurt, Bertha reached for Hanna's hand. "Go," she said, "I'll be fine."

Hanna called her mother every night. Arthur was forbidden to answer the phone. When she first moved in, he'd been a graduate student in physics at Columbia. He came by to talk and smoke pot. He had a girlfriend, or several girlfriends. She was his little sister's friend, he hardly seemed to notice her. She felt safe with Arthur. She was even fond of him. His anxiety was so enormous, when she was with him she felt relatively calm. They'd order Chinese take-out, and she'd listen to his grievances. The hierarchy in the physics department, the favoritism of certain professors, and, increasingly, his fear of the draft. Goddamn war, he'd say, and he'd make that sucking sound inhaling the last bit of his cigarette, a roach he called it. He'd stretch out on the sofa and fall asleep. She'd wake him, he'd leave, then she'd open the door to the backyard and hang out the black dress she wore to work so that it wouldn't smell of marijuana or whatever it was that Arthur had been smoking. Then one night, after Theresa called to say the new baby had arrived, a boy at last!, Arthur came by, he talked, smoked, offered her a joint. This time she took it. And just before Arthur fell asleep, she lay down next to him. It wasn't much, certainly it had nothing to do with love or desire, but there she was, different.

After that, it just became part of the routine until Arthur, one day, the day he dropped out of school, moved in. "Fucking physics department, fucking Landsdorf, Sorelli, fucking Baumann," fucking all the professors he'd worked with, but the worst of it was, he no longer could claim a student deferment, and that's when Arthur began pleading for his life. "Hanna, we gotta get married. Fucking draft board, they're not taking married men. Yet. Hanna. Please. I can't go. Fucking Nam, I can't go." He found work moving pianos for Steinway and she saw less of him, but all through the night, Arthur would talk. "They know. The FBI knows, the CIA knows, the draft board knows, you don't know Hanna. *The New Masses*, fucking commy journal in the '30s, she was a goddamn editor, don't you think they'd love to ship her son off to the jungle, give the Viet Cong target practice. Hanna. Please, I can't go," and one day in the street, he threw himself on the pavement and rolled around, pedestrians coming their way stepped into the gutter to avoid them, and she leaned down and she said, "OK, yes Arthur can you hear me. Yes, but only till the war's over. And don't tell my mother." So that after they signed the papers at City Hall, Hanna continued to visit Newkirk Avenue alone, she continued to forbid Arthur to answer the telephone, and every night they watched the escalation of the war on television.

A week ago now, a letter had come from the local draft board. ". . . report for a physical at . . ." "Hardship, 3A, Hanna if you got pregnant and stopped work, you'd be dependent, I'd be your sole support, fucking draft board they'd have to give it to me, 3A they're not taking men with children. Yet. Hanna."

"No."

"I could cut off one of my toes."

"Arthur. Arthur stop."

"Or drop acid the night before. Hanna, don't you have family in Canada."

She did. Meetings of the Student Peace Union were held these days at The Lion, most of those who attended were American draft dodgers, but she didn't think Arthur would leave, and now he had. Hanna dries her eyes and finishes her tea. From the opposite wall, a maiden and a fawn look down at her.

Time and Resolution

• • •

"But Leni, as for the news that you've once again followed your cousin into trouble, may I offer this bit of advice? You can't be good and kind to everyone, do your tasks, keep uncles, aunts, and mothers happy, be calm, and at the same time, paint good pictures. That's just the truth, I'm sorry to say. Your loving cousin, Marie-Louise." And it is, Annelene is learning, the truth. She cannot be good and kind to everyone and paint good pictures. Knowing this, however, does not determine a course of action. There is a ninety-year-old mother resting in her bedroom tonight after a cataract operation, and a ninety-year-old step-parent sitting in a nursing home in Brighton Beach, aware only of a terrifying change in his living circumstances but unable to grasp why and what. And there is a dearly loved one hooked up to life support in Beth Israel's cardiac unit. Time will resolve the situation. In the case of Mutti, a two-week convalescence will become three years of caretaking and a fourth year at the Ocean Parkway Jewish Home for the Aged. Onkel Fritz will celebrate his ninety-first but not his ninety-second birthday among the ever-changing, green clad attendants who become less terrifying as routine and medication dull his senses. And Beth Israel will contact her this evening to ask for burial instructions. Annelene is aware of time resolving each of these crises, but it leaves her little strength to understand what she is feeling and, without Emil, even less strength to transfer those feelings to canvas. Grief overwhelms, then numbs her, so that she can hardly listen to the reading of Emil's testament, which secures the practical details of her future and leaves the Galerie Bauer, Madison Avenue, *German & Austrian Fine Art*, to Hanna Silberstein.

(S)he Who Hesitates

• • •

If Hanna hesitates to accept Emil's gift, she doesn't let on. Not to Annelene, certainly not to Bertha, hardly to herself. She is just twenty-four, but she is used to coping when those who are older cannot. In this time of abstract expressionism, minimalism, pop and op art, she will manage the Galerie Bauer, adding to Emil's late-nineteenth–early-twentieth-century German and Austrian collection. And she manages well. At the time of her inheritance, the Galerie Bauer already has a loyal following. Some regard the leading figures of abstract art as charlatans, their work a surely soon to be forgotten, regrettable phase in the history of art. Others simply want paintings that tell a story. Hanna does not hesitate, (s)he who hesitates, she's been told, is lost. Losing herself, instead, in the twelve-hour work day, she finds solace following the disappearance of Arthur. Her success at the Galerie balances the sense of failure brought on by his departure. She will continue this pace of work for the next eight years until Ernesto, the Argentinian employee she has inherited from Emil, introduces her to the tango.

I Will Have To

• • •

I will have to wake her, the large Jamaican woman who is sleeping on the fold out cot next to my bed. But not yet. Although if I don't, there's likely to be. As there was the other night. The indignity of it, Mutti is thinking, the body no longer heeding the mind, and my mind as clear as ever. Although, sometimes. They say it's *Blutarmut*. Anemia. Impoverished blood. How could this be when no one in the family. But then, no one in the family had been what, ninety-two? ninety-three? I will have to wake her, the night nurse with the round brown face, the long black scar on her left cheek, the yellow-tinged eyes. We'd have taken her for a chimney sweep or a gypsy then, but that was then, and Annelene here every day now instead of painting, she has said I must speak politely to Mrs., what is her name. Smith. Mrs. Smith. I can't understand a word the woman says, it is English they speak in Jamaica, isn't it, but it's not the English I learned in 1937, of course I am polite to Mrs. Smith. A good woman, hardworking, do I really think she wants to be here, with her own children, how many are there, I think she said three, or was it four, home at night without their mother, one still a baby, of course I'm polite. I'm polite to the young red-haired woman from the Visiting Nurses, the Irish woman, I don't want her shots, they aren't doing me any good, nor her pills, nor her handholding and smiling, but I'm polite. I was even polite to that damned social worker, who tried my nerves with his whispering. The only one I was not polite to was the fat young rabbi, but then

I was at the end of my strength that morning in the hospital, a rabbi, whoever asked him, I certainly have no use for, I'll have to wake her. I cannot wait much longer. The misery of this, ninety-three, the Ocean something Jewish Home for the Aged, Jewish, and even Hanna the other day unfortunately arriving at the hour of voiding and showering and diapering, helping to lift me from the toilet, set me up with the walker, although that has become too difficult to maneuver now, no strength in my arms. I'm simply not myself and what's the point of it then when one is not. I wanted to sit with her and hear about the Galerie and her life. She was wearing the Swarovski. Her blouse, a lovely teal blue poplin, got wet with spray from the shower, she changed into one of mine, but I did want to say, How are you my dear, and You are looking beautiful, she was, she reminded me of that sister of, what was his name. This is too shameful. The sister of Hans Erich of course, the one who. But I did want to say, Hanna, I am still one of the living despite all this, you must not look at me with pity, that I cannot bear, I am Liselotte Augusta Hohenemser Dubrovsky Fleischmann and my mind is clear as, although sometimes it does slip away, a thought, something I was sure I'd known, and all of a sudden. I managed the stores, Hanna, till Krauss came and even then, in defeat, I said *Take it!* and walked away with dignity, he would never best me in character, Krauss, that he wouldn't. If the body would only slip away easily. I will have to wake her.

Letter from Nagasaki, April 18, 1970

• • •

Dear Leni,

Voices for Peace is finishing its tour of Asia tomorrow. Several people in the chorus will stay on to visit the Buddhist temples. Our guide, Mr. Hokaido, has expressed an interest that I stay as well, but after receiving your letter today, I have decided to travel directly home after the last concert. I will send this by express mail and by the time you receive it, I will be on my way. I wonder how she can be so certain, the visiting nurse, but then, I am sure she is able to predict with some degree of accuracy when a patient is failing. Strange word, "failing"—I've left your letter on the piano at the concert hall where we were rehearsing this morning, you did write "failing," didn't you? I cannot imagine Mutti failing at anything she undertakes. I would say that, from your description, if she really has had enough, she is succeeding rather than failing in making a good end. And even writing that—a good end—I can't imagine what we are thinking. In my mind, she has more strength than any of us, she will always be there, taking charge and making the important decisions. She will endure, I'm certain, there is no question of her not being there for several months after I return. Yet, I will come. I will tell Mr. Hokaido right after I post this letter. He has asked me to join him again for tea this afternoon. There is a polite graciousness I find quite charming in the way he addresses me. I believe this is part of Japanese culture. Knowing Mr. Hokaido made our visit to the memorial for those who perished in the destruction of Nagasaki all the more devastating. Schoolchildren came to our concert last night with little origami doves as gifts for our school's chorus, just little pieces of folded paper, but I will treasure mine. I will hurry to post this now before tea with Mr. Hokaido and, Leni, I do want to say how sorry I am that so much of the caring for Mutti has fallen on you, and that I am grateful that you urged me not to interrupt my work here with the chorus.

Your loving sister,
Bertha

Letter from London: Chesterford Gardens, July 1975

• • •

"Mother is very frail now and her eyes are terribly weak. I often sit by her bed and read to her. I have given up travel entirely and can get away for only a few days now and then." Hanna, visiting her mother, is listening as her aunt reads from the letter that's arrived today from Marie-Louise. "The other day, I came across one of the last letters Karl was able to send: 'you will sacrifice your life to our mother,' he wrote, warning me, 'you will never marry or make your way as a painter.' Sacrifice? I am uncertain. She is my greatest source of strength. Being needed so intensely, being useful at all, gives me some relief from the depression that has followed Canetti's betrayal."

Hanna had been told about this. On a summer day two years earlier, Quappi Beckmann entered the Galerie Bauer, elegant as always, out for a walk with her two miniature Pekingese along Madison Avenue. She seemed agitated and asked to speak in private. Hanna locked the front door before leading her to the office in the back. The two little dogs sat at attention at her feet as Quappi talked. Canetti. He'd married again, secretly, was now the father of a child. The affair with the young art restorer had begun twelve years earlier, not a word had he said to his wife who was alive at the time, or to Marie-Louise, whose home he continued to use. Shortly after the birth of the child, Marie-Louise learned of the marriage from a cousin. "Henriette has refused to allow him into the house. Marie-Louise is devastated. She refers to him as her thirty-year personal catastrophe." Quappi dabbed at her eyes and nose as she spoke and Hanna handed her an extra tissue from a box on the desk. "He'd always encouraged her work," Quappi was saying, "and as each new picture was finished, she told me, her first thought was to show it to him. So that, yes, painting is what gives her life meaning, but it was also apparently inseparable from Canetti. Since this happened, she's not been able to work. The humiliation, it's robbed her of both love and work, and the love and work she has with her mother as Henriette becomes increasingly dependent is, I think, hardly a good replacement. I've written to remind her that Max believed in her, that he valued her art. It's been eighteen months already, she must try to put this terrible nasty business behind her and begin to paint again. Perhaps, Hanna, you might consider inviting her here to exhibit." After Quappi left, Hanna's thoughts turned briefly to the matter of love and work and a meaningful life, and made a note to herself to think about it sometime later, there was a shipment of new paintings bought at auction that needed to be catalogued.

And now, in Bertha's kitchen, she listens as Annelene finishes reading the letter from London. ". . . the importance of my painting to his own life, and how essential my work has always been to him. 'Essential,' he writes, and signs his letters 'Your new brother.' Am I to be a sister to him? I think of Karl and know how impossible this would be. Problem: life without C., world without meaning—with C., endless torment. Solution: work—and I hope that it is possible—work, happy moments, that is all there is." And as the question of meaning resurfaces, Hanna decides that if a meaningful life includes love, it is best to avoid a man like Canetti.

Lafcadio . . .

When Hanna thinks of Lafcadio in the years following his return to Argentina, she sees them on a dance floor locked in desperate erotic longing, a bandoneon snapping out Piazzolla's tango, yet she knows this is not the truth. Lafcadio, although Argentinian, did not dance. Reserved, often withdrawn, and although he'd loved the music of Astor Piazzolla, he could not listen to it after news of the composer's lunch with the military dictator, General Jorge Rafael Videla, spread through the exile community. No. If desperate erotic longing was at the heart of their relationship, it was one-sided, as Lafcadio opened up in her a desire so successfully denied in the years following Anthony D'Angelo. And because those feelings lay so long unacknowledged, she was shocked by their intensity and their power. No, they never danced, but Piazzolla and tango brought them together on an evening in the first year of *la dictadura*, the fascist takeover of Lafcadio's country. Hanna had been as unaware of *la dictadura* as she was of any other political situation now that the assassinations of Kennedy, King, and a second Kennedy, and the continuing destruction of Vietnam had driven her into hiding. Her childhood friend, Carol Levine, drew her out occasionally to board a bus bound for Washington to march and chant under an assortment of banners indicting LBJ and Henry Kissinger, but Hanna was always glad to return to work. She did research, wrote articles,

ARTjournal hired her as a contributing editor. It was solitary, satisfying work. She was always glad, as well, to return to the quiet and civility of the Galerie Bauer.

But Lafcadio: it was an evening in the early fall of 1976. Ernesto, a quiet young man from Buenos Aires, carried the last shipment of paintings Hanna had recently purchased at auction down to the basement. They began closing up for the night. While she finished recording the new inventory, he showered and changed into a loose silk shirt with wide sleeves caught in tight cuffs at the wrist, tucked into narrow gray slacks. His long black hair was shiny with brilliantine. It occurred to Hanna that he looked like the portrait she'd just purchased, Otto Pankok's *Young Romany*. As they lowered the gate across the front window, she asked where he was going. And that was how she found herself on a subway to lower Manhattan and, coming up to street level, she and Ernesto entered The Lafayette Grill. A bandoneon, guitar, and double bass played from a small stage at the front of the room, and Hanna, in her staid black gallerist's dress, was whirled out onto the floor, Ernesto suddenly taking charge. The young girl who'd walked towards Anthony D'Angelo along Newkirk Avenue holding a cigarette and removing a speck of tobacco from her tongue suddenly resurfaced as Ernesto gently lowered her to the floor. Raising her again, he and Hanna glided, arms outstretched, towards a table at the edge of the dance floor where a man sat alone, a drink in hand. "Lafcadio Hernandez," Ernesto said, "Hanna Silberstein." "*Mi dominata*," he added, and the somber young man almost smiled. Gesturing to an empty chair at the table, he hailed a waiter. Piña coladas, *dos*, he said. Ernesto bowed, then headed for the bar and stayed to talk to a man with a similar wide sleeved shirt while Hanna set out to spend the last four years of *la dictadura* with this chemist from Squibb Pharmaceuticals whose mother, an

Orientalist teaching at the University of Buenos Aires, had named him for the Greek-Irish-American collector of Japanese ghost stories, Lafcadio Hearn.

. . . and Vida

Hanna has just left for work. Lafcadio stands under the shower and directs steaming water down the inside of his thigh along the scar left by the electric cattle prod. The letter from his mother-in-law lies between the pages of a report on his desk at Squibb but he knows every word of it. "We are certain it will soon be over," she has written. "The Falklands War has been an embarrassment to the Junta. While 30,000 *desaparecidos* did not move the people to rid themselves of the dictatorship, a military embarrassment will bring the generals down. We are ready to confront them, have been ready since the day they seized power. I stand with the Mothers and Grandmothers of the Plaza de Mayo. Vida's name is embroidered on my headscarf. We demand to know what has become of our sons and daughters. It has been said that the children born in prison were taken from their mothers and given to military families. The thought never leaves me, Lafcadio, that your son or daughter, Vida's child, may be here in Buenos Aires, a six-year-old in school uniform already indoctrinated by the dogs who stole him from his mother. I will stand here till they kill me but I will know the fate of my daughter and my grandchild . . ." Lafcadio turns the nozzle to his face and runs the steaming water over his eyes and mouth. He will have to go back. He will tell Hanna tonight. He will go back to the men who stole his child, the men who pulled him from his laboratory seven years earlier and brought him to the Headquarters of *Seguridad Federal*, threw him naked and bound on a table and began, but this is what comes to him in the night, in his sleep he feels the cold metal at the base of his spine where the bone cracked as his body hit the table, and as he wakes, he sees Hanna upright, her eyes open and staring, frightened, leaning over him, reaching for him, but he does not let himself in that moment be touched. Afterwards, he holds her. He tries not to think of Vida. There is a possibility she may still be alive, somewhere, unable to find him. Seven years ago, the day he was released from *Seguridad*, he'd gone back to their block of flats and, running up through the stairwell of their building, found the door to their apartment open. Every drawer and closet emptied, papers torn and scattered across the floor, books and clothing thrown on top of them. He called her name, Vida, Vida, and a neighbor appeared at the door. *Desaparecida*, she said, disappeared, they came for her, carried her down the stairs, pushed his pregnant wife into a car, drove off. He walked the streets of Monte Chingolo while Squibb, who'd effected his release, arranged for an American visa. *Desaparecida*, but where. He asked all who'd known her, bribed a neighborhood cop, it was rumored the man might know something, but what, where. Lafcadio circled Headquarters and the buildings belonging to the navy that some had begun to call a concentration camp. He hid as uniformed police and navy officers came and went, wanting to approach them, *mi mujer*, and on the day before he left for America, he stopped a guard at the navy building, a young man with a round baby face, *mi mujer*, Vida, my life, *donde*, and the guard had shrugged and walked away.

The Reagan Years

• • •

A former president of the Screen Actors' Guild is sworn in as 40th President of the United States during the last years of *la dictadura*, and Hanna, only vaguely aware of either, is struggling to hold on to Lafcadio Hernandez. She leaves work early, comes home, changes into an emerald green corset, hooks black stockings on to its garters, and pulls on black spike-heeled leather boots. The Beckmann legacy surfaces in her presentation, there is something in her disguise that is profoundly related to her Self. Her head, heart, body, and soul are functioning as one. Anticipating the sound of his key in the lock, she stands ready to lunge as he comes through the door. *Mi nene, gaucho, mi mulero*, she aspirates as she undoes the buttons of his shirt and sinks to her knees. She massages his body, kneading away the knots between his shoulder blades and the ones in his calves, finding the points in the soles of his feet that will make him sigh with pleasure. She bakes *bizcochuelo*, cooks *matambre* and serves it to him in bed wearing only her leather boots. Lafcadio is grateful. He leaves anyway. Late one night after he has returned to Argentina, Hanna goes downtown to a branch of the Salvation Army, deposits a plastic bag containing the green corset and the black boots in the doorway, and returns uptown. She will resurface over the next few years, slowly, tentatively, painfully, not quite completely. It seems, in the time she was away, the country, the world, and the people she will reconnect with, have been in movement, are changing, have changed, or are about to change, calling her to return and, sometimes, to assist. Perestroika and glasnost are no longer italicized, they've become part of common speech, and it's only a question of getting to the end of the decade before the Berlin Wall will open and tiny beige boxlike cars, *Trabis*, will stream through to the West. Heinz Seligmüller, standing with a group of war veterans, will be there to greet them. Farther east, General Secretary Gorbachev will work to institute liberal reform. Sergei Brodsky reads of the changes in *Novye izvestia*, and renews his subscription to the paper, while former Major General Vladimir Piankov sinks deeper into a state of melancholy, recalling an earlier decade in which it was necessary to divest himself of his rightfully won wartime treasures. Former Private First Class Yevgeny Mikhailov lights a votive candle in the Church of the Nine Martyrs and says a prayer for international peace. The American President does his bit for international peace as well, he lays a wreath at Bergen Belsen, and another at a German military cemetery in the town of Bitburg, either oblivious or indifferent to the implications of honoring the SS officers buried there among the soldiers. A space shuttle will go up from Cape Canaveral carrying the first female astronaut, and perhaps Sally Ride has some influence on Theresa's decision to leave four teenage children and Joey Franco in Babylon, but in a letter from Tucson, she credits Werner Erhard, the founder of *est*. "'There isn't anything to fix or change in the world,'" she writes to Hanna, "'what is, is, what isn't, isn't.'" Theresa's thrown off all false attachment, she and her *est* instructor are living in Arizona selling real estate. Nancy Reagan has sent her a citation for co-hosting the Southwest Republican Women's Caucus. Carol Levine is no longer teaching at PS192 in East Harlem, she's gone back to school for horticulture, it was the garden of their home in Brooklyn that she'd loved. She's opened Carol's Floral Design on Madison Avenue and 68th. Standing orders for peonies, hydrangea, Casablanca lilies, and hanging heliconia are delivered from her shop to the Park Avenue lobbies and homes of junk bond salesmen. Mergers and takeovers are celebrated with orchids from Hawaii. Carol investigates the possibility of artificial insemination and, later in the decade, Alejandro Levine is born. Tia Hanna will be invited to birthday parties and, occasionally, she will babysit. Farther north along Madison Avenue, the Galerie Bauer is also profiting in these years. Whereas most of the newly rich are drawn to Andy Warhol, Julian Schnabel, Jean-Michel Basquiat, others look to create a family history with a nineteenth-century European portrait or landscape, the more gilded the frame, the better. Some will even begin to explore The New Objectivity and, with reference to their student years protesting the war in Vietnam, the new stock analysts and power brokers will seek to acquire a Kaethe Kollwitz, an Otto Dix. The "decadent" art that Emil brought when he left Germany, and the pieces Hanna has acquired at auction, are now in demand. She hires an assistant, an art history graduate student whose ambition keeps pace with the decade. Ernesto wraps the paintings, delivers them. He's not looking well, he's thin, there's talk of a new illness. Stock analysts and power brokers have not yet gentrified his neighborhood, and the people who do live there don't seem to be sharing in the new prosperity. In the latter half of the decade, men and women who sleep on the sidewalk have multiplied exponentially, they lie down on cardboard in front of Ernesto's building, Hanna's as well, they congregate at the entrances to subways and in the shelter of doorways. Hanna gives them money on her way to work but she is becoming aware of what some are calling compassion fatigue. Ernesto sidesteps the drug dealers on his way home, and when his apartment is destroyed by local crack addicts searching for cash, he and Hanna turn the basement of the Galerie into living quarters. He enrolls in a research study at Mt. Sinai, he is given AZT, he survives the decade. Louie does not. Hanna stands with her mother at the grave, sadly remembering the washer-dryer, the TV console, the first four-door Chevrolet on Marlboro Road, the naive, almost quaint materialism of that decade as opposed to the voracious greed of this one. There'd been an innocence to that era of acquisition, an emergence from the war with a will to join the celebration. Hanna sees her cousins Harvey and Neil at the funeral. They've gone forth to Long Island and multiplied, grandchildren of all ages, dressed for this sad occasion and held in check by their mothers, gather quietly around Gertie. It occurs to Hanna that the years of *la dictadura* have coincided with her own child-bearing years, Bertha's late motherhood had given her the idea that there would always be time, and now there isn't. As two small children attempt to climb up Harvey's leg, Hanna cannot determine what she is feeling. It does not seem to be regret. "I remember watching while he baked," she says now as, next in line, she takes Gertie's hand. "It was wonderful, the smell of bread coming from the oven. And I remember, of course, hearing of his extraordinary kindness to my parents." Bertha and Annelene stand behind Hanna, waiting to offer condolences. They have never felt easy with Gertie and Louie's extraordinary kindness, they are not anxious to remember the time of rescue and dependency. Bertha is even less anxious to recall the days of Hans Erich's business partnership with Louie. Still, she embraces her cousin, aware of Gertie's fragility now, and the despair that loss will inevitably bring. Bertha has just returned from Toronto, she thinks of Hilde, curiously, in connection with widowhood, not herself. Hilde hasn't remarried. She continues to run the book store, a wedding reception had taken place at The Lion while Bertha was visiting. The American bridegroom, Arthur Levine, is a physics professor at the university and is beginning his third—or, did one of the guests say, fourth—marriage. The bride, a young Senegalese asylum seeker, is a physics student. Hilde seems content to host others' happiness, yet there does seem to be a man, an academic considerably younger than she, he encouraged Hilde to send her work to literary journals. She's beginning to be recognized as a Canadian poet. The young man seems quite devoted to her. Perhaps, Bertha thinks, she is mistaken, but there did seem to be, and although inappropriate to the occasion, her correspondence with Mr. Hokaido comes to mind and Bertha, confused, embarrassed, lets go of Gertie's hand. "I am sorry for your loss," she says. "He was a good man," and she draws forth a handkerchief, and wipes her eyes. Later that year, Hanna will help her mother and her aunt move to the Heights, this time Brooklyn Heights, Pineapple Street, because Annelene loved its name and the quiet elegance of the neighborhood, and because she was able to find an atelier there with living quarters. There is room to paint and northern light. Annelene is preparing for a solo exhibit at the Brooklyn Museum Art School. She will include her most recent drawings of the shops that have begun to appear along Newkirk Avenue, the Deshi Asian-Mexican-American Grocery, the Wing Fat Laundromat, the Iglesia de Dios Pentecostal Church. She will turn the drawings into paintings in the new atelier and finish her latest self-portrait. Howard Epstein, returned to her after the death of Emil Franz Bauer, will sit for his portrait as well. It's Howard she is grateful to for finding the two apartments on Pineapple Street. He lives in the Heights now, he has real estate connections, she and Bertha will continue to be neighbors. In the years that follow, Howard Epstein is their escort to the Metropolitan Opera, the Brooklyn Academy of Music, the local cinema and Chinese restaurant. Sometimes, Howard thinks, it is Bertha who listens to him, Annelene does become too absorbed in her work, she is not always aware of what he needs, perhaps Bertha, but then again, with both sisters on his arms, he feels best. And Bertha? She continues to study Japanese at the language school downtown. Mr. Hokaido's letters arrive at the beginning of each month. She has given her piano, the one Hans Erich paid for in monthly installments, to the Iglesia Youth Center and has purchased a Yamaha upright for the new apartment. Occasionally, she gives concerts at the Brooklyn Ethical Culture Society and plays for birthdays and holidays. Their piano is not a bad instrument. She insists they tune it regularly. As Hanna helps her pack, Bertha recalls the story of the crate, the first one, with the Feuerbach, Spitzweg, and Menzel. There are other paintings now, Hanna's just wrapped the one by Moritz von Schwind and a pair of Wilhelm Busch caricatures she'd found at auction. They will hang in the living room on Pineapple Street. There is something Bertha wants to tell Hanna about the paintings in that first crate, the ones that have disappeared, and the connections to, but Hanna is busy wrapping glasses and dishware in newspaper and loading them in cardboard boxes. She's brought along a Spanish man; he's taking the cartons to a truck downstairs. Another time. These years prior to cataract operations, hearing aids, arthritis, and the fall, are the Dubrovsky sisters' years of renewed prosperity. They've come late, and they're well-lived.

Content

• • •

Annelene is content. She steers a shopping cart along Pineapple Street, crosses to Willow, and passes the terracotta Bacchus who guards the house on the corner. Grapes and vine leaves tumble down the length of his chest. "Readymade pictures are lying around in the streets," Marie-Louise had written from Paris almost sixty years earlier, "you just have to take the trouble to paint them." Annelene walks carefully, the sidewalk's concrete slabs are pressed up at odd angles by the roots of large oaks. She enjoys the unevenness, the crooked rendering, angles reminiscent of a Max Beckmann painting. Another letter from Marie-Louise came yesterday. There will be a retrospective of Beckmann's work in Frankfurt at the Städel, and one of her own in Vienna at the Belvedere, will Annelene come? She considers. No. She won't. She is content to stand at her easel in the sunroom of her home on Pineapple Street. She will have a retrospective of her own, there's so little time, she will not travel. Perhaps Hanna will go, she needs a change, that's clear. There was a time, Annelene is certain, when Hanna moved as someone does who has a secret. The thought of it filled her face, it was rounder, her eyes smiling, it filled her body as well so that she walked differently, she swayed, her hips in the lead. Someone has come into her life, Annelene had thought then. And someone had gone out of it, she knew, as she watched Hanna retreat and fold back into herself, becoming once again quiet and reserved, the child she'd always been, brought up with stories of the three Muses and a surfeit of family history.

How many years ago was it when Hanna seemed to withdraw, it was as if she were grieving, and Annelene recognized grieving, recalled the time after Emil, the unbearable feelings of loss and abandonment, then sometime later, years later, a settling. Not an acceptance, never that, it was more that grief had settled in a private, smaller place, hidden but liable to appear suddenly, surprising and overwhelming. Annelene does not want that for her niece, that settling. Hanna is still young, she will urge her to go to Europe, to the Städel, and to the Belvedere. Annelene will write to Marie-Louise and let her know that her niece, Hanna Silberstein, will come instead.

Detlev

• • •

And she does. Hanna entrusts the Galerie Bauer to her assistant, and takes off for Europe. She will cover the Max Beckmann exhibit for *ARTjournal* and she will interview Marie-Louise von Motesiczky. She will visit the grandniece of Antje Schmidt, who will give her something precious, and she will attend the exhibit at the Belvedere, where she will meet Detlev Hagen, formerly Detlev von Hagen before he petitioned the court to remove the aristocratic link. He will help heal her broken heart, albeit inflicting another, smaller wound. Hanna's Detlev Hagen may bear a resemblance to the real Detlev Hagen, possibly even to Detlev von Hagen, who can say, it is only important how she tells the story to herself. Here in Europe where it all began, does she make use of The New Objectivity? Magic Realism? Say she chooses objectivity: Hanna is listening to the guest speaker at the Belvedere. They're showing fifty of Marie-Louise's paintings and drawings, coinciding with her eighty-ninth birthday. Detlev is here to interview the artist about her brother, Karl, for his book, *Wartime Resistance in Vienna*. Resistance: there's the first clue. Hanna misses it. Deliberately? Of course. Detlev's field of expertise is Resistance. Although everything that follows has the appearance of intimacy, that is only Magic Realism, invented and embellished by Hanna's fantasy. In fact, in their emotional connectedness, they will never get much further than this, exchanging erotically polite conversation, holding sekt with orange juice at the reception following the opening.

She will want to know about Karl von Motesiczky. He will want to tell her. She will want to know about the scar above his eyebrow and, later, the one below his navel. She will marvel at the loosening of her hold on sadness, and the possibility of affection post-Lafcadio for this heavyset man with the beautiful radio voice and apparent interest in her life. What she will take for interest, she will later recognize as Detlev's professionally honed interviewing skill combined with the obligatory deference of the late-twentieth-century German humanist towards the Jew. Jewess. And, perhaps, a soupçon of the century-old assumption of the Jew's (Jewess's) extraordinary eroticism. Never mind. For the moment, Hanna believes that Detlev is interested in her, perhaps he returns her affection—but is she once more moving into the realm of magic?

Better to stick with the facts: Detlev von Hagen is conceived on a furlough from the Russian front, the last of five sons before von Hagen Sr. freezes to death outside Stalingrad. Detlev has a photo of him. As a boy, he carried it in the breast pocket of his shirt. He doesn't show it to Hanna. What he does say: my father was a carpenter, a lapsed Catholic, a Social Democrat. He played the mandolin in the evening, three of his five children are old enough to remember that. Four worn pipes stood in a holder he'd carved on the mantelpiece of the family home in the East German city of Rostock. His father, Detlev had been told, would sit in a wing back chair late at night, the bowl of a pipe warming his hand. Then he was gone, and Detlev grows up anyway. Just after Soviet tanks destroy the Hungarian Uprising in 1956, Detlev, unbidden, stands up in class. He condemns the Soviet action. No one speaks. His classmates look down, studying the day's text. The cold eye of the history teacher stretches across the room, taking his measure. Detlev's knees begin to shake. "After school, von Hagen." But Detlev takes off that day, he gets on the next train to East Berlin, boards the train that still runs to the

West, and takes out of his pocket the address of his oldest brother who'd left Rostock a year earlier. Knees still shaking, he knocks at his brother's door. He is fifteen.

Detlev stays on in West Berlin, goes to the university, becomes a radio journalist and biographer of lost causes. Union leaders, Communists, Social Democrats, imprisoned already in the '30s and somehow still alive to tell of it, East German dissident poets, publishers, actors, ministers, a rabbi back in Germany after years of exile. Detlev researches the details of their lives. He knows their work and their place in history. Interviewing them for the radio, he gives his guests time to consider and reflect, listens carefully to their answers. They sense the respect, the genuflection, these old warriors, and each undoes his parcel of anecdotes containing secrets and grudges, they lay them on the table for Detlev Hagen to handle and explore. They are not yet, as they often suspect, relegated to obscurity. Here is someone who listens. As he listens to her. Hanna's hands are full of tenderness as she sits with his head in her lap and massages the folds of his large hot ears after they've made love. No. The New Objectivity: after Hanna has reimagined love.

A Kitchen in Ilvesheim

• • •

"My mother was born in this house. She left school when she was ten to work on the farm and, by the time he came to power, she was sixteen. Like so many others who'd lived through the first war and the terrible inflation, she and her family were always anxious. For them, I think the economic disaster was less terrible, farmers had food, but still they were desperate for a strong leader, someone who would be able to assure them that he was in control and would bring order to their lives. We hear his voice today, and see the film clips from the '30s, and we can't understand the cheering crowds. There's something ridiculous, even comical, about that little mustache and all that breast beating. Yet my mother stood in those crowds and she, too, was seduced. I don't think it's wrong to say seduced. Girls her age swooned when he spoke, as if he were a rock star. There are lots of theories, but what is certain is that after the war, they felt humiliated and powerless, existentially threatened, and when he came, he put words to their rage and was able to convince them that the Jews were to blame. In exchange for loyalty, he promised he'd give them order and dignity and pride, and they believed him. My mother, too."

"Your mother was a Nazi." There. The word is out. Birgit Klein-Messmer's husband has had enough. He sees no reason to protect the memory of his mother-in-law. It's the simple truth, he's said it.

They sit in a large farmhouse kitchen in Ilvesheim, and there it is, the word, it's out. The question is what to do with it. Hanna has not come to judge the Klein-Messmers or their parents. And even if she were able, she has not come to bestow absolution. She is here because the daughter of Caroline Klein, Antje Schmidt's grandniece, has made the effort to find her. A letter from Hans Erich had been found among Caroline Klein's papers after her funeral.

In the silence following Willy Klein-Messmer's remark, a Mozart sonata is heard from the next room. Although the Klein-Messmers are not much older than Hanna, they have grandchildren. One of them, their Sri Lankan-German granddaughter, is practicing the violin now. She will perform the sonata at the local synagogue, which had been vandalized but not entirely destroyed in the early morning of the day, fifty-six years ago, when Hans Erich sat in the bedroom of this farmhouse cleaning the wound of Antje Schmidt's nephew. The Klein-Messmers belong to the committee that restored the synagogue, carefully researching the interior design, collecting donations for the replicated mosaics, columns, the *mechitzah*, the *bimah*. The building is no longer a house of prayer, there are no Jews living in the area. Instead, it is a center for lectures and concerts. A Klezmer group will perform there next month. The Klein-Messmers are teachers at an anthroposophical school. With fellow members of the Green Party, they organize anti-nuclear demonstrations. This has been related over home-made apple cake in a warmly lit kitchen with hand-hewn tables and chairs and cupboards that have been in the family for generations.

The sun is setting now. Hanna can see it through the window that looks out on a tidy organic garden. She will have to be going, there is very little to be done about the word. She feels no sense of superiority in her chance connection to the victims, she doesn't hold the Klein-Messmers responsible for the past. It is true that she is uncomfortable with them, but her discomfort is hardly grand, it has no political content. It stems from something simpler, something personal, she suspects, a memory of herself as a child looking across an alleyway between two buildings, beyond a spindly ailanthus, into a kitchen. A woman, a nylon stocking tying back her hair, standing at a stove. A man coming up behind her, pressing his mustache to the back of her neck. A family at a table, a grandfather, grace before dinner. Hanna observing life as it ought to be. As she finishes her cup of fair-trade coffee now, she thinks of the cake with organic apples she does not make, the anti-nuclear demonstrations she does not organize, the grandchildren's recitals she does not attend. And although Willy Klein-Messmer is brash and unappealing, he is a man, and here is a marriage, and Hanna will go back to an empty hotel room tonight. Order, stability, continuity, discipline, belief, purpose, descriptive nouns occur to her in this kitchen in Ilvesheim. "There's nothing I can do to change that now," Birgit Klein-Messmer is saying. "I loved my mother. It's important for me to understand why she was who she was, and go on from there." Descriptive nouns bordering on caricature, Hanna reminds herself. What had she known of the lives of the D'Angelos, what can she know of the lives of the Klein-Messmers.

"It's getting late. Your train will be leaving soon. Willy will take you to the station. Before you go, there is something I want to give you. It was mentioned in your father's letter to my mother, and I believe it belongs to your family." Birgit Klein-Messmer goes to the living room and returns with a painting, a still life. A porcelain pitcher with a chipped handle, a spoon, an egg.

Marie-Louise

• • •

"I was a true believer then." Marie-Louise is speaking of the time she studied with Max Beckmann. She and Hanna are sitting in the Signature Suite of the Hotel Sacher in Vienna. A busboy has just delivered a large pot of coffee on a silver tray. Hanna sets the tape recorder to pause and pours a cup for each of them. "In the last century," Marie-Louise says, indicating the room's opulent furnishings, the crystal chandelier, "my mother and her cousins played in the family home not far from here, the Todesco Palace. Two lumps. No milk, please." Despite years of diminished resources, Hanna is thinking, Marie-Louise has not lost the bearing of a graceful, dignified, old-world aristocrat. At eighty-nine, her eyes are large and lively as they were in her earliest self-portraits. She sits quietly, stirring her coffee. The retrospective at the Belvedere had been a success. "Paintings for Eternity" and "Late Homecoming" headlined reviews in the press, Rembrandt and Dürer were cited and, following the exhibit, Marie-Louise had received Austria's Cross of Honor for Science and Art. Reparations, some grumbled quietly, while others took the opportunity to condemn Austria's complicity in its darkest past.

"For years," Marie-Louise continues now, "I repeated everything Beckmann said, uncritically, as if his ideas were my religion. We had no religious beliefs as such, you see. Certainly Mother's Jewish origins were irrelevant until they became that which was most relevant. It's odd, though. Several years after the war, sometime in the late '50s, I returned briefly to Vienna. I remember waiting at a tram stop. The tram had been delayed and I found myself observing a man who was also waiting. His face was long and thin, he was leaning on a cane, it was obviously an effort for him to stand. He looked exhausted and it wasn't the exhaustion of old age, I thought, it seemed to me that of the wanderer, the Jew, and I felt a closeness to him, a kinship. I realized it was the first time I'd spontaneously thought of myself that way. Interesting, the layers of identity one finds all of a sudden, one has only to stop, to pause and consider. That was Beckmann's idea as well." She stirs her coffee and adds another lump of sugar. "He was one of my gods. I was not at all drawn to religion, but I did have my version of the gods: Beckmann, Mother. Canetti. Each required deference and allegiance, yet all were convinced of my gift as an artist and never failed to believe in me. There were times when I knew that my work would never be valued in the art world, it was literally worth nothing, yet I knew it was good, and I knew how difficult it is to paint good pictures, to make progress, to become someone. Strange idea, though, isn't it. To become someone. As if a lack of recognition reduces one to non-existence. Perhaps this is unavoidable. However, here again, I think of Beckmann. More than two hundred paintings in the years when no one would show his work. For some, though, myself included, it did seem terribly important to be recognized, as if one were not really an artist until another said so. And no one was saying so about representational artists for several decades following the war. So there I was, a representational artist and a woman, a double handicap. The women's movement of the '60s did help with the latter. By that time, the critics, in deference I suppose to the *Zeitgeist*, had stopped referring to me as an emasculated version of Beckmann. Some even included me in the so-called revolution but it wasn't at all how I saw myself. I very much admired the young women, their radiant self-confidence and defiance of constraint, and their demands for equal recognition, but I was never one to join in marching and chanting. Every movement, I think, includes the danger of allowing another to define you. As part of the crowd, you are assumed to believe every word of the speeches and slogans. No, that kind of liberation was not for me. I needed to find my own way." Marie-Louise puts her cup on the table and sits back in the plush armchair. "Wonderful strong coffee, isn't it, I do miss that in England." Hanna pours another cup for each of them. It's late afternoon, the room has begun to grow dark, details of large, ornately framed landscapes on the walls are no longer visible. In the silence, they hear the click of the tape, it's come to the end. Hanna removes it and turns it to the other side.

"The portraits," she asks now, and Marie-Louise sits quietly as if gathering her thoughts. "The portraits," she says after a while. "Here, too, Beckmann's principles were my guide. What was most important was to gain a sense of the subject's inner life, that's what I wanted to represent, their essential truth, not simply a replication of individual features. It often landed me in trouble and I admit to feeling hurt by the rejections from those who'd commissioned portraits—the Baron Rothschild, Ursula Vaughn Williams. Canetti after the last portrait. Am I being immodest when I say that I was incapable of flattery. Iris Murdoch understood this, '. . . so sad, me with the demons,' she wrote after I'd completed the portrait, and wondered how I'd found her out. But that was always the challenge of portraiture, finding someone out. The same principle applied to self-portrait. Your aunt and I often speculated about the impulse towards painting oneself. In youth, I suppose, it is partly to record one's beauty. There I am, you think, beautiful. It is as well, though, the beginning of a desire to know oneself, to seek an answer to the question, Who am I? As we age, there is a sense of anguish in relinquishing beauty, the skin can no longer be painted with light alone, we need to fill our palette with purples and grays and jaundiced yellows to paint a mixture of bloated hills, fleshy pockets, creased gullies. We paint anguish, and that becomes beauty in old age self-portraiture as we find the possibility, finally, of seeing ourselves humbly and without pretense." She smiles. "We paint with cold-blooded authenticity. That is the gift of old age, a blessing really."

Marie-Louise leans back and closes her eyes. The success of the exhibit and the amount of attention surrounding it has been exhilarating. And she's tired. Hanna waits, then asks a last question. "The portraits of your mother . . ." Eight years earlier, the Tate had purchased a portrait of Henriette, and several have been shown at the Belvedere Retrospective with exceptional praise from the press.

"In those last years," Marie-Louise answers, "when Mother needed so much care, I sat by her bed in the evening reading to her, sometimes reading her own poems. Her large, childlike eyes lit up each time I entered the room. By day, I drew hundreds of sketches, thinking to turn some of them into paintings. Just a very few thin wisps of hair remained on her head, she no longer bothered to cover it, and the hair above her upper lip had darkened to a small mustache. If I can begin a portrait of her, I thought, without embellishment, without lies, recording her smile, the liveliness of her spirit, her intellect, and, despite her weakness, something of her joy and hope, I will have done a great thing." She pauses and looks up, suddenly remembering. "But Hanna," she says, "I seem to have come far from your original question about the search for one's self. I'm afraid I cannot give you any wisdom, my dear, as I look back over almost nine decades of seeking, finding a self here, another there. Perhaps it's correct to say that one's identity is never static, it is ever-evolving. The challenge, I think, is to discover what is authentic and to remain truthful to that. For me, that was most often the desire to paint beautiful pictures and, in doing so, to make myself and others happy."

To Castel Montero, my love

• • •

It's shortly after four AM. 4:08 perhaps, 4:09. Bertha had glanced at the clock before getting out of bed. She is lying on the bathroom floor now, unable to get up. She can shift her weight slightly, but when she does, there is a sharp pain. Pelvis, hip? Better to lie still, wait for Annelene. It happened so quickly, one minute whole, the next in pieces, lying cracked on a tiled floor, a blue and gray ceramic jug, milk and broken shards splattered over the surface, she, a small child, weeping, a servant, who might that have been, scolding. Spilled, cracked, one minute whole, the next in pieces. Annelene will call, they always talk at seven, she'll come with the key. Till seven then. Bertha reaches for the tip of a large towel on the rack, grabs hold, and pulls it down. She covers herself. The bathroom tiles are cold, the towel might help. She recalls getting up from the toilet, she'd turned, or had she, she cannot reconstruct, why bother, this is where she is, this is where she will be, when had she thought that. Long ago, but here she is, not there, and she will not dwell on, Annelene will be here after seven when she realizes there is no, "I cannot wait til seven," she hears herself say, but she must, and this will not be the day she'd planned. Cheese, bread, there are paper items on her list as well, napkins, paper towels, one other, toilet paper perhaps, the supermarket then the greengrocer, he carries better fruit and vegetables, fresher, certainly more expensive than the ones on Newkirk Avenue. Exotic fruit, too. Papaya and mango, and some of those bosc pears, and on the way home, she'd have returned a book to the library and checked out another, she's become a fan of mystery novels. And if the day is one of those warm autumn days, as it was yesterday, she'll take the new book to the Promenade and, no, this will not be the day she'd planned, and Bertha finds herself weeping for the loss of the day as she begins to imagine the sound of Annelene's key in the door, her sister's cries of dismay, strangers with a stretcher, the loud, penetrating, insistent complaint of an ambulance siren, the wait in a drafty corridor for admission. "I just turned around," she hears herself say, "and there I was, on the floor," spilled, cracked. Annelene will want to call Hanna. Yes. No. Hanna's last letter from Europe lies on the desk. Hans Erich's painting, the Hermann Adler still life, found, who'd've thought, but then, she never had trusted Antje Schmidt's niece, Caroline, how does a crate with fine housewares, Meissen figurines, valuable books and recordings, paintings—her piano music—how do such things simply disappear. Then again, so much did disappear, of course it was possible, who knew where anything was after the war, people and objects set down wherever they managed to fall, never picking themselves up again and returning to their rightful place, and it wasn't as if, after finding Hilde, and losing Ruth, it wasn't as if the objects were in and of themselves important, it was rather their connection to, and here Bertha remembers what it was she wanted to tell Hanna when they were packing and moving to Brooklyn Heights, it had to do with the paintings. The Feuerbach, the Spitzweg, the Menzel. I wanted to say, Hanna, I think I understand now. For many years I didn't, but I do now, it was not owning then losing things, even beautiful valuable things, no. For me, the paintings were not objects, they were connection. That was it. And their loss was part of the loss of all that was familiar, the loss of, what do they say here? The ground under my feet. Literally, the ground. After we left Mannheim, no home compared with the one on Elisabethstrasse, the high-ceilinged rooms, maroon and gold damask curtains drawn at dusk, our library of books and phonograph records, the paintings, the eighteenth-century music stand, the wedding vase from the Mayor's wife, the grand plush armchairs and striped sofa. The Bechstein. These were not inanimate objects. Well, of course they were but, for me, each held the spirit of someone who'd chosen them with the idea of surrounding us with beauty and with safety, with belonging, and refuge, and with love. Most came from your grandfather, Papa, and though we'd lost him ten years earlier, we lost him again when the paintings disappeared. I remember the night he unveiled the Feuerbach, how proud he was, his intention to give us the finest he had, the assurance of continuity. With this, he meant to stay in our lives, he'd always be there, his presence and protection would encompass me, that was the promise of that dark, gloomy landscape. *In the Mountains of Castel Montero*. We'd talked of Italy, of visiting those mountains, how lovely that would have been, why didn't we when it was still possible. You hardly know that side of me, Hanna, the side that loves to be out in the world, exploring, feeling myself alive with adventure. I knew it again in Japan, knew that part of myself in Nagasaki of all places. And I'd take off for Castel Montero this minute but. Ah. No. I don't think I'll be going anywhere just yet. So. That was the Feuerbach. The Spitzweg? A small painting of a gentleman caller offering a bouquet to a country lass, that was Papa's engagement gift to Mutti. As if Mutti ever resembled a country lass, but it was the sweetness of the gesture he loved, the simplicity. Liselotte Augusta Hohenemser would be his country lass, and their doorjamb ever wreathed with roses. Oh, yes. You laugh.We thought that way. Lying on another floor, the floor of the art museum in Mannheim long ago, I opened my eyes, and there was my gentleman caller, holding not a bouquet but smelling salts, and I thought he'd stepped out of the little painting I'd always loved. And the Menzel. The portrait of Clara Schumann playing the piano. She was a beautiful woman, her dark hair parted in the middle, drawn back over her ears and gathered at the back of her head in a braided bun. In the painting, her hands seem to be alive and moving across the keys. Clara Schumann had eight children, you know. She gave concerts to support the family, and composed wonderful music, songs and works for the piano and violin, all while coping with her husband's mental breakdown. Perhaps Papa wished that resilience for me. He gave me the painting just after I'd won the piano competition in Mannheim. It was a surprise. How did he know I'd win? He did. I was his first-born Muse, and the Menzel gave a permanence to my art because, you know, when you make music, you scatter the notes, you let them go, then they're gone and nothing remains. Papa knew I needed something that would always be there. Permanence. We live with the illusion that it might be possible, and every day disproves it. Now, for example. Here lies an old lady. I never did think of myself as any particular age. As the years went by, of course I saw the changes in my body, the puffy folds of flesh beneath my chin, the veins like worms just beneath the skin on the back of my hands, now and then I caught sight of my head stretched forward, the curve in my shoulders, but old, no, I never thought that, although now I think I did know. I'd even understood, although I never put it into words before now, that getting old is an exercise in letting go, and if you won't let go gracefully, the years nevertheless tear from you your walk, your sight, your hearing, family, friends. You hold on tighter because it's all slipping away while the unassailable cruelty of age mocks your efforts to hold on, so that here you lie, cracked, broken. Accept that with grace? Hanna dear, forgive me, my darling. There was so little I could give to protect you, not even cheerfulness, and this morning I am particularly heavyhearted, why is that. Oh yes. Of course. Here I lie, broken, cracked, cold. Till seven. To Castel Montero, my love, go while there's still time.

Berlin Days/ Moscow Nights

Belye Stolbi, February 1995: Sergei Brodsky massages his chest as he turns the pages of his wartime diary. Despite a heart murmur, detected just after the destruction of Tsarskoe Selo when he'd come before the draft board, Brodsky has lived to be an old man, he is eighty-three now. Tonight he's waiting for Blavatsky. It's Wednesday, they'll play chess, he's uncorked a bottle of wine from Georgia. Tsinandali. An excellent wine. Blavatsky will also have read of the exhibit in Leningrad and the one opening at the end of the month in Moscow. *Novye izvestia* lies open on the kitchen table: Degas' *Place de la Concorde*, Gauguin's *Two Sisters*, Van Gogh's *White House at Night*, finally on exhibit at the Hermitage, while the Pushkin, not to be outdone, is bringing its wartime loot out of storage as well. Brodsky's taken his diary from the hidden safe behind the bookcase. There was a time when its discovery might have sent him to the Gulag. He lights a cigarette, and turns to the first page: "Tsarskoe Selo, June 22, 1941. In desperation, we attempted to move the mosaics and carvings from the Amber Room to safety, but as I tried to lift the first panel from the wall, it crumbled in my hands. The other student interns have fled to their home towns. I cannot be the lone defender of Tsarskoe Selo. Catherine the Great's Summer Palace will be left to the advancing German army. I cannot save it. . . ."

• • •

Berlin, February 1995. Heinz Seligmüller turns to the last page of the *Tagesblatt* and considers. If he leaves the newspaper here in the day room, other residents of the Anna Seghers Home for the Aged, fully half of them senile, will take it and pretend to read. The crossword puzzle has not yet been done. Eichendorff usually gets to the paper first, pens in all of the answers, right or wrong. Today he is late. Hopefully dead in the night. Seligmüller slips the paper into the bag hanging from his wheelchair and rolls to the room he shares with two other men. An article in the news has caught his eye, something about art and the war and Russia. With his foot, he pushes open the door to Room 413. Wiener is sleeping in the armchair, Schultz staring out the window, what else is new, and Seligmüller rolls to the table in the corner where he spreads out the newspaper. There it is: *Twice Saved: Exhibit of Masterpieces of European Art Removed to the Territory of the Soviet Union from Germany as a Consequence of the Second World War.* "Thieves! *Goniffs!*" he shouts, and begins to cough. Schultz, roused, begins to cough as well, and, sensing the opportunity, hacks up a large ball of green mucus onto the floor. The two men breathe deeply. Schultz turns to the window, Seligmüller to the paper . . . *an excited crowd arrived at the Hermitage to view the paintings that, for the past fifty years, have presumably been stored in the basement of the museum in Leningrad. Curators here still adhere to the story of 'the heroic Red Army rescue' of artwork from 'damp caves' where the treasures had been stored after 1944 in an attempt to protect them from the escalating bombardment of major German cities. The artworks, according to the same propaganda, were saved a second time by Soviet museum curators and restorers who . . .* "Liars!" Seligmüller cries, activating another coughing spell. Schultz fails to respond. Dumped in this shithole now, Seligmüller thinks, there was a time, and he recalls a day in April of 1941 when he, a young adjutant then, stood at attention as the most powerful man in Europe entered the office in the Reich Chancellery. “With my very sincerest best wishes for your birthday, Heil unser Führer!” he heard Posse say, and the art dealer had bowed, his right arm stretched towards the wall. There, in ornate baroque frames, hung paintings, it was whispered, by the Führer’s favorite artists. One of mountains, that he recalls. Seligmüller’s eyes grow moist. He takes out a stained pocket handkerchief, and dries them.

• • •

Moscow, February 1995. His daughter, Sveta, has just brought dinner, cabbage soup, she’s warmed it and set it on the table. She can’t stay tonight, she’s meeting a friend. They’re off to the Pushkin, a special exhibit, she’s told him, Manet, Renoir, Goya, Daumier, paintings that were rescued during the war. Yevgeny Mikhailov fixes a cloth around his neck. A bib, he thinks, disgusted with his old man’s habit of staining his clothing each time he lifts a spoon to his mouth. As bad as Piankov, but then Piankov, he’d observed, in the field, in the canteen, even at a victory banquet, had flung food into his mouth, never attempting to avoid the consequences. Major General Vladimir Piankov, his commanding officer, bits of stew and gravy among the medals, encrusted in the buttons and cuffs of his uniform. Paintings from Germany. The war had just ended, and Major General Piankov, Mikhailov recalls now, had sent the Soviet 69th Army, his unit, to a cave on the outskirts of a village near Berlin. Orders had been given to guard the area around the cave, it was rumored that valuable art . . .

• • •

Berlin, February 1995. A seven-letter word for “property taken by fraud or force.” Someone has written p in the first square, e in the sixth. Eichendorff, the bastard. There is a clatter of carts in the hallway. Lunch. Something brown it will be, and something gray warmed over. Wurst, Seligmüller is thinking, brown bear sausage, and he imagines he feels the grainy texture, fur, he'd thought then, on his tongue. Only once but, unfortunately, memorable. It was the day they transferred the paintings from the basement of the Reich Chancellery to Hohenwalde. He had no eye for art, the loss of it was the loss, rather, of that day in 1941 when all was noble and the future assured, this he left in the cave at Hohenwalde, along with his youth. He reaches for a handkerchief again and wipes his eyes as the lunch attendant arrives. A scullery maid, Polish slut. She reached into the dessert tray again yesterday when she thought no one was looking, put a cookie into a napkin, slipped it into her handbag before leaving for the day, "*Bis morgen*," see you tomorrow, all innocence, a little wave. Bye bye. Plunder.

• • •

Moscow, February 1995. Retired railway official Pjotr Khrapchenko turns over in bed. His wife is asleep. Now and then she makes that grunting sound, in their sixty-fifth year together too familiar, could it be he'd at one time found it charming. His feet are cold, his neck and hands ache, rheumatism he's been told, and his wife's rabbit stew, the years have not improved her culinary skills, he feels it repeating in his esophagus. Something in the paper today, it's at the edge of his thoughts, he's ruled out getting any sleep tonight, damn it he'll sleep through the next day, something about German art, something saved, the Hermitage, the Pushkin. Praskovia Sokolova comes to mind and brings a smile to his lips and, remembering the lady's untimely end, a tear to his eye. German art. Saved. He sees himself standing at Moscow's Kiev Station. A winter month, 1946. He's tightened a leather belt around his trim waist, stiffened the wings of his mustache, eight boxcars loaded with wooden crates have just arrived. . . .

• • •

Rublevo, February 1995. Vladka Borkhova takes up her feather duster and slides it carefully between the figurines on the top shelf of the Biedermeier highboy in the Levinson-Volinsky dacha. Boris Levinson-Volinsky and his wife will be returning this evening from France, oil business, and his wife will no doubt bring back a suitcase of knickknacks. It will be even harder to dust the living room, and Vladka Borkhova, although no longer young, is thinking of joining her brother-in-law selling hot chestnuts in Bittsevskiy Park. She has been dusting knickknacks, she thinks, for too long, from the time poor Praskovia Sokolova, who tragically ended her life at Kiev Station, lived here; through the Khruschev years when its next tenants, Sokolova's daughter and her spouse, the Commissar, were sent to Siberia; to the present, when the dacha's latest owners, nouveau-riche Jews, petroleum wealth, moved in. It is obvious to Vladka Borkhova, they hardly appreciate what is already here, Irena Abramovna is continually adding on. Certainly she and her husband do not value her favorite pieces, she thinks, as she picks up a small porcelain figure of Harlequin, wipes it down with a soft cloth and positions it next to Columbine. It has occurred to her she might slip them into the pocket of her apron one day, Irena Abramovna would never know they were gone, and because Vladka Borkhova has never taken anything that didn't belong to her, and because the thought of it has become so persistent lately, and so disquieting, she is thinking she will have to give notice and leave for Bittsevskiy Park. The porcelain harlequin, she thinks, no one would miss it, nor would they miss the painting of the little country lass and her gentleman caller, an arc of roses framing the door where she stands, her red lips pursed in a sweet smile.

• • •

Moscow, February 1995. It has always been one of her favorites, Beethoven's Piano Sonata Number 5. There are still the original markings written in the music by her beloved teacher, Elena Siroko, from the time she was a student at the Tchaikovsky Conservatory. Natalia Seminova flexes her fingers. There's a stiffening lately and a slight swelling in the joints. She tries the arpeggio again. Later, she will join her friend at The Pushkin. Sveta will meet her at seven, there is still time to practice. Some of Siroko's markings have become illegible. It's thirty-two years since Natalia Seminova played the piece in public at the closing ceremony of a week-long celebration of Soviet/German Democratic Republic solidarity. The mayors and City Councils of both Moscow and Dresden had been there. The director of the Conservatory sat between them in the first row, the crease between his eyebrows pinched and angry, he was thinking, she was certain, of the forfeiture of Clara Schumann's portrait to the Museum of Art of the City of Dresden.

• • •

Moscow, February 1995. Leonid Kuchumov is drunk and, although this normally elevates his sense of self-esteem, he is still smarting from Irina Antonova's scolding. It occurred as they were hanging the exhibit the previous week. "Fifteenth- and Sixteenth-Century art, you fool, you idiot, don't they teach you anything at the university?" she'd said, her mouth set in a sneer, her chest thrust forward, little fists at her sides, she was half his size. Still stunned, it was a whole day later that it occurred to him to point out the paintings by Renoir, Manet, Degas, paintings rumored to have come from the collections of Hungarian Jews, the Hatvanys, the Herzogs, that now hung in the White Hall. But no words of defense had come to him as she'd ordered him to take the Feuerbach back down to the basement. Ordered him! and he'd just taken his art history degree with firsts that summer, here he was carrying an oversized, ugly landscape down to the basement like a common laborer. Illyich, or whatever the hell his name is, came to his rescue and helped carry it down the marble staircase. But that was it. Kuchumov hadn't the courage to face Antonova, director of the Pushkin Museum, he'd forfeited his internship. Choosing Anselm Feuerbach's *In the Mountains of Castel Montero* for the Saved Art Exhibit had been his undoing. Illyich helped recrate the damned thing, they nailed the box shut, and stowed it back in the corner behind boxes of Greek antiquities, and this is why Hanna Silberstein, sent by *ARTjournal* to cover the exhibit at the Pushkin, is not aware that she is standing just above Grandfather Alfred Dubrovsky's gift to the newlyweds as she interviews a smiling, gracious Irina Antonova.

• • •

Belye Stolbi, February 1995. Sergei Brodsky returns his wartime diary to the safe behind the book shelf. He sets a decanter with Tsinandali on a tray, places it next to the chessboard on the kitchen table, and takes the figures from their box. King, queen, knight, rook, pawns. He glances again at the newspaper. Irina Antonova has dedicated the exhibit to the fiftieth anniversary of The Great Victory, and called it "Twice Saved." Blavatsky is sure to have read the article, perhaps they'll speak of it, perhaps they won't. They hardly ever refer to the time when they were officers in the Trophy Brigade, and Brodsky has learned, as his academic career, his home, and his reputation disappeared, to let go of all that is painful and to find comfort in the blessed uneventfulness of an ordinary day.

"Exile"

• • •

> Three brothers, three metals, three sisters, three crates,
> Three paintings, three Muses, three mothers,

Among the papers given to her by Pavel Varschau, the executor of Hilde's estate, are several of her aunt's unpublished hand-written poems, and notes, phrases, beginnings of poems in German, Yiddish, English. Now and then there is a word in Shanghainese. Would Hanna be interested in helping him make a selection for a posthumous publication, Varschau asks, as they sit in a pub in Toronto following the morning of the funeral. Canada's Jewish feminist press has expressed an interest in the project. Pavel Varschau is now Chairman of the Department of Medieval German and Yiddish at the University. He'd been working with Hilde, helping to translate her poems. Is Hanna able, for example, to make anything of this last bit of notation, "Exile," he asks. Of course she's able to. Hanna's head is filled with family lore. Most of the action, she tells him, occurred before she was born.

Surely the Last

• • •

The seventh cervical vertebra, that's what it's called, Annelene remembers now, as she slips the nightgown over her head. It stood out on the back of the young person who'd waited next to her at the crossing yesterday as she made her way to the store. The back of his neck. Her neck. It was difficult to tell, there was a femaleness to the upswept hair but no sign of breasts or rounded hips. The carriage was feminine, an African savannah gait, a young giraffe, slow and inward turned. His or her skin was dark, burnt umber she'd use, and it looked so soft and smooth, she'd felt an impulse to put her finger just there, above the lavender T-shirt, on the bony projection of the upper spine, but, of course, she hadn't. Model for me, sit, I love your androgynous beauty, she wanted to say, but here, too, she hadn't, although she knew that Marie-Louise, who'd always led the way, had done just that. She'd invite a stranger on a park bench, for example, to her home to sit for a portrait if the face of the stranger interested her.

Annelene hangs the nightgown on a hook in the bathroom and steps out of her slippers. The seventh cervical vertebra. They'd had instruction in anatomy in Frankfurt, and although she was never certain that this naming of parts had made her a better artist, she recalls how good it had been to have mastery of something as straightforward as anatomical terms at a time when Max Beckmann's instruction had rendered her so powerless. Max would have been proud of her perseverance. Despite his severity, he'd always been generous and encouraging. The retrospective planned for her ninetieth birthday would have pleased him. She's certain he would have understood her attempt to follow the guidelines, veracity and excellence, to the last. Certainly perseverance has brought her to this point. However, there are days now when she'd just as soon not get to work, and some things, admittedly, have become quite difficult. Cooking rabbit skin glue, for example, sizing the canvas, priming it, certainly more difficult now. Exhausting. Earlier that week, she'd had to lie down afterwards. By next Friday, the canvas will be dry and, in the meanwhile, she will begin laying out ideas for a self-portrait, surely it will be the last, she is thinking, as she steps carefully into the shower. Nude, perhaps. The idea pleases her. Soaping her body with one hand, she holds on to the shower's metal bar with the other. After Bertha's accident, Annelene has developed a fear of falling. She is determined it will not happen. She'd slit her throat before having to be wheeled in a chair, she's sure of it. Carefully, she adjusts the shower head and warm water courses over the brown spots on her arms and hands, the elongated, puckered breasts, it rolls down the blue black red marbled patterns of veins on her yellowing thighs and shins. She's remembering the ridged nails and brown moles on Beckmann's hands, the deep furrow between his thick eyebrows, the pustules on Emil's eyelids, the sunken wattle of flesh at his throat, creased and ropey, so unlike the smooth skin of the androgynous young person . . . *so unlike my own skin how it was, white, pink, a circle of distinguished admirers standing around Fraülein Dubrovsky drinking tea. White. Pink. Copper and gold. The freshness of the palette I chose in those days. And I realize now, it had always been so* selbstverständlich, *so taken for granted, unquestioned, of course this is who I am, young and, yes, beautiful, and certainly womanly. Androgynous. Never. Although. I was, I admit, ambitious, which was certainly an unfeminine characteristic for the time, and work, painting, was more important than anything, or anyone for that matter. Mutti's despair, would I never marry, and I wanting my pleasure without trading who I was for protection. So perhaps there was, after all a sense of androgyny in wanting an artist's life, and now I have without a doubt joined Max and Emil, I have gotten old, and I must look at that, this is surely the last self-portrait, it must be excellent, and truthful to the aesthetic of decay. Nude, yes. But perhaps I'll throw Mutti's fur coat over me, it's chilly in the studio.*

McDonald's

• • •

Back from Canada, Hanna sorts through the mail her neighbor has collected in her absence. She's been away for three and a half months, the time in Europe extended, followed by two weeks in Toronto helping Pavel settle legal affairs and clearing the rooms where her aunt and Immanuel had lived. A small apartment, simply furnished, they'd had very few possessions. As she packed their books and letters and photos, Hanna felt how rich their lives together had been. And now, her own life sits before her in a pile of mail. Requests for donations, advertisements for concerts, plays, the Chamber Music Society of Lincoln Center, Carnegie Hall's Summer Season, the lecture series at the Y. Mailings from galleries and museums, she's missed four openings, missed five auctions as well. Fitness studio flyers into the wastebasket, she will resume walking across Central Park to the Galerie when she returns to work. Next, a letter from her editor at *ARTjournal*, Marvin Koppelstein, including an invitation to "The Spoils of War" conference. Bard's Graduate Center is hosting it. Russian and German art experts will attend. The subject is restitution, Marvin is asking her to cover it. There's a careful friendship now, a resumption of work-related cordiality. A mistake, it's taken a number of years to mend. Marvin has returned to the family he had, in truth, never left. They both should have understood this. Hanna puts the conference invitation on top of a stack of letters to be answered tomorrow and makes herself a cup of tea before opening the personal letters. There are only three, the first a birthday greeting from Theresa. "50," on the cover, and inside, "how nifty!" Opening the card sets off music and the gyrations of a group of bare-breasted female dancers in Hawaiian skirts holding glasses of what is apparently champagne. "Psst! Wake up, You! How ya' doin'? Have a good one!" Theresa's written. There's a second late birthday card, this one with hand-drawn balloons, from Carol's son, Alejandro. It includes a reminder to Tia Hanna that he has a birthday, too, he will be nine in May, and she has promised to buy him a World Wrestling Federation action figure and dinner at McDonald's. And there is a letter from Toronto. Pavel Varschau letting her know he's been able to clear his calendar in the fall. He'll take the train to New York and be there for Annelene's Retrospective. Hanna runs a bath while she unpacks her suitcase. She takes out the Hermann Adler still life and rests it against a wall in the vestibule. She'll bring it to Bertha this weekend, have the handyman put it up in the living room. Fifty. How nifty.

In fact, her birthday had passed with little ceremony. She'd taken herself to the dining room of the Hotel Sacher after the interview with Marie-Louise, ordered a glass of red wine, no champagne, she'd never liked it. And because it is customary on this sort of birthday, she gave some thought, but not a great deal of it, to herself. 1) Would she have preferred to celebrate fifty surrounded by children and grandchildren, toasted by, say, someone like Willy Klein-Messmer? 2) Was she lonely, sexually deprived, desperate for a lover or a husband? and 3) Was she unhappy? and when she had answered each of these questions with varying degrees of yes and no, Hanna ordered onion soup to start, followed by *Forelle blau* with *Bratkartoffeln*, a small salad, chocolate mousse, and turned her thoughts to the interview with Marie-Louise, then made plans: first, Frankfurt where she'd meet with Detlev Hagen, then Paris, the Louvre, Amsterdam, the Rijksmuseum, the Van Gogh, why not, before traveling to Russia for the "Twice Saved" exhibit at the Pushkin.

The River, May 1995

• • •

They make their way slowly along the Promenade. Hanna pushes Bertha in a wheelchair, keeping pace with Annelene, who is steering a wheeled walker. The afternoon is warm, they stay close to the shade of the honey locust trees. There's movement everywhere—the river, of course, and on the river, tugboats, one pushing a long, flat barge out to sea, and, despite storm clouds that have begun to gather in the distance, a pair of kayaks. There are sailboats as well, and a motorboat followed by a tail of white foam. The Circle Line is heading east, and now Annelene is recalling the *SS Gneisenau*, the journey from Europe to Shanghai, the storm on the last night of 1938, New Year's Eve, that left no one standing with the exception of herself and the ship's captain. His delighted, champagne welcome as he opened the door to his cabin. His blond mustache, the swastika on his lapel. She smiles, remembering her emerald evening gown.

They stop in front of a bench. Hanna parks Bertha's wheelchair next to it, and closes the safety lock. Annelene takes a handkerchief from her pocket and wipes her brow. It's become a long walk from her home on Pineapple Street to the Promenade. The three women sit now with their backs to the trees, admiring the yellow and orange striped lilies growing in the shade, surrounding the base of a wrought iron street lamp. Flecks of rust lie on its surface, Annelene notes with satisfaction, preferring the aesthetic of decay, and not only the aesthetic, she thinks, but the veracity, even the justice of metal returning to air, to earth, and in the middle of this somehow comforting thought, she thinks she hears Bertha, "not at all as it used to be," but perhaps she's imagined that, their dialogue of almost ninety years.

It's not at all as it used to be, Bertha is thinking, not, however, with reference to the rusting lamppost. She is thinking of the wheelchair and the Brazilian aide who sleeps next to her at night, the Jamaican woman during the day, meals taken with strangers. No, it's not at all as it used, and now Hilde. She turns to Hanna who is looking out at the buildings across the river. She'll have to ask. She puts her hand to her ear and begins turning the little wheel, why can't she get the hang of it, it's infuriating, this absurdly expensive, worthless piece of plastic. It begins to emit a piercing sound.

Hanna covers her ear. As soon as they've rested, she is thinking, her mother and aunt will ask about the funeral. She'll turn so that they see her lips, she'll enunciate clearly, repeat what hasn't been understood. And it's not as if it's quiet here. Below the Promenade, trucks and cars are streaming to and from Manhattan, Annelene and Bertha can hear that, and Hanna's aware of sounds they no longer hear, the scrape and shuffle of a man jogging past them, the patapat gait of another, the release and pull splat of flip flop sandals as strollers amble by. The sounds of babies in carriages, teenagers on bicycles. Parents calling to their children in Japanese, Spanish, Hindi, Finnish perhaps, or maybe that's Hungarian, all the languages of Brooklyn Heights, English as well. Eros is not absent here on the Promenade, a pair of pigeons, the male stalking a seemingly reluctant female, fanning out his feathers in ritualized lust, and a pair of young Indian lovers, apparently released from the restraints of home, he's pulled her onto his lap on the next bench over.

Bertha, Annelene, and Hanna sit quietly, resting, taking it in, the lovers, the babies, the boats, clouds, the long glass and steel rectangles of Lower Manhattan. An old man wearing a business suit and tie, a member of the neighborhood's Jehovah's Witnesses, rides by in a motorized wheelchair. In one hand, he holds up a magazine with the cover facing them: "Awake! Is There Life Beyond the Grave?" and Bertha turns to Hanna.

The Retrospective, September 1995

It is almost fifty years since Emil bought the building on Madison Avenue, scraped the faded paper from the walls, painted them fresh, tore up the carpets, sanded and stained the floors, and polished the chandelier. He bought a grand piano and a long mahogany table, and had them installed in the largest room. Stepping down now from a ladder under the chandelier, Hanna throws two used bulbs into the wastebasket, and flips the switch. The Galerie Bauer is lit, ready for an old-fashioned vernissage. A pianist will play softly in the background, and the retired head of the Brooklyn Museum Art School, Annelene's former colleague, will deliver the address. The table is set with plates of pâté, caviar, cheese, cold cuts, olives and gherkins, bread, bunches of red and green grapes, fresh figs. Tumblers and wine glasses stand ready next to bottles of mineral water, sherry, sake, Chardonnay in buckets of ice, and there is a large rectangular cake in the middle of the table decorated with marzipan commedia dell' arte figures, a Columbine, a Harlequin. It is a birthday cake, for this is Annelene's ninetieth, and this is her Retrospective. Howard Epstein has ordered a limousine for the evening. He'll bring Annelene and Bertha, and Howard's offered to have the chauffeur swing by Newkirk Avenue to pick up Mr. and Mrs. D'Angelo, although they're uncertain as to whether they'll come, they hardly ever go out in the evening. Gertie might come if Harvey or Neil will accompany her, and Carol will bring Alejandro and her mother, and perhaps her latest lover. Marvin Koppelstein will stop by, a critique will appear in *ARTjournal* a week from now, and Gronewicz, the grandson, he's in town for a show at the Armory. And Pavel Varschau, on the train now from Toronto. Hanna touches the letter in her pocket, one of Hilde's poems, the last he's sent. It came this morning. Letters are coming more frequently now. 6:18, Penn Station. Hanna checks her watch. The guests are not due for another hour. She takes a look around the Galerie. There are seventeen paintings, including three self-portraits, and six charcoal drawings. The sketchbook of the *SS Gneisenau* lies open in a vitrine at the far end of the room. As for color, Payne's grey is dominant, along with cadmium orange and red, phthalo blue, dabs of gold. Hanna walks slowly through the exhibit, straightening a painting, wiping dust from the frame of another, checking titles: *Model with Tattoo* from the time with Beckmann. *Mutti on the Gangplank of the SS Gneisenau. Bertha at the Black Cat.* More Shanghai paintings, three on loan to the Galerie, purchased after Annelene's work had been included in the St. Louis exhibit "Max Beckmann's Students." *Boy with Rickshaw* from the St. Louis Museum of Art, and two from a grandson of Ostropovich, he'll be here tonight, *Bubbling Well Road* and *The Honey Cart Driver.* Sassoon, now in London, is unable to come, but he's loaned four of the charcoal drawings, Shanghai street life and skyscrapers lining the Bund. An anonymous loan next, also in charcoal, newly arrived refugees sit among suitcases at the *Hongkew Refugee Quarters*, laundry hangs on a rope suspended from the ceiling. And a last charcoal, their Newkirk Avenue neighbors, small, crouching in a dark hallway, a shawl covering the woman's head, a six-pointed star on her breast pocket, *Polish Jews in America*. Two paintings from the subway series: *Women Ascending the Stairs at 34th Street* and *Straphangers*. Portraits hang on the last wall. From a photo of their visit, *Hilde and Immanuel.* Hanna remembers now holding a cloth doll in her lap and turning to look at the man in the strange chair with wheels. He wears black gloves, and when he smiles at her, she turns back quickly to the precious doll, holds it tightly to her chest. She is aware that her heart is beating, it is one of her earliest memories. That, and Hilde holding Immanuel's hand, bending to rub her cheek against his. Hanna has not seen this before. She is curious, excited, even a bit anxious. She is unable to sort out these feelings that are so, she checks her watch again, 6:14. Hanna is smiling as she continues along the wall. There is Mutti, a last portrait, in bed, Mrs. Smith behind her, holding a tray with small bottles of pills. On loan from the Brooklyn Museum, *Onkel Fritz in Brighton*, the old man on a boardwalk bench, his eyes fixed on the Atlantic. *Emil Franz Bauer*, seated like royalty against a maroon curtain. *Howard Epstein* (on loan from Howard), athletic, graying, a red, white, and blue background. *A Maiden and a Fawn.* The self-portraits are last. *The Two-Headed Horse*, Annelene standing between both heads, caressing them, pressing them to her breasts seen through the thin cotton of her nightgown, her face tilted back, her mouth open, the horse clicks the hooves of its back legs together while a carousel of color spins overhead. Next, laughing, she is standing in *The Red and Gold Dress*, the silk with the Mandarin collar. Her face is in profile, something is sparkling just beneath the surface of her chignon. At the end of the wall, the oil barely dry, *Pineapple Street*: Annelene wearing a long fur coat and a wool paisley scarf wrapped around her head. Little wisps of gray come out from under it. She holds three brushes in her left hand and peers from behind a canvas. The fur coat has come undone, one bare breast and thigh are visible as she leans to catch sight of herself in a mirror. To her right is a vase with daffodils, no longer fresh.

Hanna turns back to the portrait of herself. *A Maiden and a Fawn.* 1957. Private Collection. She is thirteen, her love for

Anthony D'Angelo is on the wane, she is Anne Frank waiting to hear from Hunter High School. Her bare arms and legs are long and thin, her eyes wide, searching. A fawn with long thin legs and wide eyes as well, stands close to her, testing its stance. The two figures are hesitant, fragile, on the cusp, about to begin. Hanna smiles and turns from the portrait. From her pocket now, she takes the letter, and unfolds Hilde's poem.

Waking alone to light through the slats,
knowing you left again in the night,
Wrapped in the pain of parting,
I go to the kitchen, strike a match, touch it to the gas,
a dahlia springs from the flame, orange, blue, pulsing.

Steam rising from its dented spout,
the cast iron kettle calls to me to
tip it to the filter, and liquid
streaming brown and fragrant
fills the blue chipped mug.

The day's begun as every day,
the dented spout, the blue chipped mug,
the past is past, what's lost is lost
and what I saved is who I was
and it's enough, it's just enough.

References

• • •

The following historical, biographical, and autobiographical works were invaluable in helping me understand the world of the Dubrovskys and all whose lives intersected theirs:

Akinsha, Konstantin and Kozlov, Grigorii with Sylvia Hochfield. "Spoils of War: The Soviet Union's Hidden Art Treasures" *ARTnews*, April 1991

Akinsha, Konstantin and Kozlov, Grigorii. *Beautiful Loot: The Soviet Plunder of Europe's Art Treasures*. Random House, 1995

Beckmann, Mathilde Q. *Mein Leben mit Max Beckmann*. Piper Verlag, 1980

Chelala, Cesar. "A Musty Old Apartment in Argentina" *New York Times*, October 22, 2008

Eisfelder, Horst Peter. *Chinese Exile: My Years in Shanghai and Nanking*. Ayotaynu Foundation, January 2003

Hoeffel, Paul Heath and Montalvo, Juan. "Missing or Dead in Argentina" *New York Times Magazine*, October 21,1979

Kallir, Jane. *Saved From Europe: Otto Kallir and the History of the Galerie St Etienne*. Galerie St Etienne, New York, 1999

Keller, Volker. *Jüdisches Leben in Mannheim*. Edition Quadrat, 1995

Lloyd, Jill. *The Undiscovered Expressionist: A Life of Marie-Louise von Motesiczky*. Yale University Press, 2007

Ross, Alex. *Escape to Shanghai: A Jewish Community in China*. Free Press, December 1993

Schlenker, Ines. *Marie-Louise von Motesiczky: A Catalogue Raisonné of the Paintings with a Selection of the Drawings*.

Marie-Louise von Motesiczky Charitable Trust in association with Hudson Hills Press, May 2011
Zellers, Hanna. "What I Remember" Unpublished Memoir.

Note: In researching the life of Marie-Louise von Motesiczky, I used two excellent sources, Jill Lloyd's biography and Iris Schlenker's *Catalogue Raisonné* (listed above). Both volumes contain the authors' translations of the artist's correspondence, and in constructing the fictional voice of Marie-Louise, I have incorporated details and phrases that are the work of Lloyd and Schlenker. My sincerest gratitude to both for many days of fascinating reading.

Here is the place, as well, to credit the authors Konstantin Akinsha and Grigorii Kozlov (likewise listed above) for their recounting of the role of the Soviet Trophy Brigade in the plunder of European art. *Beautiful Loot*, which reads like a mystery novel, gave me the groundwork for the journey of the Dubrovsky paintings, and some of the authors' language and descriptions have been used to reconstruct that time in history.

And Other Characters,
some historical, some invented

• • •

The Germans

Ruth Silberstein, Hans-Erich's sister
Dr Gustav Hartlaub, Director of Mannheim's Museum of Art
Siegfried Oppenheimer, textile manufacturer
Max Beckmann
Mathilde "Quappi" Beckmann
Heinrich Simon, editor, *Frankfurter Zeitung*
Frank Morav, former employee of Hohenemser's, soldier
Antje Schmidt, housekeeper to the Silberstein family
Caroline Klein, Antje Schmidt's niece
Birgit Klein-Messmer, Caroline Klein's daughter
Samuel Didner, doctor in Shanghai
Heinz Seligmüller, adjutant, Hitler Youth Corps
Dr. Hans Posse, Hitler's art agent for Special Assignment Linz, the Führermuseum
Fritz Fleischmann, attorney, born in Mannheim
Emil Franz Bauer, art dealer and gallery owner, born in Leipzig
Detlev Hagen, radio journalist

The Russians

Sergei Brodsky, art historian, officer in the Red Army Trophy Brigade
Serafim Druzhinin, curator at the Tretyakov Gallery, Trophy Brigade

Alexander Voloshin, Director of The Moscow Circus, Trophy Brigade
Yevgeny Mikhailov, Private First Class, Red Army
Vladimir Piankov, Major General, Red Army
Pjotr Krapchenko, railway official, Moscow's Kiev station
Praskovia Sokolova, wife of a Red Army general
Vladimir Blavatsky, art historian, archaeologist, officer in the Trophy Brigade
Natalia Seminova, pianist
Irina Antonova, director of the Pushkin Museum
Leonid Kuchumov, Antonova's intern

The Americans

The D'Angelo Family—Theresa, Anthony
The Levine Family—Arthur, Carol, Alejandro
Howard Epstein, sports equipment manufacturer

The Internationals

Marie-Louise von Motesiczky, Viennese expressionist artist
Henriette von Motesiczky, mother of Marie-Louise
Josef Gronewicz, art dealer, Amsterdam
Ostropovich, Russian-Jewish owner of real estate and The Black Cat Night Club in Shanghai
Elias Canetti, Bulgarian émigré intellectual and author, Nobel Prize winner
Pavel Varschau, Canadian biographer of Immanuel Häring, Toronto University professor
Ernesto, Argentinian employee, Galerie Bauer
Lafcadio Hernandez, Argentinian chemist
Mr. Hokaido, Japanese guide, Nagasaki

Acknowledgments

• • •

For their generous gifts of time and expertise while I was writing and researching *Just Enough to Start Over*, I am very grateful to the following:

Gerard Aalders, Netherlands State Institute for War Documentation; Noah Brozinsky, Washington, DC; Carola Cribari, Heidelberg; Claudia Dausch, Kunsthalle Bibliothek Mannheim; Peter Heuss, Claims Conference Frankfurt; Saul Kagan, Founding Director Conference on Jewish Material Claims Against Germany; Jane Kallir, Galerie St Etienne, New York; Marilyn Kaggen, New York; Marion Kaplan, German-Jewish History, NYU; Horst Kessler, Kunstsammlungen/Haberstock-Archiv, Augsburg; Caroline Klemperer, Indiana/New York; Lena Leuci and Tim Riley, America's National Churchill Museum, Missouri; Lucia Malamud, Buenos Aires/New York; Frank Moraw, Heidelberg; Konrad Mueller, ESOL, Heidelberg; Sean Rainbird, Staatsgalerie Stuttgart; Birgit Schwarz, Kunsthistorikerin, Vienna; Gerald Tulchinsky, History Department, Queens University, Canada; Tom Weiner, Vietnam War Draft Stories. And for technical support: Jenna Bornhöft, Joelle Bornhöft, Adam Kwapich, and Irwin Cohen.

As most of the research was completed almost twenty years ago, many of the above have since retired, and some are, unfortunately, no longer with us.

Now, twenty years later: Sincerest thanks to Paul Dry Books—to their very fine staff, including Julia Sippel, whose careful and insightful editing and creative suggestions made our work together a real pleasure, and Mara Brandsdorfer, for her work on the book's design and for sending it far and wide. Special thanks belong here as well to Sarah Kafatou who shares the talents of all three Dubrovsky sisters and who enthusiastically recommended the manuscript to her own publisher, Paul Dry; and, most especially, thanks to the novelist Steven Bloom who read and weighed in on the manuscript, and was endlessly encouraging.

Sara Gothelf Bloom was raised in Brooklyn, New York, and spent much of her adult life in Germany, working at the Heidelberg Opera and as a freelance concert singer. For more than twenty years, she toured the country as a soloist with a small ensemble doing concerts of Yiddish songs for German audiences. Today, she lives in Brooklyn, and *Just Enough to Start Over* is her first novel.